SHORT HAIRED WIG

and Other Stories

BY NEIL D. MARTIN

Produced by:

FriesenPress
Suite 300 – 852 Fort Street
Victoria, BC, Canada V8W 1H8

www.friesenpress.com

Distributed to the trade by The Ingram Book Company

For Connor; He who prevails.

ACKNOWLEDGEMENTS

It has taken me 'way too long to put this collection of stories together and it would have taken a good deal longer without the generous help of a few special people.

I know I'm going to forget someone but I can't forget to thank Doug Jamha for his time and his kind advice.

Thanks to Myrna Kostash, who generously took the time to read some of my pages and pointed out that what I was writing was fiction. Thanks, also, for using the word "gripping" to describe my prose. You have no idea what that meant to me at the time.

Thanks to Garrison J. Pon who, after reading a very early draft of the Liz Lyons story gave me what has to be the most economic critique ever when he said, "Wordy." You were right.

Many thanks to the good folks at Friesen Press who waited patiently as I dithered and dawdled and fussed with my manuscript when I could have just sent the thing in and gotten the help I needed.

Thanks to Len Wyatt for generously spending holiday time reading what I thought was a final draft and saving me from doing these stories damage by trying to pack them into novel form. Also for the good scotch.

Lastly, thanks to Sandra, my rock in stormy seas, for putting up with all my silly foolishness, all these years.

TABLE OF CONTENTS

Short Haired Wig

The first time I entered the lobby of the Ritz Hotel I was wearing a disguise. The year was 1970. I was fifteen years old and I needed a job.

My buddy Gary worked at the Ritz as a bellhop and he told me they had an opening, so in I went. But I couldn't go as myself.

The minimum hiring age at the time was sixteen, so I knew I would have to lie about that. Gary told me it'd be cool. The management apparently had a pretty laid back attitude about it, as long as you went by the hotel dress code, which included things like no mini–skirts for chicks and no beards for the guys.

Unfortunately, it also banned long hair for men, and that was my problem. My hair was well past my collar and I had no intention of cutting it: thus the disguise, which consisted of a wig designed to hide my long hair and make me look like I had short hair. A short haired wig.

NEIL D. MARTIN_segment>

Not that I had any political beliefs about it, or anything. I was no hippy; I just happened to like my hair long. A lot of people thought you were a hippy if you wore your hair long. I suppose there were guys my age who didn't mind being labeled like that, but not me. At fifteen, I didn't know what I was, but I sure as hell wasn't a hippy.

If I was to identify with any group of people it would have been the beatniks. I was a baby when the beat generation emerged from the fringes but from what little I knew about it, I thought I'd like to have taken part. Something about the way they spoke, calling people "cats" and "groovy" just turned me on, along with the clothes they wore. A chick in a tight black leotard with a bobbed hairdo really caught my eye. Jazz was something I had yet to discover, so I suppose it was more the way the beatniks looked and sounded that I liked.

Near as I could figure, the hippy "movement" was something that happened in San Francisco in the summer of '62. It was over 'way before anybody in Canada even heard about it, but it left an enduring echo in our lives. Ripples from the "summer of love" continued to lap our shores in 1970, in ways the real hippies would have been horrified to see.

Corporate America was doing its best to capitalize on the baby boom, taking any hint of a trend from the hippies and mass-producing it for the consuming public. Beads were big. Vests of any description came back in style, provided they were not worn with any matching jacket.

A shopping trip through downtown took us through boutiques and 'head shops', stocking items from a hundred places that our parents had never heard of.

Soft muslin shirts with Nehru collars, alpaca serapes from Peru, saris from the Hindu Kush, hand carved incense burners of teak and sandalwood, sandals of hemp rope and rubber, and a thousand things of bamboo and wicker, were just the tip of the iceberg. And the fashions were just the start.

The bookstores were not immune.

The Beats gave us Hinduism, Zen Buddhism, Yoga, Tai Chi, Chi tea, kung fu, Transcendental Meditation and Sufism. The Koran, the Vedas, the Kama Sutra and the Bhagivad-Gita. Kahil Gibran and Omar Kayam, the I Ching and the Egyptian Book of the Dead all came home in the beatniks' tattered rucksacks and found themselves vying for shelf space with LSD, UFO sightings, Mexican scorcery & peyote séances, Scientology and God knows what else.

The result was a heady witches brew of arcane spirituality, which people my age inherited. We were left to wander the bookstore aisles and ponder what possible relevance Carlos Castenaneda and Lobsang Rampa could have to our lives.

There was nobody around to explain it to us, unless we wanted to join one of the dozens of cults that came out of the sixties.

The Church of Scientology almost got me once.

I'd been grooving down the street one bright summer day, minding my own business, when a chick about my own age approached and started rapping with me.

2

She was foxy enough that I didn't even stop to think about what a weird thing *that* was. L. Ron Hubbard may have been as crazy as a bagged cat but he knew something about most fifteen-year-old boys; they are all about fifteen-year-old girls.

She invited me back to a building that the 'church' occupied downtown, and before you could say 'indoctrination' I found myself chatting with a well-groomed cat about twenty five. He was easy going and pleasant and very skilled at leading the conversation. It was only much later that I realized how easily he'd dug a lot of information out of me without making me freak out. I was such an easy mark, he must have thought he'd hit the jackpot.

Maybe the idea of fulfilling his recruitment quota for the day with so little effort made him get over-eager. I'll never know, but I'm eternally grateful for whatever it was that caused him to slip up.

He asked me what I had planned 'career-wise' and I told him.

"I'm a musician," I said.

"Oh, good!" he replied, "I love musicians."

Then he excused himself for a moment to go get someone he 'wanted me to meet' (no doubt the senior recruitment guy. I can still imagine the conversation they had;

'Hey Phil, I think I got a live one for you-a musician, even. Want to check him out?')

But by the time he and Phil got back, I'd split. I sat there thinking to myself about the wording he'd used.

"I love musicians."

Who the hell says, "I love musicians?" No one says that.

You'd say, "I love music," or "What instrument do you play?"

"I love musicians?" No way. There was something creepy about that. It sounded like he *ate* them, or something. Anyways, it just *felt* wrong, so I was out of there by the back stair and I give thanks to a benign providence that I did not hang around.

Of course, on the other hand, it's entirely possible that I might have found inspiration in their whacked out teachings and gone on to a career like Tom Cruise or John Travolta. Who knows? Not me. That's the thing; nobody knew.

It was like walking down the midway at some bizarre carnival with hawkers on both sides, each one with their own brand of truth to sell, soliciting your attention.

The hippies were gone, but they'd left all their stuff around. All, except the how-to manual.

It was up to each of us to make up his own mind about what bits of cultural flotsam we would adopt into our particular image. This made for some pretty eccentric life styles, not to mention décor, as people chose wildly divergent elements of fashion, architecture, career choices, etc., but there were a couple of things that were pretty much universally accepted if you wanted to be a cool guy in 1970;

Rock and Roll, and long hair.

Both had come into my life at the same time.

I'm talking about the Beatles' first appearance on the Ed Sullivan show, February 9, 1964. I was nine years old.

Just that year, my Dad had finally given in and bought our first TV set; and not a moment too soon. It was an enormous black and white RCA built into a handsome hardwood cabinet. That's the only way they could sell TVs back then; they had to be furniture, too.

I don't know where life might have taken me if I'd missed that show, but looking back it's clear that seeing those boys with their dark suits and mop-tops cavorting before a crowd of hysterical females was a pivotal moment. I'd never seen anything like it and I wasn't alone.

I must have heard the Beatles' music on the radio by then, because the few rock and roll stations of the time were playing little else, but I wasn't aware of actually listening to it. Up until then my listening habits were pretty much restricted by the availability of music in the house, or rather, the lack of it.

My sister had a portable record player that I was under threat of death not to touch, so of course the second she left the house I spent every minute I could listening to her small collection of Paul Simon & Oscar Brandt, Kingston Trio and Elvis Presley records. I loved Elvis but even he didn't prepare me for the Beatles.

Not that I heard any of their music on Ed Sullivan, either. Nobody did. All you could hear, from the moment Ed swept his hand toward the stage and yelled "THE BEATLES!" were the screams of the girls in the audience.

The camera guys were obviously aware of this and as the boys gyrated through the motions of playing "I Wanna Hold Your Hand" they kept switching to the crowd. For minutes at a time, the TV audience was treated to shots of tear-stained teenage girls swooning and fainting. Then they would switch back to the stage for a close-up of one or other of the band who would obligingly mug for the camera.

The thing that most impressed me was that it didn't seem to matter what they did—the effect on the audience was the same. John would look into the lens and smile and the noise would explode. George would join Paul at the other mike for an inaudible "Ooo" and another pre-pubescent girl would keel over unconscious. Even homely old Ringo could render several bobbysoxers senseless with a simple waggle of his head.

By the end of the broadcast it was clear to a generation of boys who were about to enter their dating years that, whatever these guys had, we had to try and get some.

At nine I was just starting to get curious about the dating thing. The parties we went to had started to become boy-girl affairs and the idea of asking a girl to go to one had been alarmingly stressful for me. I finally played it safe and asked the girl from across the lane.

Teresa was a nice girl and we'd known each other forever. Her parents were a little straight-laced and would probably have never allowed her to go if it had been anyone but me asking.

I put on my clean white shirt and combed my hair and walked across the alley to get her and together we walked a couple of blocks to the party. When we got there, everybody was downstairs listening to—you guessed it—the Beatles. Some one broke the ice and started dancing and after a couple of songs went by with us watching, I asked Teresa if she wanted try it. To my enduring surprise, she asked me to take her home, instead.

I went upstairs to get her coat from the bedroom and once I was alone, I found that my confusion about the situation had brought hot tears to my face. I struggled to regain control long enough to walk her back home.

I managed to find Teresa's coat and my own and when I turned around to leave, who should be standing there but Ronnie Palmer; the hottest chick in school and my wildest fantasy crush.

"Are you crying?" she asked, astonished. "What for?"

"I don't know, just...I have to take Teresa home. I don't know why I even brought her. Her parents..."

"You *are* crying. Boy, are you weird, Ward."

So I took Teresa home and put the dating thing on the back burner for a while. Funny thing was, all the way back to her place, as miserable as I was feeling, the songs kept going through my head.

All the next week I had "Love me Do" and "Twist and Shout" stuck in my head. I started thinking about saving money for a Beatles album when my best friend Myles told me they were going to be on Ed Sullivan. I thought I was tuning in to hear the music.

I'd love to see statistics, if it was possible to gather them, on how many young men asked their parents for guitar lessons that night. It's easier to look up the sales records of the companies that sold electric guitars for that year and the following ones.

I think it is fair to say that the Beatles were almost single-handedly responsible for an entire crop of teens deciding that, whatever else they might do, they were going to play an instrument. And not just any instrument would do.

The catalogues of guitar manufacturers that year showed a mad rush to bring out models that looked identical to those played by the Beatles. The classic case in point was the oddly teardrop–shaped bass played by Paul McCartney. At the time of the Sullivan Show appearance, that style was exclusive to the Hoffner Guitar Company. By the end of that year, no fewer than nine manufacturers were offering look–alike models in their lines.

It didn't end with the instruments, though. Virtually every nuance of the band's appearance that night became marketable overnight. Boys who couldn't have cared less what they wore to school that day suddenly were refusing to go if they didn't have black slacks with the right fit. "Beatle Boots" became the only acceptable footwear.

A style of cap that Greek fishermen had worn for centuries suddenly became known as the "Johnny Ringo," to be worn with a black turtleneck. Those who couldn't afford black turtleneck shirts made do with something called a 'dicky,' which looked like a black lobster bib with a turtleneck and was made to fit under your shirt. Trouble was, of course the shirt had to be white, so the dicky would be clearly outlined under it. It lasted about a week.

Long hair, however, was here to stay; that and the music. Lying on my belly on the hoop rug in front of our big new TV as the show wound down, it was nothing short of a revelation.

I'd always known I was a drummer. I'd never given any thought as to what kind of music I wanted to play. Up 'till then, if it had a beat, it was good enough for me.

When I was little, my folks had an antique Edison record player in our rumpus room. It was an elegant thing of brass and walnut scroll work that played cylindrical wax records, of which we owned about fifty, kept on the shelf above. Mom must have shown me it one rainy day, and it wasn't long before I'd learned how to make it work.

It became the center of my day. I would pull a chair over so I could see the names of the recordings, etched into the rims of the cobalt tubes, make my choice and pull it out of it's cardboard case, then slide it onto the shiny steel drum. Cranking the brass handle around to wind the motor up and releasing the stop to set the record spinning, dropping the needle down onto the grooved surface, I thrilled with anticipation when the scratchy sound came out of the big, bell-shaped speaker.

There were recordings of symphony orchestras and singers from the turn of the century, narrated stories (my favourite was "Uncle Josh and the Honey Bees"), and even one record of someone doing birdcalls.

And then there were the marches. There were six or seven of them, mostly military bands doing Sousa compositions. I loved them. I started off just marching around the basement floor to them, but soon I found that what I really wanted was to play the snare drum parts. By the time I was four I'd established a routine. I would run through a couple of the other records for fun and then get down to business.

I had no drums, of course, but where there's a will, there's a way. A pair of HB pencils and a copy of the World Book Encyclopedia served me well enough, though I doubt if my mom quite approved.

In grade one I got thrown out of class for drumming on the sides of my desk during quiet time. When the teacher, a nice grey haired lady called Mrs. Brindle, told me to stop that noise, I answered; "What noise?"

She assumed that I was being a smart aleck but she was wrong. I was honestly not aware of the racket I was making. The other kids all laughed but Mrs. Brindle was not amused. I had to spend the rest of the period standing out in the hall, and later I had to apologize to the class. I didn't mean it and they all knew it. They all knew I was like that.

In 1965, I was ten years old when the school ran Canada's new flag up the pole for the first time. I played snare drum to "Oh, Canada" on the front steps.

I learned every drum beat I heard on the radio, every record I could get my hands on, from Motown stuff my big sister bought to borrowed Elvis 45's and rock-a-billy stuff from my mom's old lacquer 78's. I even learned to play Bolero from a classical recording of "Carmen."

It was all grist for the mill but until that magic night in February, watching the rings on Ringo's fingers glint in the stage lights, I didn't have a clue what I would do with it.

Everything changed that night. I became a man with a mission. I approached kids at school; kids I didn't even know, if I heard they had an instrument. I started dragging my drums down the street in my dad's wheelbarrow on Saturday afternoons for the "jamboree" session at the teen drop in center. I put together a couple of ensembles that didn't last, then finally hit on a pretty good combo with three buddies from my neighborhood, and it wasn't too long before we'd learned enough songs in my folks' basement to actually play a dance.

Well, sort of. We played "Hey Joe", "Gloria", "House of the Rising Sun" and "Twist and Shout" (we thought it was by the Beatles). Then, for the second set, we did them all again as instrumentals. Third set, we put the lyrics back in and extended each one with a lengthy jam in the middle. For a grand finale we did "Wipeout" featuring me on drums. It didn't matter. It was great. We were on stage, playing music and there were girls watching.

We held 'band practices' three nights a week, plus Saturdays. We worked hard, learning songs by listening to records on my sister's portable player. When we thought we had a new tune rehearsed to the point that we could play through without any major mistakes, we would invite some girls over to the practice.

After rehearsal we'd sit and rap about all the other stuff we needed to be a band, like a name. There was currently another group on the north side, calling themselves the "Undecided Suggestion." We thought that sounded a bit negative, so we became the "Four-gone Conclusion."

We played on the weekends at the local community league halls, collecting dollars at the door, and occasionally got hired to play an evening dance at a local youth club. It lasted almost a year, and then our lead player's parents decided he had to concentrate on his schoolwork.

The band split up and I was back looking for players. It was grade ten before I found a new lead guitar guy and a bass player, and when I convinced our old keyboard guy to try it again, "Joyband" was born.

We were showing a lot of promise, putting together a repertoire, even playing a couple of gigs at local restaurants when Percy, the guitar guy, said he felt like he was taking on too much playing both rhythm and lead, and suggested a second guitar. He had somebody in mind, and when he brought Gary over for a try out, the chemistry was perfect.

We knew we had a sound going, and prepared to get really serious about things, but I had a problem. The cheap little drum kit my dad had bought me had given up the ghost and been replaced by a slightly less cheesy set of second hand drums that were already coming apart under the constant use they were getting. If we were going to go pro, I needed a set of professional drums.

I had no money, so when Gary told me about the opening at the hotel, I really had no choice. The only hurdle to applying was the hair, and the answer was the shorthaired wig. Gary had one. He told me where to get mine, just down the street from the Ritz at a hairstyle place.

It was called the Ritz Hair Stylists, one of a half-dozen businesses in the vicinity of the hotel that shared its name. There was the Ritz Flower Shop, the Ritz Dry Cleaners, Ritz Travel and the Ritz Shoe Re-New. They clustered about the hotel like chicks around a hen.

At one time, there had been a Ritz Smoke and Gift (now replaced by the news stand in the lobby), and the Ritz Haberdashery for Men, as well. Everything that the well-heeled guest might need to make his stay at the hotel convenient could be found within a short stroll down the avenue.

Ritz Hair Stylists was inhabited by a dapper little man wearing horn rimmed glasses and a snappy fortrel suit. A tiny silver bell was attached to the door and he looked up from a magazine at the sound of it. He took in my shoulder length hair and a look of eagerness came into his eyes.

"May I help you?" he asked hopefully.

"Yes, I'm looking for a...a wig, actually."

"Ah." Some of the warmth left his smile. "A shorthaired wig, I suppose."

"That's right. My friend got his here. I'm applying for a job..."

"Yes, yes. Just step this way, please." He was all business as he ushered me to the back of the shop. There, along the shelf on the rear wall were a number of Styrofoam busts, each wearing a wig of a different color.

Sitting me down in the barber chair, he took a measurement of my skull using a fabric measuring tape like my mom used for sewing. Then he turned to the shelf and selected a wig from one of the heads.

He'd chosen one that closely matched my natural color, and after he showed me how to tie my hair into a ponytail and flip it forward to be trapped under the wigs elastic cap, the effect was just like seeing myself with a modest haircut.

It made me look older, to my surprise. The wig was designed to cleverly mask the mass of hair it hid. It looked quite natural and felt light and comfortable on my scalp. I was relieved and pleased at the prospect of wearing it.

"Wow, that's great." I said, "how much?"

"Three hundred and fifty dollars."

I almost choked.

"Are you sure? The guy who sent me here said he paid fifty bucks for his."

"Ah." He whipped the wig off my head and replaced it on the shelf. Without another word, he disappeared through a curtained doorway at the back of the store. He was only gone a few seconds when he returned carrying a small cellophane bag, from which he pulled another wig, he handed it to me.

"I think this is the model you're looking for," he said, and crossed his arms.

I took the wig from him and examined it. It lay there in my hands like a little dead animal. It was nothing like the first one. This one was a mousy brown color, not even close to the color of my hair. It seemed to be constructed of some kind of nylon netting, like a cross between a cheap bathing cap and a hair net that you see dishwashers and kitchen help wearing. It was reinforced in places with a light wire framework, evidently designed to keep the thing in place, but as I tried it on I could see that it failed miserably.

The wires dug into my scalp here and there, not actually hurting, but not very comfortable, either. Instead of masking my ponytail, this wig actually seemed to accentuate the mound of hair beneath it, giving the impression that my scalp was malformed. I looked like I'd suffered some horrible head wound that had healed over badly.

The worst part was the sideburns. The wig was just a bit too small for me, and the tight fit created tension in the wire frame that extended down into the sideburns. The wires that were supposed to keep them nice and snug against my temples were being pulled inside out, so that the sideburns stuck out at an angle on either side of my head like a pair of little wings.

Looking in the mirror I could see the shop owner standing behind me, his arms still crossed. He looked impatient.

"Seems a bit tight," I said to his image in the mirror, "do you have one a little bigger?"

"One size," he said with a smirk, "fits all."

"You're kidding."

"May I suggest..." he said, and he reached around me to pick up my glasses where I'd put them on the counter. He placed them on my face so that the arms held the sideburns down. It was an improvement, all right, but still—the overall effect was horrific.

"So this is the best..."

"I'm afraid that's all we have in that price range."

I looked wistfully back at the wig on the shelf. Three hundred and fifty bucks! If I got the job I'd be making about ninety-five dollars a week, plus tips. I sighed.

"I'll take it."

"Fine. Will there be anything else?"

"No, that's it, I guess."

"You understand, there is no return on these items."

"Right—no, I guess not, eh?"

I paid the man and he put my wig in another bag, along with the receipt. I went directly home and barricaded myself in my room to try it on again. I hadn't noticed how big it made my nose look. What if someone I knew saw me in it? Other than Gary, of course, who had to wear one, too. I'd never live it down. But then what were the chances of anyone I knew going into the Ritz? And even if they did, how would they recognize me? I looked completely different with the wig on. I only hoped it would fool the manager.

The next day I arrived a few minutes early for my appointment with Eddy Cymbaluk, the hotel manager.

As I turned in under the big neon-lit marquee over the front entrance it occurred to me that I'd never actually been inside the Ritz. The thought surprised me. I had always known the building. I was aware of the reputation the hotel had.

Where once had been a high society hot spot, frequented by the moneyed class, now stood an old and aging relic. Doomed to fall further into disrepair and disrepute, like a fading beauty who finds she must compromise her dignity in order to maintain herself, the Ritz had fallen on hard times.

The grand façade of the building had been marred by the addition of a glass and aluminum entrance, flanked by dimly lit showcase windows, which advertised the entertainment for the week on poorly crafted poster boards.

Sometime in the fifties the ownership had decided to add a garish neon marquee sign over the doors, complete with backlit "read-a-trons," the acrylic letters frequently misspelling the names of the acts in the lounge, or welcoming the weekends' banquet guests in several mismatched colors.

The sidewalk in front of the hotel was the busiest red light walk in the city. The girls leaned up against the old brick and sandstone walls, they and the old hotel supporting one another.

Around the corner, the entrance to the tavern was usually flanked by a pair of drug dealers, who would melt back into the shadows to let a patrol car go by and then re-materialize as it turned onto the avenue; business as usual. Downstairs, they hired good bands to lure the kids in but it was common knowledge that you drank there at your own risk.

The place was a dive, but once inside, if you looked closely you could still see some vestiges of the way she had been. The height of the ceilings, the width of the halls and the grand sweep of the staircase all told a different story.

And there were things left over from her glory days that hadn't changed. The Ritz occupied a place in the city's society even still.

The Elks club and the Shriners still held monthly meetings there. Weddings and Bar-Mitzvas were booked into the banquet room, along with graduation balls and conferences. Members of the legislative assembly, when in session, could save a few bucks on their expense accounts by staying at the Ritz without appearing to slum it too much.

Outside, the sixties had altered society forever, but a lot of things in the Ritz remained unchanged. There was a time warp there that had somehow frozen the place in another era, although it was difficult to put one's finger on just which one. The hotel was a place that allowed the people there to live each in his own epoch, unaffected by the passing of time outside its doors.

Eager as I was to partake of the wonders of the seventies that were unfolding all around me, I had no idea, as I stood there in my shiny new loafers and black slacks, that I was first about to take a tour through a curiously preserved world of the past.

"Eddy's not here right now," Gary told me, "but he'll be right back. You can wait in the coffee shop if you want."

"Naw, I'll just hang around here, I guess."

"OK, well, I gotta be on the switchboard, so…"

I could hear an angry buzzing coming from behind the desk.

"Sure, man, you go ahead. And, Gary…" he paused and looked back, "thanks, man."

"Hey, de nada, amigo. Good luck." He went back to work.

I stood there feeling like an idiot in my unfamiliar outfit. After a couple of minutes I was wishing I'd taken Gary up on the coffee shop idea.

I began to take stock of my surroundings. I gradually became aware of the scale of the lobby. My eyes travelled up to the ceiling, twenty, twenty-five feet over my head, and took in the finely wrought masonry work along the top of the four massive arched columns.

The focal point of the room was a gigantic marble fireplace at one end, now set with an electric fire behind glass doors. In front of it was a pair of leather couches that must have been twelve feet long. Two matching armchairs closed in a square area of the marble floor that was covered by a thick rug.

An elderly woman occupied one of them, reading a magazine. We seemed to notice each other at the same time. She put her reading down and turned slightly to match my curious gaze with one of her own. I looked away, and felt my cheeks flush.

I let my eyes wander to the far wall and along it to the door across from the front desk. A demure brass plaque on the wall stated simply; "Lounge." Further along the same wall was the elevator door. Past that, a curving marble staircase descended from the floor above, resplendent in hand carved mahogany rails, which ended a pair of ornate finials.

It was a warm day and the lobby was stuffy. I began to sweat, whether from the temperature or nerves. My new white shirt was clinging to my back. I could feel my scalp growing moist under the wig, which didn't breathe at all. The sweat began to accumulate at the edges of the thing where the wires held it in place. I could feel them starting to slide upwards under the pressure, the sweat acting as a lubricant.

I reached up self-consciously and gave the sideburns a tug, but I could feel it immediately begin to slide up again. The old woman in the chair had abandoned her magazine entirely and turned to watch me steadily.

It felt like I had been standing there forever when the door to the lounge crashed open to admit a man in a hurry. He was wearing a rumpled brown suit and smoking a cigar, holding it between his teeth and dragging on it as he advanced across the room, emitting puffs of smoke behind him as if he was steam driven.

He spotted me standing there and came puffing over.

"You Rick?" he asked, blowing cigar smoke in my face.

"Yes, sir." This must be Eddy. I struggled not to cough for fear it might dislodge my wig. Eddy examined my face closely. Close up, I could see, to my surprise, that I was taller than he was by a couple of inches. He had curly light brown hair, thinning on top and blue eyes that looked like they didn't miss much. His suit was a little baggy on him, like he'd lost some weight recently. His tie was askew.

"How old are you, Rick?"

"Sixteen, sir"

"Yeah? What year were you born?"

"Nineteen-fifty, uh…four, sir" I thought I'd blown it. The sweat began to really pour.

"Uh-huh. All right. Can you start tomorrow?"

"Yes, sir. Tomorrow is fine." *Please leave before this wig slips anymore.*

"All right. Gary will show you the ropes. Be here at eight."

"Yes, sir. Thank you." *Please God, don't let this stupid wig let go until he turns around.* He turned around. In the same instant the sideburns of my short haired wig cleared the arms of my glasses and silently sprang out to either side of my head.

Eddy turned around again. His eyes went to the sideburns, first the left one, then the right before settling on the left. His eyes narrowed and one of his eyebrows lifted. Without taking his eyes from the curious sight at the side of my head, he spoke.

"You got a social insurance card?"

"Yes, sir."

"Good. Bring it tomorrow."

"Yes, sir."

He hesitated, looking like he was trying to decide what to say. His eyes never moved.

"All right," he said finally, as he wheeled about and strode brusquely off towards the coffee shop.

Watching him barrel through the door to the café, I had the sudden impression that, if there hadn't been a door there, he would have just gone right through the wall, leaving a little Eddy-shaped hole, like in the cartoons.

I stood still while it sunk in; I was hired! A sense of relief washed over me, followed by one of panic as I realized that I didn't have a clue what it was that a bellhop did.

I didn't care, though. I had a job. I was in.

The Wars

My parents came out of the Second World War with a deep and abiding certainty that, having done their part to defeat Hitler, they were now entitled to live out the balance of their lives without any more unpleasantness. It was an attitude shared by many of their peers.

My dad had signed up the day war was declared. Never mind that his contribution to the war effort had involved little more than sailing to England. He enlisted with a will to do his part, to caste his fate to the winds of war ready to lay down his life, if need be, for the greater good.

Dad, who'd been forced to leave the farm he'd grown up on because of severe allergies, arrived in England just in time for spring. The verdant English countryside promptly attacked him with such an effective variety of pollens and other airborne irritants that he was overwhelmed and soon became so ill that, as a soldier, he was deemed redundant.

The British did what they traditionally had done with the incurably ill; they sent him to the seashore, where he spent the balance of the war guarding a nice, quiet beach in Torquay.

Still, he'd volunteered and he'd served.

My mom had been a paymaster sergeant, stationed in Halifax, meeting the 'boys' as they came off the boat with their back pay.

They had done their duty to God and country and were now riding a wave of post- war optimism so potent that it convinced them they could afford a new house.

North American builders were reveling in the demand for housing and investing in the new model of the commuter city. A house in the suburbs and a car, and you'd be ready for whatever the new society was about.

It turned out to be about having babies, for one thing. The baby boom was on and, like it or not, I was part of it, even if I barely qualified.

In a lot of ways, I guess, their retreat to the suburbs was also a retreat from reality. My folks couldn't really afford a new house on my dad's wages. They'd planned on having a little extra income from my mom's sewing, and if that wasn't enough, they could always take in borders.

It wasn't, and they did—but that's another story.

In the wide streets and generous sidewalks of the new neighborhoods like ours, there was a general agreement that life was going to be better. In fact, they insisted on it. It was so important to them that nothing disturb the Shangri-La dream they had of life, that if anything unpleasant happened they all just ignored it.

I can remember awful things that occurred when we were growing up in the 'burbs that our parents just don't recall.

There was the dad who was regularly seen taking his belt off as he escorted one or other of his grade school-aged kids into the garage, wherefrom the sounds of a severe thrashing would emanate, only to fall on the deaf ears of his neighbors.

One of our neighbors hung himself from the rafters in the basement of their house when I was five. I remember being horrified and frightened and then, in the end, just being mystified as to why no one talked about it. It just fell into the category of stuff you weren't supposed to mention.

They wanted so much to have it be some kind of utopian dream that they were willing to ignore almost anything that told them otherwise. A neighbor could drink intemperately, abuse or neglect his wife and children, beat his dog and write bad cheques, but let him allow dandelions to take hold in his front lawn, and the wrath of an indignant community would descend upon him.

We were given the illusion of being safe, growing up in those wide streets. We walked to nice new schools a few blocks away and enjoyed the use of well-attended community halls and sports facilities. If our families went to church we wouldn't even have to leave the area to find one of our denomination. The local mall (also a new phenomenon) provided us with the necessities. There was hardly ever a need to go anywhere outside our happy, safe little neighborhood. It was a great place to be a little kid.

When we first moved in, our house was so new that it was the only one on the block with anyone in it. The main road out front had yet to be built, so my dad had to negotiate a twisting muddy gravel road out to the city streets, but that was nothing to a farm boy.

One by one, the houses filled up and playmates were found. Friendships were born and routines established. Early memories are always populated by the same faces playing 'kick-the can', 'red light/green light' and 'hide & seek' in the twilight, hopping over hedges and running over newly seeded lawns.

Mike Randford, tall and freckly like his dad. Dwayne Robins, abrasive and arrogant like his, and my best pal, Myles MacKay.

Myles and me had something in common growing up, and that was a love of military stuff. Myles came by his honestly, as his father was a colonel in the army.

Both his older brothers were starting careers in the forces as well. Mrs. MacKay was a war bride. She had a cool British accent and a wistful air about her that I thought was because she missed her home. I have the distinct impression, looking back, that Canada hadn't quite met her expectations. I think maybe she'd assumed being a colonel's wife would mean more than a house in suburbia.

I guess it didn't help that her husband's career kept him travelling so much, leaving her alone to look after the kids. He was often gone at Christmas, but he always made sure there was something under the tree for each of the five kids. Myles liked to collect things, so he almost always got a set of stamps or coins from wherever his dad was stationed. He became an expert philatelist at a young age.

I used to think that Myles' military family was the reason we spent so much of our childhood playing war games, but I can see now that it was like that for everyone. The war had been such a life-changing thing for our parents' generation, it was just a part of the times we lived in.

Almost everyone knew someone who'd lost somebody in the war. My mom told us about a "boy" she'd been dating before she met dad, who'd been "torpedoed in the North Atlantic." That was the phrase she used. For years I thought she meant that he'd personally been hit by a torpedo while swimming, which I supposed would certainly have ended the relationship, it just seemed like an awfully extravagant use of explosives.

I read about the two world wars in a few books we had on the subject. These were about the only books in the house, besides the big Encyclopedia. There were a few old National Geographic magazines, a half-dozen Readers' Digest Condensed collections and the war books.

They were mostly accounts of Canadian heroes and their exploits. Billy Barker, Wop May and the famous battles at Vimy Ridge, Ypres and Ortona were covered in exhausting detail, along with their American counterparts; Sgt. York and Patton and the Battle of the Bulge. In the sixties there was a sad vacuum of any literature written for kids.

I was so desperate for reading matter that I used to drag the big World Book Encyclopedia down from its roost on the mantle and pour through the definitions, admiring the beautiful color illustrations until I'd read the whole thing.

My mom noticed and attempted to remedy the lack of books by joining the "Book of the Month Club." She let each of us choose one book and I picked "Robin Hood", only to discover when it arrived that it was the Old English version and therefore almost unreadable.

I did my best, wading through pages of 'thee's and thou's and 'zounds and gadzooks,' until I was walking around talking like some pint-sized escapee from a Shakespeare company.

I remember having arguments with my classmates in grade three about whether or not there were two ways to spell "night" and if one of them could mean guys on horseback with suites of armor. It almost ended in fisticuffs when I called Dwayne Robins a "blackard." I think if I had called him one of the standard things he would have beaten me senseless but the word stopped him.

"Boy, are you weird, Ward" he said.

Myles and I went to school together and became the teachers' pets in grade four. Our teacher, Miss Breeze, was the most beautiful woman in the world and we struggled with the fact that only one of us would be able to marry her when we grew up. When she came back to grade five as Mrs. Johnston, we were devastated.

By grade six, we were double trouble; a couple of smart alecks that fed off each other in a never-ending, two-boy comedy act. The other kids loved us and most of the teachers put up with our antics as an alternative to spending the whole class dealing with us. We achieved a certain status among our peers, one that saved us the bother of having to win spots in the pecking order by that other timeworn method of fighting.

The television brought a lot of things into our homes. There were lots of "Variety" shows, talk shows, sitcoms and the like during the day, but in the evening we tuned in to the war shows. There were other things on in the evening, of course, but the writers in Hollywood seemed to really excel at the war shows. Maybe they had all been enlisted.

Most nights of the week we could take our desserts into the living room and sit on the rug, just in time for the opening credits of something like "Combat," in which Vic Morrow played the stoic Sgt. Saunders of an American infantry platoon fighting the "krauts" in Europe. These shows ran according to formula, so each episode was much like another.

The platoon would go walking through the woods on some mission or another, usually just vaguely referred to as "the objective." All would be quiet until Sgt. Saunders got out his map and checked it, saying something like; "our objective should be just over that next ridge."

Anytime somebody said something like that, we knew it meant trouble. Before they got anywhere near their objective, they were going to have to deal with about a million and a half German troops, who usually came riding along the road on a "halftrack."

The halftrack was an armored vehicle, sort of a half tank, half truck affair, which had the advantage of being obligingly open on top, so that the Americans could chuck a grenade in with the Germans for a splendidly noisy opening to the inevitable battle.

There would ensue a firefight, in which the German troops could always be relied upon to fire promiscuous amounts of small arms ammunition without actually hitting anyone (although, gosh they came awfully close), while the G.I.s picked them off with deadly accurate return fire, occasionally lobbing another grenade in for effect.

Once in a while, just when it looked like our heroes were getting the upper hand, one of them would hear something. Then they would all hear it; a metallic squeaking sound, accompanied by the roar of a massive diesel engine that could only mean one thing;

"A tank!"

It was almost always a German Panzer tank.

Crashing through the pines like they weren't even there, blasting more trees with their 88mm gun while peppering the area with withering salvos from it's two machine guns, these behemoths were the sure antidote to a lag in the action.

Whenever the Panzers showed up we knew it meant that one of the good guys was going to die. That was the price for knocking out the tank, and it was always the same. One Panzer=one G.I. It seemed like a fair exchange, even if the Panzers never actually killed anyone else. It was plain that they would if somebody didn't do something, and somebody always did; usually the new guy who'd just joined the platoon that week.

He would take a hand grenade out, pull the pin with his teeth and, sneering in contempt for his own safety, somehow climb up on the top of the tank to one of the hatches. It never occurred to us to wonder why, if they were going to build something as impregnable as a tank, the German army hadn't thought of putting locks on the hatches.

But, there you go, and maybe it was just this kind of over-confident omission that had lost them the war. Anyways, the inevitable would occur, and the guy who killed the tank would himself be killed, and that was the end of the show for the week.

Watching "Combat," we might easily have come away with the impression that the Americans had fought the war in Europe all alone. We never saw any Canadians or British troops, much less any of the other allied armies that were involved. Very rarely the French resistance would put in a cameo appearance, usually acting as guides to the "objective." Of course, it was an American show, and bound to be bit biased.

"The Rat Patrol" was another favourite. This one was about the 111th Armored Recon Battalion, fighting the war in the deserts of North Africa against Rommel.

The weapon of choice in The Rat Patrol was the Willis Jeep, and its fifty-caliber machine gun.

These would be driven hell bent for leather across the desert, *Vrooming* over dunes that must have been twenty feet high, kicking up great clouds of sand and all the while mowing down hordes of Afrika Corps troops with the 50 cals. How they managed to aim them whilst bouncing around in the back of a jeep was not clear but, then again, we never asked.

The thing about these shows was the attention to detail. Uniforms, vehicles and weapons were no doubt surplus and therefore accurate, but the real work went into re-producing the sounds. Each weapon had it's own distinct voice. From the 'pow' of the M-1 rifle to the 'bup-bup-bup' of the Schmeiser sub-machine guns, battle scenes were painstakingly overlaid with sound-scapes that left no doubt as to who was shooting at whom, and with what.

This was carried over into the comic books we read. Titles like "Sgt. Rock," "Captain Savage," "Blitzkrieg" and the immortal "Sgt. Fury and his Howling Commando's" all contained imaginative descriptive words for the purpose of expressing just what a noisy thing war was.

The writers would make up words to describe the sounds generated by a 500 lb. bomb going off (WRRAAM!) or the different sounds that bullets made as they struck various surfaces. 'Ping ping ping', if the submachine gunfire was hitting the steel plated side of a vehicle, whereas the same ammo stitching it's way up a sandy embankment would go 'thwupthwupthwup.'

There was a big difference between the sound of a Tommy gun and the sound of a Browning Automatic Rifle. Just ask the experts. The kids who watched the shows and read the comics all knew the sounds so well we could reproduce them at will.

As we ran through the back alleys and through the yards, attempting to replay the shows we'd seen the night before, it was of the utmost importance to get the sound effects right. You could pretend that the Winchester cowboy rifle left over from your Hop-along Cassidy days was a modern weapon, or use a stick, for that matter, as long as you got the sound right.

We invented the game as we went, usually starting off with a scene from a TV show as a jumping-off point to a lethal improvisation where anyone could introduce new elements to move the game along. The rules were not static and were affected by who was playing at the time. Those of us who excelled at the game were granted the privilege of inventing some of our own sounds, within reason, but you were taking the risk of having your sound challenged if you went too far.

"Oh, man that's phoney!"

"What?"

"Smoke grenades don't go 'whoosh'!"

"Sure they do! Didn't you see 'Combat' last week? Saunders threw one into the bunker so Manelli could get close enough to take it out with the bazooka!"

"Sure I saw it."

"Well?"

"Well, it didn't go 'whoosh'."

"Did too."

"Did not."

"C'mon, you guys, you're holdin' up the game."

"Yeah, I gotta be home early."

"Ok."

" OK, let's play!"

"Not if you're going to go around shoutin' 'whoosh', we're not."

" All right, smartass, what sound did it make, then?"

"It was more like "Whoom!"

"Whoom?"

"Yeah, Whoom."

"Yeah, 'Whoom' sounds right."

"Let's just play, all right?"

It was important. You had to get it right, and even the best of us could take things too far. One day Myles, who was generally recognized as the best sound effects guy in the platoon, learned the limitations of style.

It was the day after a particularly vicious scene had been portrayed on "Combat", involving a German sniper. He had the platoon pinned down in the ruins of a French village. He'd already killed two recruits and wounded the corporal, who lay in the open, clearly vulnerable to the next and fatal shot, but the fiendishly clever kraut held off, hoping to lure yet another target out into the open in a rescue attempt.

Sgt. Saunders had taken refuge behind an overturned jeep and kept drawing the sniper's fire, by way of trying to pinpoint his position. Every time he peered far enough around the cover, the high-powered rifle would bark it's 'Ka-chow!" followed by the ricochet (Beeyow!) of the bullet off the metal of the jeep. But every once in a while, the bullet seemed to hit the cobblestone street as well, and give off a different sound; a double ricochet.

As we recreated the scene on the front lawn of Mike Randford's house, the tension grew as we eagerly anticipated Myles' oral rendition. When it came, the battlefield fell silent.

"Cock-a-Zineeow!"

We looked at each other. Who would raise the challenge? Perhaps emboldened by being on his home turf, Mike did.

"Cock-a what?" he enquired, his voice dripping with scorn.

"Cock-a-Zineeow," replied Myles confidently, "you know, the double ricochet."

"No way."

"Whattya mean? Sounds just like it!"

"Naw, it's wrong," said Myles' little brother Jim.

"What do you know, squirt?"

"You can't use *that*. It's got *cock* in it."

"Yeah, and besides, it ain't accurate." Dwayne decided to weigh in.

"Well," said Myles, "what is, then?" Ever the pragmatist, he could see he was up against a united front. He'd clearly gone too far. He'd transgressed the unwritten code.

"I don't know—just 'Beyoebeyow,' I guess."

"All right. Mine was better though."

The thing was settled, and we could get on with the game. For nine-year-olds in the sixties, these were weighty matters.

The toy companies knew. They had been trying to get boys to play with dolls for years with little success until Mattel came up with "G.I. Joe."

Up until then the closest any of us got to playing with dolls were the molded plastic "army men" figures. These came in boxed sets, each containing a company of soldiers from one or other of the armies that fought in the war. There was the American infantry, British infantry, German waffen corps, Afrika corps, even regiments of Gurkas, all modeled with incredible attention to detail.

They came in various sizes but the ones we liked were the smallest, HO scale, about an inch high. The thing about HO scale was that it was one of most common model train sizes, so there was lots of other stuff available to accessorize your armies. They made tanks and military vehicles in HO, too.

Myles and I collected armies and spent hours setting up little battlefield dioramas in the back yard. Sometimes we'd buy tiny firecrackers called "lady fingers" and bury them in strategically planned locations throughout the battle ground, to be lit after we finished placing the last man in his exact location, giving us a mini artillery barrage to begin the battle.

Then "G.I. Joe" hit the stores. We wouldn't have been caught dead playing with a Ken doll but we had to admit, with "G.I. Joe," they'd finally hit on something.

Even then they seemed to realize that the idea was only as good as the hardware was accurate. This was obvious by the painstaking detail of the tiny little weapons that each doll came with. Making molds for an M-1 rifle two inches long is not easy, or cheap.

Some of us received "Joe's" as gifts and while we could appreciate the gesture, on our block it was still about the role-playing.

There were lots of toy weapons in the stores, some more popular than others, but the most coveted line was the Mattel "Shootin' Shell" models. They included kid -sized plastic replicas of the Winchester 98 lever action carbine (the iconic cowboy rifle), and the famous Colt 45 six-gun, complete with plastic holster. These were wonderful toys which, in addition to firing caps for the sound effect, would actually shoot little red plastic bullets about ten feet. Wow, were they cool. Most of us had one or the other of these, but I remember the excitement when Mattel announced their new line of "Shootin' Shell" World War Two models.

They put out copies of the M-1 carbine, the Thompson Sub Machine gun, and the Colt 45 Automatic, all standard issue arms for the allied forces in WWII. No one I knew asked for anything else the following Christmas. There was such a

demand for them that our parents actually started to become concerned about the amount of violent play we did.

There were conversations over the fence about whether it was "healthy" for us boys to be spending so much of our energy re-enacting wartime dramas; crazy talk like that. It never amounted to much, though and common sense prevailed.

We amassed a huge arsenal of caps and bullets, and each of us were outfitted with one or other of the "Shootin' Shell" guns.

Before long, we discovered that the caps just didn't sound right. Besides, they were always misfiring. The little bullets, with their limited range, made a poor substitute for our imaginations. I soon found that, nice as it was to have realistic *looking* guns to play with, I'd just as soon provide my own sound effects, thank you very much. Some of the other guys were maybe more interested in the way things looked. For me it was all about the sound.

Around this time we all grew out of the play acting thing and began to look for more mature ways of passing the time. Our love of weaponry and things that go bang stayed with us, though, and we retained our admiration for explosives.

Inevitably, some of us began to aspire to creating the real thing. Not that there was any lack of real weapons in our lives-almost everyone's house had a gun of some sort in it. Myles' basement housed a respectable armory of expensive hunting rifles and shotguns, all displayed in a locked glass case in the rumpus room.

Like a lot of enlisted men, my dad had brought home the rifle he'd been issued when he joined up. There it sat in the back of the hall closet; a British made Lee Enfield Mark V 303.

These were the standard issue infantry rifle for all Commonwealth countries from 1895 through 1957, making them the longest used bolt action rifle ever. They were sturdy and reliable weapons and accurate enough for use as a hunting rifle, although they weighed a ton.

My dad carried his all the way back to Edmonton and found no more use for it there than he had on the beaches of the English Riviera. He told me that he and another guy had taken turns trying to set off an unexploded bomb that a German Henkel had rudely deposited on the beach one day, but it hadn't worked out. They'd finally been obliged to call the sappers to come and deal with it. Still, the rifle had been fired with the intention of inflicting harm on the enemy and that was something.

We were encouraged to take an interest in firearms and such, as part of our heritage. After all, it was not so long since our forefathers had homesteaded this wild country and relied upon the gun for protection as well as to fill the pot. Hunting was still popular and at a certain age we were all expected to take part.

Dad would take the old rifle out before a planned hunt and diligently clean it at the kitchen table. We would all gather round in awed fascination. Dad would take the opportunity to teach us the basics of gun handling, as he'd been taught by his father. He told us to always store ammunition safely and separately and to leave the gun unloaded until the hunt began. He showed us the safety catch and admonished us never to point a gun at anything we didn't want to kill. It was heady stuff to a young kid, and would have been more exciting if any of dad's hunting trips had ever been successful.

Other than a duck hunt with a borrowed shotgun, the only time my dad ever came back from a hunting expedition with something to show for it was the time he and my uncle brought home about a hundred pounds of frozen meat wrapped in butchers' paper. There was an assortment of steaks and chops, a twenty five pound turkey and thirty pounds of hamburger in handy five pound packages.

It seems they'd gotten lost in the bush and stumbled onto an oil rig camp that had just closed up shop. The only person left in camp was the cook, who was emptying out the larder and disposing of all the leftover food in the freezers before they turned off the generators.

After the hunting party had enlisted his aid in disposing of some rum they'd been carrying (in case of emergency), the cook had forced the meat on them in a gesture of brotherly generosity and given them a ride back out to their vehicle, to boot.

We knew that taking Dad's rifle out of the closet was strictly forbidden; a crime that carried the most stringent of punishments, but that didn't stop us from trying to make our own weapons. We'd all been given bows and arrows at a young age, as the terrified squirrel population of the local ravine well knew. It went unsaid that each of us would receive a 22 cal., good for plinking at squirrels and rabbits, but we yearned for more. We wanted to create those sounds for real.

Myles came close to the dream when he found out that a certain kind of 22 could be made to fire full automatic by just removing a key part. He and Barry Ewaniuk took theirs out to the fields on the outskirts and terrorized the local rabbits for a while, but it seems that as the day wore on they got tired of that and apparently felt a need for something more exciting. They began pretending to shoot at each other, aiming at the ground to kick up clouds of dirt, confident in their marksmanship until Barry missed his aim and shot Myles in the foot.

It must have been at fairly close range for a 22 to do as much damage as it did. Myles was limping for weeks and bandaged for a long time. They both lost their guns for an indeterminate time and were grounded for the rest of the summer. It didn't matter to us. It wasn't what we really wanted, anyways.

What we really wanted was explosives.

My brother Lyle caught the explosives bug when he found a recipe for gunpowder in a Boy Scout training manual. We lost no time gathering the ingredients. The sulphur was no problem, but the lady at the drug store looked skeptical when we ordered a five pound bag of salt peter. What really tripped us up was the activated charcoal. We weren't even sure what the difference between activated and non-activated charcoal was.

The activated kind proved impossible to buy, so we tried using BBQ briquettes instead. After watching the sixth or seventh of our homemade bombs just fizzle out on the driveway, we gave up the whole idea.

A more accessible explosive weapon was the Molotov Cocktail. They even used them on "Combat" once, when the Resistance bailed Saunders out of a tight spot.

We all had access to gasoline. Every garden shed had a jerry can full for the lawn mower. Beer bottles were in good supply around the neighborhood. In the days before recycling, they used to pile up in the garage until spring cleaning. Ditto rags. We were set. We lost no time putting a few Molotov Cocktails together.

We took the first ones down to the school where we could use the central courtyard of the building as a proving ground. It was enclosed on all four sides except for a narrow access and there was nothing flammable in the area. We chose a night when our parents were out visiting and arranged to meet at the entrance; Lyle, Myles, Mike and me.

The bombs were in a burlap sack. Lyle let me carry it on the unspoken understanding that I needn't bother even asking to throw one. We went around to the sheltered enclosure of the courtyard and got ready. Lyle made sure everyone knew to stay behind him. We had no way of knowing how long to keep the bottle upside down before lighting it, or when to throw it once it was lit, so we decided that one person would throw, another light the fuse.

Everything went smoothly the first time. Lyle held the bottle inverted for a few seconds until he could see the fuel wick down the fabric, then Myles lit the rag with a match. As soon as it caught Lyle threw it into the center of the square about twenty feet away.

The result was a little anti-climatic. The bottle arced through the air and landed with a crash, followed by a "whoof" of the gas catching fire. Flames sprang up a foot or so high over a small patch of tarmac and burned merrily for thirty seconds or so, until the fuel was exhausted. All that was left were the few bits of beer bottle glass scattered over a dark stain on the pavement, which Mike proceeded to find out were too hot to pick up.

This was not at all the result we had anticipated. On TV, the Molotov Cocktails had produced tremendous bangs and erupted explosively, sending the German soldiers cart-wheeling out of their half-tracks. Something was missing.

"We'll save the other ones until we figure it out." said Lyle. It was his project. We plodded back home, disappointed. Lyle hid the remaining bombs under an old wash basin in the yard until he could work out what the problem was.

It was springtime and we all had plenty to keep busy with. Before long the unused Molotovs were forgotten.

Myles and I were excavating my folks' back yard, with an eye on building an authentic World War One trench, until we were discovered by my mom, who'd apparently been thinking more along the lines of a vegetable patch.

It was strange how much longer it seemed to take filling the thing in than it had digging it in the first place. Myles said he thought it might have something to do with relativity, which may have explained why he was relatively hard to find after he went home for lunch.

Several days passed before the chance came to pursue the testing agenda, and I could tell my brother hadn't come up with any theories as to why our Molotov Cocktail had failed to go boom. When our parents announced that they had planned an evening out, we knew we couldn't pass up the opportunity. Lyle told us he thought it would go better if we let the rag soak a little longer, which sounded dumb but, desperate for some excitement, we all went along.

When we got to the school, we were disappointed to find the courtyard occupied by a group of model car enthusiasts who showed no sign of leaving. After a hurried conference in the soccer field we agreed on an alternate test sight; the alley behind the Wasic Café.

Looking back, it's easy to see why the location appealed to us. It was close by the school. There was a "T" intersection in the alley there, providing three possible escape routes if things went wrong. The spot was screened by the shopping plaza on the south and the United Church to the east.

I don't know if we even considered that the café was right on the "T" and would be the closest to the test. In any event, we failed to take two things into account when we decided on the place, one of which was Joe Wasic.

Joe was well known to us, as we all frequented his restaurant when we could afford to. It was the only café within walking distance of school, so it was something of a hang out for the local kids, a fact of which Joe was well aware.

In addition to the lunch counter and the half dozen booths, he kept a fully stocked candy counter at the front of the store. Here we squandered our allowances on "sweet-tarts", "lick'emade" or licorice pipes. There were gumballs, wine gums, ju-jubes and gummy bears by the scoop, and two-for-a-penny mojos if you really needed to stretch a dime. Joe had little copies of 45 records made out of licorice and "Bazooka Joe" bubble gums with baseball cards and a cartoon in each pack. If we were feeling expansive, we could blow our entire fortune on a wax whistle or a giant jawbreaker, guaranteed to last three days.

We used to agonize over our choices, trying to maximize the pleasure we could glean out of fifty cents. On special occasions, or if one of us came into some extra money, we might order French-fries to go, served in a wax paper bag into which we could add as much ketchup and salt as we thought we could get away with. The trick then was to eat them fast, before the combined cooking oil and ketchup would make the bottom too soggy. Many were the boys who let themselves get distracted from the task at hand and had the bottom let go, dropping the remaining chips on the parking lot, where the gulls made short work of them.

When we got a bit older and began to claim our right to occupy one of the booths, ordering fries and cokes, we would test Joe's patience by dropping sweet-tarts into our coke bottles to make them erupt onto the table. When our shenanigans got too noisy, or too messy, Joe would come over, wiping his hands on his apron and regarding us through his wire-rimmed bifocals.

"Boys," he would say, in his odd accent, "there is a time for coming, and a time for going." He'd pause for effect... "And the time for going is coming!"

Nobody knew anything about Joe's past. He was a strong-looking man of about fifty, who spoke with an Eastern European clip to his voice, but no one knew where he was from. He had a wine colored scar over one eye and two tattoos on his forearms that no one had been able to read because he never stood still long enough.

There was speculation that he had been a sailor, and maybe that's where he learned how to cook, but nobody knew for sure. If we'd given those tattoos a little more thought, we might have reconsidered our choice of test sights but then again, we never expected the test to be such a success.

The other thing we failed to take into account was the effect that a week of abnormally high temperature could have on a pint of gasoline in a sealed glass container.

The fumes must have been building up, exerting tremendous pressure on the inside of that bottle. We didn't know it but we'd solved the mystery of how to make the Molotov Cocktails explode.

We proceeded as before, with one person holding the bottle while another lit the fuse. It's a good thing that Lyle lost his nerve and threw it right away because this time the bottle didn't even hit the ground before the flame found it's way inside and ignited those pent up vapors. It was still a foot off the ground when it went off with incredible force.

THOOM!—The explosion occurred about ten feet from the back door of the restaurant and it still blew the window in. The shock wave hit us, ruffling our clothes and singeing our hair. A huge fireball rose fifteen feet in the air, like a pint-sized model of an atomic blast. We stood gaping in shock.

"Holy Shit!" someone yelled. That pretty much summed it up.

Then the scorched back door of the Wasic Café flew open and Joe appeared in the doorway holding a meat cleaver in his hand. Bits of glass sparkled in his hair as he looked wildly about him. One look at his face was all we needed.

The four of us took off running in four different directions. Lyle and Mike, standing four feet apart and facing each other, ran straight into one another. The collision knocked them both to the ground, where they would have been easy for Joe to collar but, for some strange reason, he decided instead to chase me.

I was fourteen years old at the time and I could run. I'd almost broken a provincial record in the one hundred yard dash that year at the intramural games, coming short by 3/100ths of a second. I thought I'd run my best that day but now, pursued by an angry man with a cleaver, even on broken ground I'm sure I set a new personal best.

There is a sound a person's feet make when he's running on gravel; a combination of your feet hitting stones and then the stones that you eject in your wake hitting the ground behind you. Chuff-clatter-clatter.

When you are being chased down a graveled alley there is a third sound added. It's the sound of the person behind you swearing as the stones hit them on the shins. And here's the thing; the closer they get to catching you the more stones hit them on the shins, making them angrier as they close on you.

25

Any kid knows that if you are being chased on gravel, it's best not to get caught.

As I sped down that alley with an angry Joe Wasic in hot pursuit, I remember being a bit angry, myself. I was angry that, out of the four of us, he'd chosen to take off after me. It just wasn't fair.

Secondly, I was pretty cheesed off that I couldn't seem to out distance the man. Any other guy his age would have been thirty yards behind me by the time I got to the end of the block but, judging by the sounds of it, Joe was staying right with me.

"To heck with this," I thought, "No old guy is going to catch *me* on my home turf."

I knew where there was a new house under construction the next block over. The basement was still surrounded by a moat-like ditch, waiting for the weeping tile to go in. The workers had laid planks across to access the interior. We'd been playing there earlier and I knew the safe path through. I could be in the front door and out the back while Joe was trying not to fall through the holes in the floor.

As we left the alley onto the paved street the sound of our progress changed, becoming at once more defined and serious. I had to get through this block and over to the next avenue, which was easily done by turning left through a little walkway between two lots. A brief return to gravel as we crossed the alley brought fresh oaths from Joe, then we were between the houses on the other side of the block and out onto the street with the construction site.

As I came to the lot I gave no hint of my intention to turn until the last second, then leaped the sidewalk onto the bare earth of the yard and made straight for the front door. The soft earth under my sneakers slowed me down, but I knew it would slow Joe, too. I approached the spot where the planks were at breakneck speed, confident in my knowledge of the terrain, looking for the light sheen of raw pine in the moonlight. I never considered the possibility that the workers would remove the planks at night until it was just too late.

I made a last-second try at jumping the gap, but the dirt gave way under my foot and I felt myself sliding even as my momentum carried me into the concrete basement wall. My solar plexus hit the edge of the cement with a sickening force. The breath left my body and I slid limply to the bottom of the ditch.

The next thing I remember was Joe Wasic's face, full of concern, as he reached down to pull me out of there.

"Jesus Christ, kid," he said, "Are you all right?"

Joe Wasic turned out to be about the best friend I could have had. After he picked me up out of the dirt and helped me back to his restaurant, Joe sat me down in one of the booth seats and went into the kitchen. When he came back he was carrying a bottle of vodka and two shot glasses.

He sat down and poured two shots, sliding one across to me. Seeing my hesitation, he frowned.

"Go ahead, I won't tell your mama," he said, "What, you think it's too early in your life for you to have a drink? That's the trouble with you Canadians. You have so much of everything, you think you have so much of life, too. You all think you are going to live forever, so you put off living until it's too late. Drink."

I took a sip of the fiery stuff, choking on the fumes. The pain in my chest where I'd hit the basement wall blended with the burning sensation in my stomach until, overall, I began to feel better. Joe swallowed his vodka in one gulp and poured himself another.

"You owe me some money. Take a deep breath."

Again I hesitated.

"I said, take a deep breath. Sharply. Now."

I did as I was told.

"You don't have to hold it in. At least you didn't break any ribs. Now, you owe me some money to fix my window."

"I don't have any money."

"You think I don't know this? You're going to have to work it off. I have dishes that need washing, floors that need mopping. Plenty of things around here for a boy to do, believe me."

"Ok, but how much..." "I don't know how much until I talk to the window guy." He downed his second shot of vodka. "There's some painting to be done, too. Maybe you can do that. Tell me; what the hell were you trying to do, anyway?"

"I don't know. We were just messing around with some gas and stuff."

"Gas and stuff. Molotov Cocktails. Don't look so surprised! Whose generation invented them, do you suppose? The Grateful Dead? I know more about Molotov Cocktails than you want to hear. You're lucky nobody blew his arm off."

"We didn't mean to do any damage. We were just messing around. We were originally going to do it over at the school, but it was taken."

Joe stared at me for a moment, then suddenly he laughed. He took off his wire-rimmed glasses and gave them a wipe with a napkin from the stainless steel dispenser. His shoulders continued shaking with mirth. He glanced up at me and shook his head in disbelief. I almost started to laugh with him, in relief, but something told me not to.

"All right. Whoever the other part of 'we' is, I don't want to know. You I caught, you will work off the damage." Joe stood up and picked the bottle and glasses up off the table. "You come in most days after school, anyways—instead of goofing around and making a nuisance of yourself, you can work. Yes?"

"Ok."

"Good. You can start on Monday, right after school."

And that's the way it started-my first job. Everyday after school I went to the restaurant and worked for Joe.

At first I washed dishes, mostly, but after Joe saw that I wasn't going to wreck the place he started finding other things for me to do. I helped unload delivery trucks and put stuff away in the freezer. I refilled the salt and pepper shakers, ketchup bottles and napkin dispensers. It was light work and I only stayed a couple of hours a day. Before I went home for supper I mopped the floor.

I didn't tell my folks about our arrangement at first, 'cause they'd have wondered why I wasn't getting paid. After a couple of weeks, Joe told me that the bill for his window was paid. I went in on a Saturday to paint the back of the café. I finished up around lunchtime and while I was cleaning brushes Joe came to the door.

"Come in and have some lunch. You can finish that later."

I went inside where a cheeseburger deluxe sat on the table at the back booth, accompanied by a coke and a side of fries. I was hungry after the mornings' work and tied right into it.

Joe came out of the kitchen and joined me. He put a fried egg sandwich and a glass of milk on the table but for a minute he just sat there, watching me eat.

"You ever been hungry?" he asked.

I stopped chewing, surprised by the question. Before I could think of a reply, Joe went on.

"I don't mean hungry like you are now, with a good appetite for food that's in front of you. I mean *really* hungry. I mean the kind of hunger you have when you haven't eaten for three days and you don't know when you might eat again. You ever go a day without food?"

I thought about one time when I skipped breakfast and went out on Dad's boat without a lunch. We started catching fish and got so into it that we stayed out until suppertime. When we got back to shore, my Mom had made up a big pot of stew over the Coleman stove and I must have eaten a quart of it, I was so hungry. I didn't say anything, though. I didn't think that was what Joe meant.

"No, I guess not," I said instead, "have you?"

Joe picked up his sandwich and studied it in his hand.

"There was time I would have killed for an egg." He looked at me and smiled. Then he took a bite and, chewing slowly, he said, "People say that; 'I would kill for a burger—I would kill for an egg'. They don't know what it means to be so hungry that you would actually kill another human being for some food. No one knows—until you've been there yourself."

"Were you there?"

Joe didn't answer right away, just kept chewing his sandwich. He gave a little shrug.

"Yah, I was there. I was there for almost a year. Warsaw. You know where is Warsaw?"

"Poland, right?" I said, "You mean in the war?"

"The war." Joe said it like he'd never heard the word before. "Yah, it was in the war. In the ghetto. You heard about this; The Warsaw ghetto?"

"I read about it. The Germans walled off a section of the city and put all the Jewish people inside."

"That's right. Inside the walls, we were hungry. Sometimes no food got in for weeks. People ate leather, glue. The cats disappeared after the first month. After that, the rats." He paused, took another bite of his sandwich and washed it down with a sip of milk.

"We knew that the German soldiers carried food with them. They all had these little cylinders, like lunch boxes. In case they had to stay away from their barracks and missed a meal. Some of them would put in treats for themselves—sausages, or ham. There were times when, standing in a lineup a block long for a loaf of bread that was half sawdust, you would find yourself beside one of them standing guard. And the smell of what he had in his canister would drive you mad."

He took another bite of sandwich, a sip of milk. I'd lost interest in my fries.

"The joke was; they were there in case a riot started. But the smell was enough to start one!" He laughed sharply. I tried to smile, but I didn't make it.

"We weren't supposed to do anything against them, for fear of retaliations. The civic leaders forbade any attacks on sentries or patrols. They got lost, sometimes, wandering around in our ghetto, smelling like that. What were we supposed to do? Just let them go? When we were starving?" Joe took the last bite of sandwich and drained his glass of milk. His eyes focused again and he smiled at me.

"Sometimes the patrols never got back to the barracks. And yes, there were retaliations. Small at first; ten Jews for every soldier, then a hundred. And when the big one came—when they brought in the tanks to finally end it, some of us wondered if it was us that had brought it on, just for a few sausages."

Joe shrugged. He stood, picked up the dishes.

"You want to keep working for me? I will pay you." He turned back to the kitchen.

"Let me know."

Next day I showed up as usual and just started doing the dishes. Joe came into the kitchen with a bus tray full of dirty plates, stopped and said "Good." And that was that. I didn't ask him how much he was going to pay me, or how many hours a week I could expect to work. That wasn't the way Joe did things. We just carried on like nothing had changed until two weeks later, when Joe motioned me over to the back booth as I was leaving. He handed me an envelope.

"Payday." He said.

"Yeah? Cool!" I opened the envelope immediately. Inside it were four ten-dollar bills. I'd never had so much money before. Joe saw the look on my face.

"Don't look so shocked," he said, "this is what comes of honest labor. You weren't expecting more, were you?"

"Oh, no! This is great, Joe. I just never thought what it would feel like to have some real money, for once."

"Well, don't spend it all in one place, unless it's here. See you on Monday."

"See ya'." I started for the door, then I stopped.

"Joe?"

He looked up.

"Thanks."

Joe inclined his head a few inches to one side.

"You are entirely welcome."

I fell into a routine of school, working at Joe's and practicing on the drums. It didn't leave a lot of time for hanging out with the other kids from school but school had begun to lose its' appeal anyway. About the only class I really enjoyed was English.

The teacher, Mr. Forbes, was an odd sort of person, an American ex-pat who had left a career in the states and started again at the bottom of the pecking order because of the Vietnam War. He was given to grand gestures, like parading down the halls each 4th of July with a union flag in his jacket pocket and a three-corner hat on, whistling "Dixie".

He won our hearts on the first day of class when he picked up the teacher's copy of the English text, holding it between two fingers at arm's length like it was a skunk, and dropped it into the wastepaper can with a loud clang.

"That will be the last time we see that," he told us, "Now let's get on with some learning."

Mr. Forbes had some unconventional opinions on things and he wasn't afraid to voice them. This endeared him to the students and many of the other staff but some were not impressed. A few treated him with outright hostility.

The story goes that he was at a staff meeting when the topic came round to how teachers could be encouraged to follow the curriculum more closely. It was no secret that Mr. Forbes didn't bother following any curriculum but his own instincts in his classes, so he didn't have anything to say. One of his detractors, however, an unpopular math teacher by the name of Mrs. Soams, decided to get in a dig. When Mr. Forbes declined to rise to the bait, she pursued it further.

"What's the matter, Mr. Forbes? Are you uncomfortable with a little sarcasm?"

Forbes gave her an even gaze over the rim of his glasses.

"Ah, Mrs. Soams," he replied amiably, "let's see; 'sarcasm'; from the Greek 'sarcasmus', literally, 'the tearing of flesh.' More colloquially referring to the tearing of flesh by dogs. In your case, obviously, a female dog."

It took a moment to sink in but Mrs. Soams apparently got it, as she abruptly left the meeting, sputtering incoherently. Now that's what I call an English lesson.

His class was the high point of the day for me. You never knew where he might lead us in a given class. He usually started off with some sort of reading. It could be poetry, or an excerpt from a novel. Sometimes it was something out of that day's newspaper.

Mr. Forbes always sat at his desk to read, with his reading glasses perched on the end of his nose, occasionally glancing up at us, peering over the rims to see if an especially salient quotation was being properly received. When he was finished, he'd put down the reading matter and take his glasses off, all the while looking from face to face, giving us all time to digest before he began to ask for comments.

From there, the conversation could go almost anywhere. Mr. Forbes encouraged us to debate things and to explore topics that were controversial. He liked to get us going and just step back and let us go at it, only occasionally interrupting to make sure everyone who wanted to take part got a chance to speak their mind.

We talked about everything from war to legalizing marijuana to abortion. Nothing was out of bounds unless it was pornographic or had nothing to do with the topic at hand.

One day Mr. Forbes read us a piece of poetry from some great tome; an ode, I think it was, after which the class was silent.

"Well? Hasn't anyone a comment to share?"

Dead silence. A fidget here, a quiet cough there.

"Oh come, now," Mr. Forbes said, "Surely someone has something to say about it?"

"Poetry is boring." Rod Waddington dared.

"Boring? Oh, no, Mr. Waddington, poetry is many things, but boring it is not."

"Prove it." Rod challenged, pushing his luck even in this relaxed forum.

"Very well, I shall. Your assignment this class will be to write me a poem. Any form, any length; no holds barred but it has to have at least two lines. Haiku are acceptable, provided they conformed to the rules."

We looked at each other in mild shock. Once we realized he was serious, after a chorus of moans and groans, we got out notebooks and went to work.

I stared at the blank paper in front of me for twenty minutes, while images of what I wanted to write drifted through me, coming tantalizingly close to forming themselves into words. Finally, with five minutes left in the period, I started frantically dashing off whatever came to mind. A rhyme scheme appeared and the words began to flow of their own accord onto the paper. I was just finishing when the bell rang. I had to hand it in without even reading it through. Mr. Forbes had noticed.

"Some of the greatest writers do their best work up against a deadline." He remarked as he took my paper from me.

I was shaken a bit by the experience. It had felt a little like being possessed, or like that "automatic writing" that clairvoyants and mad people do. I took refuge in the drama room to mull it over.

We only got drama once a week, so the classroom was empty a lot of the time. I found I wasn't alone, though. Several of the girls from my class had gotten there first, including Vivian Ghiles, who was a friend. She had dated Myles a bit in grade seven and I had to admit I was bit smitten with Viv. We made small talk and I tried to put the poetry thing out of my mind but I think I came off a bit distracted by the looks I got from her and the other girls.

It wasn't long before the whole thing got lost amid the hubbub of the rest of the day. I didn't think about it again until next English class.

"I want to thank you all for your assignments last class," Mr. Forbes began, "there was a great range of effort put into this work. Some of you submitted poems that showed an earnest effort. Others of you—and you know who you are," he fixed his stare on Rod Waddington for a second, "Obviously did not take the assignment seriously. Rest assured, such lack of initiative will be reflected in your final mark."

As he spoke, Mr. Forbes strolled up and down the rows of desks, handing back our poems. He hadn't bothered to mark them on scale, only adding little editorial comments to each-"good rhyme scheme" or "excellent effort."

"You should all be proud of your work. Poetry is not an easy thing. We do not write good poetry from the mind, as some of you came to realize doing this exercise. Good poetry comes from the heart, which is why so many of the good poets' work is romantic in nature. Great poetry comes from the soul."

He'd pretty much finished handing back the papers, in no obvious order. There was only one sheet left in his hand, which had to be mine as I was the only one without. Mr. Forbes walked right past me on his way back to the front of the class.

An icy hand gripped my heart.

"There were many fine poems handed in but one in particular stood out from the rest." He sat down behind his desk and took out his reading glasses. I slid down in my seat, trying to become invisible.

"This piece, while not as polished as one would expect from a mature poet, is *real* poetry, in the sense that it was written from the heart and therefore must be measured on a different scale. I'm going to read it to you now, as I have no doubt that the author would be intimidated if I asked him to."

I was wondering about the relative merits of jumping out the window when he began.

Ode to what's Right
by Rick Ward.
See the young soldier, standing there,
A light wind ruffles his hair,
Sword gripped tightly in trembling hand,
Thinking, most likely, of his homeland.

The land so distant it seems like a dream,
His homeland, his own land,
Which he must redeem.
He and the others-they'd all been so gay
As they rode from the city
(He remembers that day.)

And what of the others who tarried behind;
the mothers, the lovers, the old and the blind?
Their fates fall to him now, their lives in his hands.
He must win the battle, or forfeit their lands.

No thought to his own future can he afford,
The tale will be told on the point of a sword.

And if he should fall, like the others who'd died,
His sleep will be sound knowing only-he tried.

But, no time for thinking-the battle draws near,
No doubt in him now, as all things are made clear.
His grip on the pommel of fortune grows tight,
Eager to do what he must-for what's right.

Mr. Forbes read the poem with style. I was amazed at how he was able to smooth out the bumps in the meter by adding the right pause, or rushing over a clumsy phrase. He made it sound a lot better than it was. When he was done he peered at us over the rim of his glasses and spoke into the silence.

"That," he said, "is poetry. Well done, Rick."

I mumbled something, squirming in my seat. A couple of the other kids were looking at me curiously, as if it had just been revealed that I had some incurable condition. Vivian, who sat just across the aisle from me, turned and stage-whispered to me.

"You wrote that?"

I shrugged miserably and nodded.

"Wow," she said, "you are so weird."

"Hey Ward," Rod Waddington called as he walked past, "I knew you were a homo, but putting it out there so everybody knows—that takes guts, man."

I swore never to write poetry again.

Down in the rumpus room I spent all my free time on the little drum kit. I worked harder learning to play the drums than I'd ever worked on anything.

Paradiddle, paradiddle, five stroke roll. Slow, then faster and faster until I lose control then start again, building proficiency and pushing my limits until, little by little I make progress. Every day something is a bit easier than it was the day before. Slowly but surely I built a repertoire of skills on the drums, one rudiment at a time.

Then it was time to try using them on some music. I had my sister's portable record player down there and I listened to any record I could get my hands on, trying to discern the drum parts through the scratchy tracks of LP 78's or 45 singles.

It was an eclectic mix of music, but I didn't know the difference. If there were drums on the recording I would try to copy them. Of course there was no way I could hear the recording and play the drums at the same time, so I'd listen a few times through and then rely on my memory for the arrangement and play it through. When I forgot what came next, I'd go back to the record, trying to drop the needle at the spot where memory had failed me. I became an expert at that, anyways.

How many hours down there practicing, pushing myself to do better, working until my hands wouldn't hold the sticks anymore? I'll never know, but I know that it was never enough. It was all I wanted to do. It was my passion and my obsession. When I wasn't playing I was thinking about playing, dreaming about having a band to play with, planning to be a musician whatever it took.

At night I thought about how much money I could save toward my dream. At twenty bucks a week, even if I only saved fifteen I could put away seven hundred a year or more, almost half the price of a new set of Ludwig drums. Maybe I could find a good used set, so I didn't have to wait so long.

I'd fall asleep promising myself to save every penny I made.

Of course, it didn't work out that way. As the year wore on I found more and more excuses to dip into my savings for things I thought I needed at the time.

My Dad helped me find a used set of professional looking drums, lots better than my cheap Japanese set, even if they weren't Ludwigs. I had to agree to pay for half.

Clothes had suddenly become important.

My first attempt to put a band together had resulted in an invitation to play at a house party. We needed a microphone so somebody could sing. That 'somebody' turned out to be me, mainly because nobody else in the band had the nerve.

I found a used Asian copy of a good mike in a pawnshop and talked the guy down to seventeen bucks for it, but I couldn't find a used mike stand anywhere. We were scheduled to play at a party the following week and I had to do something. A new stand was fifty dollars or more, and that was just a straight upright one, designed for someone standing. I needed something that I could use while I played drums.

In desperation, I took a wire coat hanger and bent it up until it fit over my head and rested on my shoulders with the mike cradled in the hook part. It worked great until I moved.

When I played drums, the mike would start to wave back and forth in time to the beat. If I had to turn quickly to hit a crash cymbal, I ran the risk of getting smacked in the teeth.

It was the best I could do in the time we had, so after a couple of practice sessions, we took it to the party for my first gig in public. It worked OK for the first song, but half way through "Hey Joe," I discovered that the grounding in the house was faulty, resulting in my getting a shock from the mike each time it touched my lips.

Luckily, "Hey Joe" was originally a blues song. I doubt if anyone had ever delivered a more tortured rendition than our audience was treated to that evening. We finished the show instrumentally.

At the end of a year working at the Wasic Café I had saved a grand total of fifty bucks. I had to use that to rent a sound system for my second band's debut concert in the local church basement. The band was a big hit with all the neighborhood kids and I felt that it was money well spent, even if our take at the door was only forty bucks.

I had vowed to do better in grade nine and for a while I did, but that year I met a girl and started dating regularly and it wasn't long before my savings were gone again.

By the time the year was half over I was borrowing money from my Dad to put new skins on my beat up old second hand drums, in the hopes they would sound good enough for our first school dance. We got hired to play the year-end dance too, so I guess it had paid off, but I was still no closer to having a set of real professional drums

My Dad understood, but there wasn't much he could do. We just barely got by on his salary—not even, 'cause my folks had to take in borders to make ends meet. There was no way that he could come up with fifteen hundred bucks for a set of drums. The best Dad could offer was that he would co-sign a loan for me at the music store so I could buy my drums on time.

"You'll have to make the payments, though. I can't help you, and if you default, the store will take the drums back and you'll be back to square one."

The payments would be about a hundred a month, which was more than I was making at Joe's. I went to him and asked if he could let me come in a few more hours a week, or maybe on weekends, too.

"Listen, I know how important this is for you, but what can I say? I don't need anyone helping on the weekends. I don't really need you most evenings as it is."

We sat at the back booth, like always. Joe had brought us a couple of cokes. He took a sip of his, clunked the heavy bottle down on the table. Condensation dewed the outside of the glass, made rings where the bottle sat.

"To tell you the honest truth, buddy, there are days when that forty bucks I pay you could also go to pay a bill or two around here, you know? If you wasn't such good company, I don't know if I'd have kept employing you as long as I have."

He smiled, but I knew that he was only half joking. I told him about the job Gary had mentioned at the Ritz.

"It's just part time, though I guess I could go full time. I'd have to quit school. My Mom would have a bird."

"What Mom wants stopped mattering when you learned to cross the street. What do *you* want?"

"I want to play in a band."

"I know. It's all you talk about. You know, you are a lucky guy, to have found your passion in life so early. Most people go their whole lives without ever knowing what it is that would make them feel the way you do about your music. Mind you, if it was me, I'd have picked another instrument-maybe something a little easier to carry- harmonica, maybe? Just kidding."

"I know what they'll say—that I should wait until I've finished grade twelve."

"Wait! Wait! What poor advice to give to a young man, especially one that already knows what he is. Listen; the secret to happiness in this life is to follow your bliss. Once you know where your passion lies, the rest is easy! Don't do what I did!"

"You?"

"Ya, don't look so shocked. I was young once and I knew what my destiny was. But I took their advice. I put it off. Waited. And one morning I woke up and there was a German tank parked outside and they were building a wall at the end of our street.

Listen to me, buddy; don't wait for anything. You know what you want—go get it."

"I wouldn't be able to keep working here, you know."

"Sure I know. Why do you think I'm telling you all this? I'm trying to get rid of you." He smiled. "It's Ok. You will come in for a cheeseburger deluxe sometimes."

"Sure. Maybe I'll mop the floor, for old times sake."

"Careful, I might take you up on that. Go now. Tell your friend you'll take the job, before somebody else does." He finished his coke and stood to clear the table. I stood there awkwardly. Joe put a coke bottle back down on the table and wiped his hand on his apron. We shook hands.

"Now go," he said.

I turned and walked to the door of the restaurant, stopped and turned around.

"Joe?"

He stuck his head out of the kitchen door.

"Ya?"

"What was it?"

"What was what?"

"The thing you waited on. Your passion."

"None of your business. See you."

"See you."

And I left.

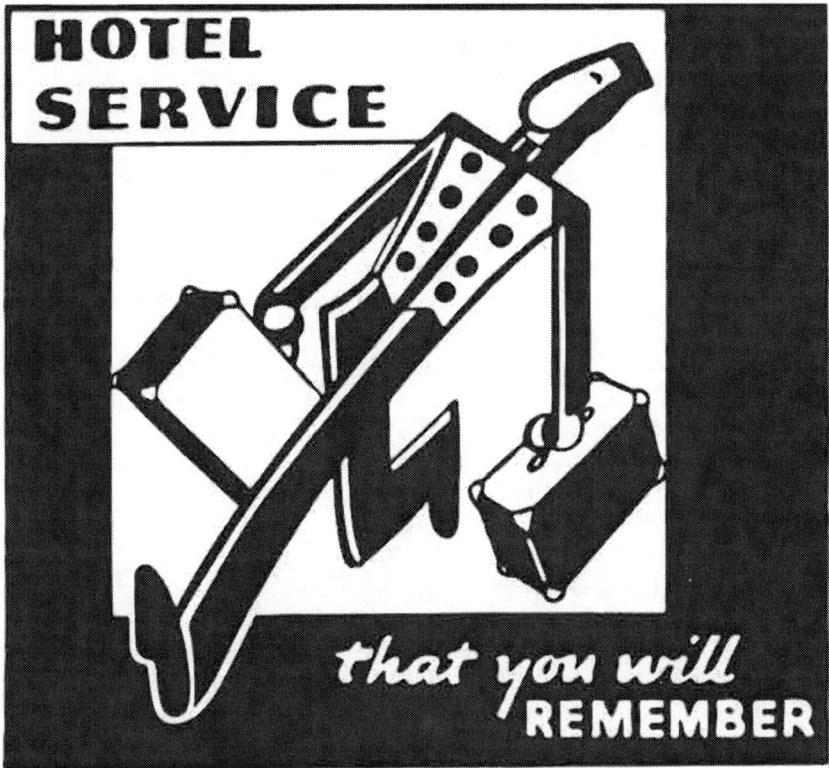

HOTEL SERVICE
that you will REMEMBER

GUNS AND DRUMS

I don't recall whose idea it was to join the Army Cadets. It seems like something Miles would have come up with, but I don't think he was the one who convinced me. I remember thinking about it with mixed feelings.

On the one hand I liked the idea of wearing a uniform and getting free training in the arts of war. There was the added bonus of getting our hands on some real weapons.

On the other hand, the army dress code was very clear on the hair issue. Regulation hair length for men was "not touching the collar or the ears." Sideburns, beards and bangs were not allowed. If I wanted to join up, the hair would have to go.

Of course, the short haired wig was the answer to all that, but that wasn't the clincher.

The clincher was the band. I had been taking drum lessons for over a year at the ABC School of Music, just two doors down from the Wasic Café. It was handy to school and I could go straight from my weekly lesson to my job at the café without losing any time. My parents liked it because it was cheaper than the big music store in the mall.

My instructor there was named Vic and he made no secret of the fact that the drum kit was not his first instrument. I suspected it wasn't his second, either. He was a pretty cool guy and he'd done a good job of giving me the basics of playing the drum kit but as time went on I was increasingly aware that Vic didn't have a lot more to give me. The lessons had started to be repetitive and took me no time to master. It was time to move on.

My brother and Myles were intending to join up at the upcoming intake session over at the old Armory. It was the home to the local branch of the infantry militia and army cadet wing of the hometown battalion.

I talked to my Dad about it and he was the one who pointed out that the Army Cadets would have a band. Dad had played trumpet in the army band during the war, so he'd seen the rigors of military drumming first hand. He told me about it.

"Those military drummers have to be sharp, because everybody is marching to them. If they go off time, the whole parade goes off. They were always practicing, trying to tighten it up. I tell you, you learn to play military drums and the rest will be easy. Where do think all those jazz players got their chops?"

He was proud of the fact that we would all be joining the cadet version of his old regiment.

Plus, the lessons would be free. So when we went to the information night at the armory, I went over to the table with the sign that read "Band."

There were a couple of older guys lounging around behind the table. They seemed surprised to have someone take an interest but, once they figured out that I was serious, they were very helpful. It turned out they would have an opening soon for a snare drum player and someone with prior experience would definitely get consideration.

We signed up; Lyle, Myles and me, and were given a date to return for "orientation," along with a list of stuff we would need to bring with us. Turned out the army supplied our basic uniforms, which were surplus "battle dress" worn by all Commonwealth counties since the thirties, but left certain items up to the cadets to purchase.

The uniform was the same one we'd seen British and Canadian troops wearing on TV, which made us all happy. There was a short tunic and matching slacks in khaki twill that buttoned together at the waist to keep the top from riding up. Suspenders were issued, which alleviated the need to get the sizing accurate.

The list of peripherals that we had to buy wasn't long but it seemed to have been written in another language. I spent some time on the bus home pondering the meaning of the term "puttees" and wondering why we would be expected to bring our own "weights." I wondered aloud what they meant by "cadets will be issued webbing, however, each cadet will be required to supply "webbo" appropriate to same." Myles was a wealth of hand-me-down information.

"Webbing is the belts and shoulder straps you wear with the uniform to hang stuff off. It comes in khaki, so you need to buy this paint, called "webbo" so you can paint it the right color. If you're going to be in the band you're going to need white."

"Putees" turned out to be the long strips of material that they wound around the top of the boots and half way up the leg, originally designed to keep the cooties out in hot countries. Worn by themselves, they ruined the look of the trousers so that's where the "weights" came in.

"Weights" were tubes of cotton about two feet long with little metal ball bearings inside. You tied them loosely around your ankle and pulled them up to your knees until you had your puttees wrapped up and when you shook them down your leg, they pulled the bottoms of your trousers down around the puttees and straightened out the crease in your slacks.

We could have gotten official army weights at the quartermaster store but Myles had a better idea. His brothers in the service had shown him how they made their own weights with nothing more than a pair of used skate laces and some marbles.

This information was treated as classified in order that we could get the money for the weights from our parents anyways and spend it on chocolate malts and hot dogs after parade on Saturday.

We all had been issued one pair of slacks and a tunic, one pair of boots and leggings and two shirts and ties. To be properly in uniform we all were going to have to learn to tie a full Winston knot and to shine up our badges and buckles with "brasso."

The thing I liked best about the uniform was the beret. It was forest green with the regimental badge on the front, worn with the right side pulled down. I thought it gave the uniform a jaunty touch of informality but it did present a problem for me, because I had to wear it over my short haired wig.

The beret had an elastic cord around the rim, which kept it firmly in place against the jolting rigors of marching, providing you had the right size. Mine seemed to fit fine but with the berets' elastic putting more tension on the wig, its tendency to ride up on my skull increased with the amount that I sweated. It looked all right at home in the mirror. I just prayed for cool days on the parade ground.

One day after school, we all went down to buy our stuff at the SOS store. It was a favorite haunt but I hadn't been there for a while and I'd forgotten what a wonderful place it was.

Tables overflowing with surplus army gear filled the floor space, while the walls hung heavy with more arcane military stuff. Rubber gas masks with flexible hose linking them to their charcoal canisters vied for room with mess kits and canteens. Empty ammunition boxes in various calibers were stacked beside folding "entrenching tools" (army talk for shovels) and helmets from both sides of conflicts back to the Boer War.

There were Ghurka knives with their cruel curving blades and three-foot bayonets from the trenches of Belgium but my favorite was the standard infantry bayonet of the WW1 British Army.

They were little swords about 18" long with hardwood handles and a deep blood gutter along the top of the blade. They rang musically if struck against one another, which was a sure indication of good steel. Some even came with the original scabbard, complete with the big brass button for mounting it onto one's belt. You only had to feel the weight of one to understand why our webbing belts came with shoulder straps.

We could have spent hours in there and typically did, until the owner got tired of us and told us to buy something or scoot.

He was a kind of rough looking guy with a gimpy leg that he said he'd gotten in Korea from artillery shrapnel. The other guy who worked there said that was bull. He told us that the boss had been born with the bad leg and had never been able to get into the services because of it.

That seemed to make sense and was certainly more believable than half of the crazy war stories the owner told us when we went in. We listened politely and said 'wow' in all the right places, knowing that if we did, he'd let us stay longer, even though none of us ever bought anything.

His surprise was noticeable when all three of us actually purchased a can of webbo.

"Did you guys join up, or something?"

"Yep. Army cadets. First parade on Saturday." Lyle answered.

"Good for you. That ought to keep you guys off the streets, eh?"

We exchanged looks. We hadn't thought of that.

Around about this time something happened that made me reconsider my obsession with guns and stuff. Myles and me had been hanging around the local Catholic school hoping to get to know some of the cute girls that went there. We got to know some of the guys, too.

One of the cooler guys there was Gerard Fulton, tall and good-looking with a reputation of being pretty tough, as well. His girlfriend Connie was one of the hottest girls in the neighborhood and naturally had two or three friends that were also hot. Gerard lived close to the school and his parents were almost never home, so we'd gotten into the habit of going over to his place after school.

The house had an unfinished basement, but they had kind of a living room down there with an old sofa and a couple of chairs. The other side of the basement was Gerard's dads' place where he kept all his guns and hunting stuff. We weren't supposed to touch any of his stuff, but of course we did.

This one day, we're all down there waiting for Gerard to rustle up some snacks when Myles ambles over to the other side of the room and picks up the 12 gauge shotgun that's lying there on the table. He takes hold of the slide and racks the action.

"Wow, did you break it?" asks one of the girls.

"No, no-that's the way you load it. Here, I'll show you." Myles says and, picking up a shotgun shell that's lying there, he slides it into the slot.

"Now it's in the gun, but it's not in the chamber until you rack it. Like this." He repeats the sliding action.

"Then if you want to unload it, you rack it again."

Once more he works the action, causing the shell to eject from the chamber and catching it neatly in his hand.

"Can I try?" asks the girl.

"Sure." Myles slides the shell back into the gun and hands the weapon to the girl, who holds it clumsily.

"Here, let me show you how," says Myles. He moves around behind the girl and puts his arms around her to help her get the grip right.

"Smooth move, buddy." I'm thinking.

Just then Gerard comes down the stairs with a platter of chips and pop. He sees the shotgun and immediately grabs it from Myles.

"Hey, man—what the hell? You guys know we can't touch the old man's stuff. You want to get me grounded for life?"

"Hey, careful man—it's got a shell in it."

"Ya, sure. My old man keeps all the ammo locked up. You think I'd fall for that?"

"No, really, Gerard. There was a shell on the table. I just put it in the slot."

Gerard is grinning and laughing, certain that Myles is putting him on, trying to get him to take the warning seriously so he can get a laugh on him. He racks the action.

"Don't fuck around, man," says Myles, backing away nervously, "I'm not joking."

Everyone else starts to try to convince Gerard the gun is loaded, which convinces him more that we are all in on the joke. He points the gun at Myles' chest. His finger is on the trigger. A chorus of panicked warnings from all of us only makes Gerard's grin grow wider.

The barrel of the shotgun swings around the room, making us scatter like startled minnows in a stone-dropped pond. Ever the pragmatist, Myles dives behind the furnace.

"You guys think it's loaded? Maybe we have to test it. Who wants to be the test dummy?"

The gun barrel points at one after another of us, pausing on each cringing target before coming to rest on me. The hole in the end looks huge. It seems to grow until it encompasses the whole of my vision.

"What about you, Ward? You want to be the test dummy?"

My knees are turning to water. I can see that Gerard is sure the thing's not loaded. Flop sweat pours down my face as I frantically try to think of something to say that won't just make him try to prove it. He wiggles his eyebrows up and down at me and pulls the trigger.

Nothing happens. Gerard looks at the gun, lowering the barrel.

"Shit, the safety's still on, anyways..."

BLAM!

The sound of the 12-gauge going off in the cement confines of the basement is deafening. A cloud of acrid blue smoke envelops both Gerard and me for a few seconds. Neither of us moves as it dissipates, revealing us to each other again. The color has drained completely from Gerard's face as I imagine it must have from my own. Someone is crying.

"Gerard?" comes a tiny, frightened voice from the upstairs, "Is everything all right?"

The sound of his mother's voice shakes Gerard out of his shock. He racks the gun again and catches the empty shell as it ejects. Putting it in his pocket, he replaces the shotgun on the table.

"It's OK, mom," he shouts, "I dropped a sheet of plywood. I'll clean it up."

Myles emerges from behind the furnace, staring at the spot where the blast hit the concrete floor. There's a puddle of molten lead embedded into the floor like a tiny meteorite had landed there. Smaller blobs describe the force with which random shot had bounced in a spreading pattern outward from the initial impact.

Gerard moves quickly to open all the windows and get a fan going to clear the smoke. The two schoolgirls are hugging each other, in tears.

"Gerard, you are such an asshole..." Connie begins.

"Not now. Take these two home, will you? I have to re-arrange the furniture."

"We can give you a hand."

"No, you guys better just clear out. I'll take care of it. I'll see you later."

Myles and I walked home from Gerard's place together.

"Were you scared?"

"What do you think?"

"Man, I thought I was going to crap my pants when he pointed that thing at me."

"Me too. But then, just before he pulled the trigger, there was this second when I wasn't afraid anymore."

"You mean you knew about the safety?"

"No, before that. I was sure he was going to shoot me. I knew I was going to die. And just for a split second, I wasn't afraid."

"Weird, man. You going to tell your folks?"

"No way! I'd be grounded for a month. You can't tell either-OK?"

"I guess. It's going to be all over school tomorrow, though."

"Yeah. Oh, well—just so long as the parents don't hear about it."

Something changed between Myles and I after that. I didn't share his love of guns and stuff anymore. I didn't care if I ever saw another gun after that, which was just as well because it was a long time before we got to handle any guns at Army cadets.

First we had to learn how to march.

We showed up as ordered in our full uniforms with our boots polished and our brass shining. There were about twenty of us, milling about on the parade square including a couple of guys from our school we hadn't expected. Myles and I were goofing around with Rodney Waddington when a voice bellowed at us to line up.

We did our best to form a straggly line across the tarmac and soon became aware that the voice belonged to a guy about twenty, wearing the rank of corporal. He informed us that we didn't know how to line up properly because we were all a bunch of worthless worms.

Over the course of next half hour the corporal, whose name was Dunn, proceeded to show us how to form ranks and space ourselves out correctly by extending our arms out to our sides, all the while berating us for being hopelessly ignorant and too stupid to learn.

The secrets of marching in time and stopping together, of turning in rank without losing formation and the all important three-count which is basic to the parade of all commonwealth armies were revealed to us, along with information regarding our ancestors and upbringing of which we had not previously been aware.

The corporal wasted no amount of hyperbole in his attempt to have us understand our lowly standing in the world, occasionally singling out an individual for special abuse. We all took it in stride, so to speak, until he gave Rodney Waddington a particularly rough tongue-lashing.

Now, it was a well-known fact at school that Waddington was a resourceful and talented lad. The first time I met him, Myles and I were standing on the grassy lawn of our Jr. High school chatting with Judy Boyle. We couldn't help it.

Judy was regarded as the knockdown, drag-'em-out, no-holds-barred foxiest chick in the school and that day she had worn her new micro-skirt to school. It was hemmed about 11 ½" above her shapely knees and left little to the imagination, but our thirteen-year-old fantasies were making the most of it. We were kidding ourselves that Judy hadn't noticed us ogling her legs, when Rod Waddington joined us.

Rod was big for his age and had an easy grace about his movements. Loping sanguinely over, he hopped the little steel fence between us and seemed about to say hello when suddenly his eyes rolled up into his head and he performed a kind of rude pirouette before collapsing on his back at our feet.

He hit the turf hard enough to bounce a bit but, curiously, his eyes stayed wide open. I thought he must have been having some kind of fit, until I saw him look over at me and wink. Judy saw it too and realized that Rod had a perfect view right up her skirt. She screamed and covered herself, then wound up and kicked him hard in the solar plexus. I felt the impact from five feet away.

After Judy left, we waited until Rod started breathing again and helped him up.

"Geeze, man; she really put the boots to you." Myles observed.

"It was worth it," replied Rod, between gasps.

Even if we doubted his methods, we had to admire his tenacity.

Rod was one of those rare and gifted individuals who, for reasons unknown, could swallow air almost endlessly and use it to produce burps at will.

Not only did he have the means to accomplish this, he'd honed it to a fine art. Like someone who is born with a pleasant sounding singing voice and who then takes the time and puts in the effort to learn how use the instrument skillfully, Rod was a virtuoso.

He could let out low rumbling basso-profundo burps that made neighboring dogs sit up and look around and seemed to go on for minutes. He had learned to form his burps into speech sounds at an early age and could do the entire alphabet uninterrupted on request.

Waddington had developed such a level of performance in the art of burp-speech that he no longer bothered to display his skill in public. Such mere parlor tricks, while handy for entertaining the younger set, were really beneath the true artist.

But Rod was not a person to rest on his laurels.

Always seeking new challenges, he'd come upon a training manual in a joke shop on the little-known science of throwing one's voice.

We'll never know how many hours of grueling practice he went through to learn how to speak from one area of a room and have the sound seem to emanate from another place. This alone would have satisfied a less ambitious performer, but not Rod. In a flash of genius, he realized the potential of combining the two skills into an entirely new discipline.

Back into the basement he went and did not come out to perform again until he had successfully combined the art of burp-speech with that of voice throwing so seamlessly that those of us who witnessed him doing it could hardly describe the experience. There weren't a lot of us. Rod knew that he'd come up with something very special and that nothing would devalue it faster than over-exposure.

He once reduced a substitute gym teacher to tears. The poor man was fresh over from Sweden and his grasp of the language was tenuous at best. This became obvious when he first took our grade seven class out to the soccer field and then decided to take attendance.

When he asked Jim Gracey what his name was, Jim answered with a straight face.

"Fuck," he said.

"Fuck vat?" the hapless victim enquired. Jim knew a good thing when he saw one.

"Yomamma," he replied.

The teacher bent over his clipboard, dutifully recording the information on his attendance form. As he went down the row asking everyone's names, we all tried to outdo Jim's creativity with equally profane and increasingly bizarre aliases of our own. We couldn't believe our luck.

It hardly seemed possible that this guy could have learned English without coming across at least one or two profanities. We did our best to try them all out. It took about ten minutes for him to fill the form with an impressive selection of the worst language a class of grade seven city kids could think of, looking hard into our faces in an earnest attempt to memorize the names of his charges.

He really should have twigged when we were choosing sides for a game of shirts vs. skins and the two captains had to resort to pointing when they couldn't remember who had given what blasphemy as his name.

As the game got underway and the sub began to yell instructions and words of encouragement from the sidelines, things just got too good.

"Fuck! Move up in your zone. Mudddafucka; cover your area. Now you go on defense Sonobitch. When the ball turns over, you need to get back to your defensive zone, Twatface. Vat's so funny, you guys?"

It went on for some minutes before the girls' Phys. Ed. Teacher overheard what was going on from the other side of the field and came to his rescue. She took the clipboard and studied it for a second, her ears turning deeper and deeper scarlet as she read.

"OK, you guys. Let's see how clever you think this is after 30 laps around the field. That's right, everyone. There will be written apologies from you all before the end of the day."

We wrote our apologies and the poor guy took a moment before our next gym class to congratulate us on having put one over on him and assure us that he harbored no hard feelings.

Not so Waddington, however. An artist of Rod's stature had his pride. *Nobody* made *him* run 30 laps. He would have his revenge.

The soccer field presented a major challenge to Rod's burp-speech throwing techniques but he was up for it and motivated by the still-sore muscles in his legs. He mounted a psychological attack on the sub, designed to confuse and bewilder.

Rod began with subtlety, using the bass voice/burp to its best advantage. In the open air, amid all the ambient street noises, it was difficult to tell if there actually was a sound at all. It was like the rumbling of a distant thunderstorm.

"Motherfucker." The word seemed to emanate from the very air itself. The teacher glanced about himself, puzzlement on his face.

Rod waited a good five minutes before resuming. He knew the gym class was forty minutes long. He was in no rush.

"Cocksucker." Came the voice—but from where? Or was it just the truck rumbling by on the adjacent road? Minutes passed. Then...

"Sonofabitch." This time Rod made it sound like the voice had come from directly behind the teacher, who whirled about to find no one within twenty feet of him. He scratched his head and peered at us, rushing past with the ball. A dark suspicion had begun to form in his mind.

Rod left him in peace for almost ten minutes this time, playing the unfortunate innocent like a trout in a stream. When he went back to work, he threw subtlety to the wind. The burp/voice erupted with all the volume and force Waddington could deliver, aimed to originate from the clipboard in the teachers' hands.

"FUCK!"

"SCHEISE!" Rod's victim yelled, throwing the board to the ground. He stared at it, then at the class, all continuing to play like nothing had occurred. His eyes narrowed. He attempted a smile but it didn't take. He was visibly shaken.

Rod returned to a more measured approach, mixing his strategy for maximum effect. This time the sound seemed to waft on the breeze from no particular source, at all.

"Aaashole…"

The substitute decided he would try to not react. He made a show of concentrating on the game. Rod brought out the heavy artillery. He added a personal touch by bringing the voice out of the innocent mouth of Manly Jones, who happened to be standing close to the teacher at the time.

Manly was a popular victim of all the boys and a frequent subject of Rod's performances who, besides having the worst name in the universe, was the son of the grade nine math teacher and the arts teacher and therefore pretty much doomed. God only knows what they were thinking, having him enrolled in the same school they both worked in.

"Baglicker." Manly seemed to say, then clapped his hand over his mouth in horror. The two of them stared at each other. It was too much for Myles, who collapsed on the turf in laughter.

Then it was his turn to be Rod's instrument.

"Eat my shorts!"

Waddington blended his burp/voice so skillfully into Myles laughter that even Myles thought he'd actually said the words somehow.

The sub had had enough. He threw the clipboard to the ground again, this time in pure frustration.

"You boys!" he shouted, his voice breaking with emotion, "You are cruel and nasty. I have only come here to be mit you in good spirit but you—you have no pride to act dis vay. You should be all ashamed of yourselves! Gym class is over. Go to showers and I hope you drown dere, you spawn off the devil."

Next gym class we had an older man from the high school who took no prisoners.

Having both witnessed the gym incident first hand, Myles and I considered ourselves members of the privileged few and never dreamed we might be able to see Rod in action again. We couldn't believe our luck, standing at attention with the other cadets on the parade square when Waddington decided to go to work on the corporal for dressing him down in front us.

Once a reasonable amount of time had passed after Corporal Dunn's verbal assault on him, Rod started his response. He began again with the bass burp/voice, so low as to be almost indiscernible.

"Duuunnn…"

But the corporal was no innocent immigrant. His understanding of the psychology of his charges was complete. He issued the halt command and walked around to the front of our ranks.

"Who the fuck just made that noise?" he demanded.

There was no answer. We stared stonily ahead.

"All right. I'm going to let that one slide. Any repeat of that behavior is going to result in some serious disciplinary action. Platoon-right...Face! March!"

Almost immediately, Waddington pursued his case.

"Duuuunnn..."

"Right! That's it. Platoon, fall out and give me twenty laps around the parade square. We'll keep that up until someone confesses to producing those disgusting sounds. On the double!"

For the next half hour, Corporal Dunn mercilessly ran the whole platoon around the square while Rod continued to pepper the air with burp/speech. Dunn knew he would find out who the culprit was sooner or later and in the meanwhile he carried on conversing with his unseen opponent.

"OK, wise-ass. Go ahead and enjoy yourself. I'll tell you what; you and me are going to have some good times once you get turned in by one of your buddies. You are going to wish you'd never bothered to join up."

The threats sounded real to me but Waddington wasn't cowed. He kept up his assault, although the strength of his delivery seemed to be flagging. We were all getting tired and some of the less fit were in real distress.

Some of the others did reach the end of their ability and lay about the ground, unable to take another step. One guy developed a cramp in his leg and limped off to the infirmary. Another one abruptly began projectile vomiting into the rose bushes that bordered the square. Dunn did not waiver.

I was hanging in, out of breath but not in real discomfort except for the feeling that both of my homemade puttee weights had come undone, freeing all the marbles inside to bounce about inside my trouser leg as I ran.

There were only three of us that knew Waddington's identity; Myles, myself and my brother Lyle. None of us would willingly expose him, least of all Myles and I who would then have to avoid running into him at school for the rest of the term. I could tell Lyle was holding out on general principles but we were all reaching the limit of our pain thresholds. It seemed only a matter of time before one of us caved and gave him up.

Dunn began alternating the running with pushups, either in an attempt to up the pressure on us or to prolong the torture. The result for me was that one of my puttees started to work it's way free of the winding and unravel, while the sweat was making my short-haired wig slip up to the top of my head. I was going to lose one or both at any second.

Then, Waddington made a mistake. He must have been so tired he wasn't thinking straight. When he tried to throw another voice/burp rendition of the corporals' name he forgot to throw his voice at all. The sound came directly from his mouth just as he was staggering past the corporal, no more than three feet away.

"Platoon-Halt!"

It was the final straw for my loose puttee. When I came to a halt and stomped my right foot down, it let go completely, releasing my pant leg from it's confines and allowing the marbles to go cascading noisily across the tarmac. Dunn completely ignored it, so intent was he on finally confronting his tormentor.

The Corporal advanced on Rod like a predatory cat who'd finally cornered his helpless prey. He placed himself directly in front of him with his nose about an inch away from Rod's. They were about the same height, so Dunn was able to peer threateningly out from under the brim of his cap.

"So; cadet Waddington isn't it?"

"Yup."

"You mean 'yes Corporal,' don't you?"

"Uh...OK, yes corporal."

"What do you mean by disrupting my parade like this?"

"Um...nothing, corporal."

"Nothing. You mean nothing by it. You just decided it would be fun to waste everyone's time when we could be learning to march like soldiers. Is that it?"

"Pretty much, corporal."

"You know, there isn't any room for jackasses like you in the cadets, Waddington. Some of these cadets want to take the thing seriously and a few mean to go on to a career in the regular Army. Why should they have to put up with you wasting their time? Why should they have been subjected to this nonsense, eh?"

"Don't know, corporal."

"Don't know. Well, know this, Waddington. After today, if you stay on here you are not going to be enjoying your time in the cadets. You are going to have extra duties every meeting, which will start with cleaning the toilets in the armory and get steadily more unpleasant from there, do I make myself clear?"

"Yes, corporal."

"So why don't you do yourself a favor and just march over to the quartermaster and return those items of uniform that the regiment was so good to have loaned you, and just piss off home. On second thought, don't bother to march. Marching is what soldiers do. We both know that you'll never be a soldier, now don't we?"

"Whatever you say, Corporal."

"Yes, well—that's what I say. What do you say? No sense in prolonging the agony, is there? Do the right thing and bugger off home to mommy so these men can get on with the business of becoming soldiers, all right?"

"All right."

"Good boy. The rest of you are dismissed. See you next week."

As he left the parade square, Corporal Dunn walked past me and spoke in a quiet voice, just for me to hear.

"Cadet Ward."

"Yes, Corporal?"

"You seem to have lost your marbles."

"Yes, Corporal."

That was the end of Rod Waddington's military career, much to the benefit of both himself and the army, I suspect. I kept going weekly, slowly absorbing all the moribund little details of parade. We learned to salute in the Canadian fashion, which I was surprised to learn was different from either the British salute or the American.

I was waiting for word from the band that I had been picked for the snare-drum spot but so far nothing.

The day was fast approaching when we would finally get our hands on some military weapons. I found myself looking forward to it in spite of the incident in Gerard's basement.

When it arrived, we were marched into the cavernous expanse of the armory and over to a door in the corner. All the doors in the armory were impressively thick and solid, made out of heavy oak. Each had a sign over it engraved in a solid brass plaque. This one said "Small Arms Ordinance."

We waited in single file until the Sergeant Major came to unlock the big padlock on the rifle racks and the Corporal began handing out the firearms one at a time, reading out the serial number of each for the Sergeant to record beside our names.

"The FNA1C2 is a Belgian made, gas powered, semi-automatic rifle chambered in standard NATO 7.26mm. It has a ten-round magazine and a carrying handle at the point of balance and is capable of being altered to fire full automatic in the FNA1C1 designation, which is mounted with a collapsible bipod on the front stock. It was the standard issue infantry rifle for all NATO troops from 1955 to the present mainly because, to use the vernacular, it is a sweet shooter."

We had been drilled on the characteristics and proper handling of the weapon in class but this was the first time we were allowed to actually touch one. We were higher than kites, knowing that if we handled the rifles responsibly this time, we might be taken downstairs to the firing range and get a chance to fire them regularly, so we tried our best to contain ourselves even though, inside, we were giggling like schoolgirls.

"The plan is for us to clean the rifles this first time out and then hand them back in to the Sergeant. We have all witnessed the demonstration given by the Corporal," shouted the Sergeant.

It seemed like a simple task.

"The first thing to do is to neutralize the gas pressure that is stored in a cylinder in the front stock. This requires opening the bleeder valve on the end of the stock, which has to be done carefully so as not allow all the gas to escape at once.

The valve knob is attached to a steel rod that runs the length of the cylinder and is spring loaded, as well. If the valve is opened too fast, the out-rushing gas could blow the rod out the end of the rifle with lethal force, so the procedure is to hold the rifle between one's bent knees with the barrel pointed up and away at a 60 degree angle."

We formed into a circle, facing outward so that no one was in front of another as we all waited for the order to loosen the valve. When it came, the silence was unbroken as everyone concentrated on un-screwing the valve knob as slowly as possible. We were supposed to hear a tiny "click," which told us we were within a quarter turn of releasing the pressure. I never heard it.

To this day, I swear I turned that knob as slowly as I could. I could hear others finding their "click" and proceeding to turn until the area was full of the gentle hissing of escaping gas. I kept going, listening for that click and wondering to myself why it was taking so long, when suddenly my rifle gave out a "POW" like the sound of a pellet gun and the valve let go.

The sound got the attention of everyone in the platoon and we all watched together as the valve stem from my FN sailed up and up towards the thirty-foot ceiling of the armory, turning a lazy about-face in mid journey so that the pointy end was first when it hit the oaken roof beam with solid "Thunk."

There was a second of appreciative silence before the platoon cracked up.

"Nice shooting, Ward," said the Corporal.

That week I received my posting to the band and I've never touched another military weapon since.

Thirty years later, when I learned they were going to tear the venerable old building down to make way for some fashionable new condos and a Starbucks, I took a lunch break to drive over and found the door open to the demo crew.

There it was, my valve stem, hanging from the roof beam, as it had been that day in 1970, where I suspect it stayed to the very end.

THE HOTEL

My first day of work at the Ritz, I was up at six, too excited to sleep. I had a quick breakfast of fruit and toast and set about getting ready.

The new black slacks I'd bought looked OK until I put on my cheap brown loafers and saw how they clashed. Note to self; first payday, buy black shoes.

The white shirt was left over from my grade nine graduation. It fit all right, but when it came to putting on the shorthaired wig, I just couldn't bring myself to do it.

I stood there looking at myself in the mirror, holding the wig in my hand and thinking dark thoughts.

"Come on, man. Think about a new set of Ludwigs, just out of the box." I told myself.

That did it.

Catching the bus with my wig on was an educational experience. The normally surly look from the driver was replaced with a big smile and the offer of a transfer pass. Even the grouchy old guy who always seemed to be on when I got on gave me a friendly nod as I sat down.

I got off across the street from the hotel and looked over at the place while I waited for the crossing light. I must have walked past the doors a hundred times and not taken notice of it. Viewed with the knowledge that I'd be working there, it looked entirely different to me. I was nervous and excited as I crossed the avenue.

The lobby was busy. People were coming and going through the different exits and entrances. Maids were trundling trolleys loaded with rags and towels, bottles of cleaning fluid and ashtrays. The smoke shop man was cleaning his windows industriously. There was a general air of hustle and bustle.

I went over to the front desk. A woman was behind the desk, calmly dealing with a small crowd of customers who were apparently not familiar with the idea of waiting their turn. She was in her mid forties, I guessed, with red hair piled up in a beehive and icy blue eyes framed by cat's-eye glasses.

As she juggled conflicting priorities, keeping mental track of who wanted what, occasionally reprimanding the most impatient while insisting that the shy ones state their needs in turn, it was clear she'd been doing this a long time. I was so impressed that I failed to notice when my turn came.

"What can I do for you, kid?" she asked in a nasal monotone.

" Oh! Uh, I'm here for the bellhop's job, uh, that is-I've already been hired, I think, so I'm here to start."

"You Rick?"

"Yes, ma'am."

"I'm Betty. You're late. Next time don't wait in line. Gary is upstairs. When he comes down he's going to show you around. Have a seat. I don't suppose you know how to operate a switchboard, do you?"

"No, ma'am, I don't. Sorry." I sat where she had indicated, in front of the confusing looking maze of wires and circuitry.

" 'Sawright, just don't touch anything, then."

Betty busied herself sorting all the paperwork created by the flurry of activity, leaving me to examine the switchboard. It was built into a structure like a desk with an instrument panel on top of it, made of some black material, the same stuff the old phones were made of; Bakelite, I think it was called.

Evenly spaced rows of stereo input jacks covered the face, while corresponding plug-in jacks adorned the horizontal front of it. I was familiar with these. They were the same as the ones used to plug an electric guitar into an amplifier. Each one sat upright in a little socket, ready to be pulled out and plugged into the right hole. I theorized that the cord would be spring loaded and, making sure Betty had her back turned, I tried one. Bingo.

On the right side of all this was a rotary dial, housed in a little formed hemisphere of the same black material. There was a pair of antique-looking headphones hanging on the side. The thing looked ancient. The whole other side of it was scorched and half melted looking, bubbled in spots.

When it looked like Betty was free for a moment, I asked her.

"Somebody have a fire?"

"Whaat?" She tore herself away from a magazine she'd picked up and took her cigarette from her lips. I indicated the burn marks.

"Looks like someone had a fire."

"Oh, that. Yeah, there was fire, all right. About fifty years ago."

"Fifty years?"

"Hyup." She took a drag off her smoke and inhaled the word with the smoke. She went on, blowing smoke out her nose as she spoke. "Nineteen twenty, I think it was. They had just converted the place over to a hotel from a boarding house. Not near as fancy as it is now. Anyway, the city was putting in natural gas lines out in the alley, and some guy left a pipe open, or something."

Betty took a quick glance around the lobby to see if anyone was headed to the desk. Satisfied that she wouldn't be interrupted, she took another drag and plucked a flake of tobacco from her tongue before she went on.

"Somebody sent the bellman down to the basement for something and, while he was down there, he heard a funny hissing sound. 'Course, back then, they hadn't figured out that natural gas had no smell. Hadn't started adding the smell so's people would know if there was a leak."

"There was a leak?"

"Hyup. But the poor sap had no way of knowing that. All he knew was that something was hissing down there in the dark, so he does what anybody would have done back then."

She paused again, this time to grind her cigarette out in the big cut-glass ashtray. She selected another smoke from the package and placed it between her lips. Taking the lighter from the top of the cigarette package, she flicked it open and struck a flame.

"He lit a match?"

"You got it, kid." Big drag from her smoke, exhaling with her words, "He lit a match."

"Jeez...what happened?"

"What do you think happened?"

"He blew the place up?"

"Hyup. Well, half the place, anyhow. The rest was on fire from the explosion and burned to the ground, they say. Funny thing is, the guy—the bellhop—was OK. Not a scratch on him, although I guess he never heard too well after. He was the one that helped the manager haul the burning switchboard out of the building. After that, they rebuilt the place."

"The way it is now?"

"Pretty much, I guess. And you know what? They hired him back on. The bellhop. I heard he worked another twenty-five years in the hotel."

"Wow. I hope nothing like that happens to me."

"Blowin' the place up, or working here for twenty five years?"

I was still working on an answer when Betty spied a man coming across the lobby with a suitcase and started clearing things up in front of her, swiping ashes into the ashtray and giving her beehive a plump.

"Well, look on the bright side, kid. As long as you don't burn the place down, you're doin' all right."

I was still thinking about that when I saw Gary coming down the stairs. He was wearing his red vest and carrying a big metal hoop with at least a dozen keys threaded onto it. They jangled as he came across the lobby.

"This guy giving you any trouble, Betty?"

"Not so far," she replied dryly, "Why don't you take Mr. Hasting's bags up to 324. Maybe Rick wants to go with you and see how the pro's do it."

She skidded the room key across the desk to Gary and handed the guest some paperwork.

"There you go, Mr. Hasting, the bellmen will see you to your room."

Mr. Hasting, a middle-aged guy in a tan leisure suit, took his receipt and folded it up. He turned to Gary, who was already picking up his suitcase.

"Is there any more luggage in your car, sir?"

"Nope, that's it. I took a cab from the airport."

"I bet he charged you five dollars," said Gary, heading towards the elevator. He gave me a nod. I hurried ahead and punched the 'up' button.

"Five fifty," said Mr. Hasting.

"Let me know when you're checking out and I'll get you a seat on the shuttle from the travel agency next door. Two bucks, no tip allowed."

"Fine! Thanks a lot."

"You're welcome. Just call down to the desk when you've confirmed your reservation with the airlines. Ask for Gary."

"Will do."

The elevator arrived. Picking up the suitcase, Gary addressed me.

"First rule; Elevator up, stairs down."

"Got it."

"First day on the job, son?" Mr. Hasting asked amiably.

"Yes sir."

"Well you watch this guy close," he nodded at Gary, "He knows his stuff."

"Yes sir."

We stopped on the third floor and the elevator door opened.

"One through twenty on the left, twenty two to thirty on the right. Which way?" Gary said.

It took me a few seconds to realize that I was being quizzed.

"Umm, 324, so...right. Right?"

"Right on." Gary turned down the hallway. "I just wanted to see if you remembered the room number."

He led the way around the corner, down the wide corridor. Opening the door to 324, he stood back and allowed Mr. Hasting in first, then plunked the suitcase on the floor of the little closet and swept past to the window where he opened the curtains with a flourish.

"Here you are, sir. The air conditioning controls are just here, under the panel. All the way left for cold air, all the way right for heat. The TV is equipped with remote control, which you'll find here in the bedside table, along with our room service menu. Room service is available from seven a.m. until nine o'clock p.m. and the coffee shop off the lobby is open until ten. Just pick up the phone to reach the switchboard at the front desk. It's manned twenty four hours a day, so just let them know if you need an outside line, or to reach the operator. I hope your stay will be a pleasant one, and if there is anything we can do to make you more comfortable, please don't hesitate to ask."

He said it all briskly, but not so fast that it sounded rushed, just business-like and confident. I was impressed. What happened next impressed me even more. Gary waited until Mr. Hastings started to answer.

"No, that will be all, thanks," Mr. Hasting said, and put his hand in his pocket.

And just as he finished, as Gary moved past him, the hand came out of the pocket and passed a bill off to Gary's hand. There was no hesitation on either part. The thing was done so smoothly you'd think it had been choreographed.

The bill disappeared into Gary's pocket as quickly as it had been produced. Gary winked at me on his way past and I followed him back out into the hall.

"That," he said, as we proceeded to the stairs, "is how you get a tip."

I'd known that tips were an important part of the job, but I hadn't imagined there was a technique involved.

" Wow. You made it look so easy."

"It is easy with a guy like that. Nothin' to it."

"What do you mean?"

"Mr. Hasting has been around; stayed in hotels lots, I bet. You get so you can spot the type. It's mainly about how comfortable a guest is."

"Comfortable, so he knows how it's done?"

"More like he knows *that* it's done. There're still a lot of people who don't think they need to tip. You learn to spot them, too."

"I guess that could get awkward. How do you know?"

"They usually want to carry their own bags up. That way, they don't feel like they owe you anything."

" So, what; you just don't put your hand out, or...?"

"Naw. Don't sell yourself short, man. Pretty rare to find somebody that won't give you *something* if your hand is out. It's expected."

"I don't know. I guess...it would feel like I was *begging*, or something."

We were half way down the stairs to the lobby. Gary stopped, turned around to look at me.

"Look, it ain't like that, man. This job pays minimum wage. If you work full shifts that gives you a hundred and ten bucks a week. Think you can live on that?"

"No, I guess not."

"Damn right, you can't. So you need to make the tips count. We're lucky here; we don't have to pool our tips like some places. You learn how to pull good tips out of guests, you can double your income."

"Double? A hundred a week in tips?"

"Not right at first, of course. You gotta learn the ropes. But after a while... look; you're on days, right?"

"Right. So?"

"So, weekdays, between five and fifteen people check in to the hotel. Weekends more. Two bucks being the going rate, even if you only average that much per, that's between ten and thirty bucks a day just in check ins alone."

"Ok, but I don't get all the check-ins."

"Pay attention. You came in late today. Tomorrow you start at six."

"Six?"

"Oh, yeah. You don't want to miss the breakfast room service. Usually there's a half-dozen trays go up between six thirty and nine, average tip on room service is five bucks."

"Five bucks? Right on!"

"Right on, indeed. Of course, you gotta hustle. Nobody tips that well for cold eggs. Once you get that going, it's another thirty, forty bucks a day. Then there's check out time, starts around ten."

"Sounds like you keep pretty busy."

Gary started down the stairs again.

"Idle hands are the devils' workshop, man. You'll be rich in no time. C'mon, I'll introduce you to Mel."

Mel turned out to be the guy at the smoke shop in the lobby. He was there, putting packages of cigarettes away on a shelf when Gary and I entered the shop.

"Hello, Gary," he said, without turning around, "who's that with you?"

"Hey, Mel. This is our new bellman, Rick. Rick, meet Mel; the only guy who really knows what's going on in this zoo."

"Oh, I wouldn't go so far as to say *that*," Mel said. He stopped what he'd been doing and turned around. Smiling in my general direction, he stuck out his hand. I hurried to take it, a bit surprised.

"Pleased to meet you, Rick. Say, that's a pretty good grip you've got. Calluses, too. Let's see..." he held on to my hand for a few seconds and I could feel his hand moving in mine, measuring, gauging. He let go just as I was starting to feel uncomfortable and looked at the ceiling thoughtfully.

"Drummer?"

"Right the first time." Gary said.

"Hah! I knew it. You play the drums professionally, Rick?"

"Hold the phone! You knew I play drums just by feeling my calluses?"

"You'd be surprised what you can learn from people's hands, Rick."

"Come on," I said to Gary, "You must have told him."

"Nope."

"It isn't magic. It's just paying attention."

"Far out."

"Hi Mel!" a feminine voice from behind us. "Hi, Gary-who's your friend?"

I turned to see a lovely young woman approach the counter. She was dressed in a pair of silver lame short-shorts and a tight fitting halter-top that left her midriff and shoulders bare. Her dusky blond hair was piled up in a sixties style with wisps let down on the sides. Heavy makeup failed to conceal the fact that she was very pretty.

"Hey, Carol. This Rick, the new bellman."

"Hi, I'm Carol."

"Hi."

"Pack of DuMaurier, Mel. Thanks. So, are they treating you OK so far, Rick?"

"Sure. I guess."

" You always this chatty, or you don't like girls?"

"Rick's just speechless after Mel guessed that he plays drums just by shaking his hand."

"Hah! Still doin' them parlor tricks, Mel?"

"They're not tricks, it's just…"

"Paying attention, I know. So, you're a drummer, eh?"

"Yeah."

"That's so cool. I love the drums. Thanks, Mel. Maybe I'll get to hear you play sometime?"

"Sure, that'd be cool."

"Let me know when you're playing downtown. See ya. See ya, Gary. See ya, Mel."

"See ya."

"See ya."

Gary and I watched her walk away, across the lobby to the lounge door, in mute admiration.

"What a babe."

"And she loves drummers. That can't be bad, eh, Rick?"

"No shit. You hear that? I think she digs you, man."

Carol had reached the door to the lounge and disappeared inside, breaking the spell.

" Well, we better get going. Got a lot of hotel to cover. See you, Mel."

" Ok. See you guys—nice meeting you, Rick."

"Nice to meet you. Mel."

"Come on, we'll do the parking next. I want to be finished down here so we can be back upstairs at my break time."

"Break time?"

"Right, I guess nobody's filled you in, yet. Every two hours you get a fifteen minute break. Every four hours you get a half hour lunch break. That's rule number two—never miss a break."

"Never miss a break. Got it."

"Not even if the place is burning down."

"About Mel; I was wondering; how does he know to make change? I mean…"

"How did he know Carol handed him a ten and not a one? I don't know. Did you see him feel it? There must be a mark, or something."

"And how does he know where the right smokes are? Of course, he puts them away, I guess."

"Tell you what. Don't spend too much time trying to figure Mel out. Just don't underestimate him. For a guy who can't see fuck all, he's got a lot on the ball."

I got through my first week at the Ritz without any major problems, mainly due to Gary and Betty watching to make sure I didn't screw up. I learned how to operate the switchboard, which turned out to be easier than it had looked. It was really just a matter of getting the right cable plugged into the right socket.

I achieved some humorous results at first, connecting the wrong parties and having to sort out who was talking to whom, but after a couple of days I got so I could handle three or four calls at a time. It was at peak times, when ten or twenty calls came in back to back, that the task began to resemble a wrestling match with an angry octopus.

Betty always seemed to sense when I was getting into trouble and would appear at my elbow, giving advice.

"Ok, kid, just slow down. You're doing fine, just don't get rattled. Take a deep breath. Now, tell the next two calls to hold. Good. Now, who can you get rid of in a hurry? Just tell them the line is busy and to try again later. There, now—think you can handle it? Jeez Louise, kid—you tense up too easy. Just calm down, you'll do fine."

She never offered to take over, no matter how confused things were. She insisted that I do it but she never left until I had a handle on things. With her help I was soon borderline competent at it and my worst worry became making sure my wig didn't get caught when I took the headphones off.

Gary took me with him any time he did something I hadn't seen yet, as long as we weren't needed at the desk. He showed me all the chores that the bellhops were expected to do, from ushering guests in and out and taking care of their luggage, to sorting laundry and taking room service orders up to the rooms.

We were in charge of changing the plastic letters on the marquis out front, which advertised the lounge entertainment and any special events in the banquet rooms.

We were also in charge of assisting with banquets.

The banquet manger was a portly middle-aged guy with a bad comb-over named Mr. Graves, who was always in a frantic hurry. He had an odd way of speaking in big words and convoluted sentences that made it hard to understand him. I guess he thought it made him sound intelligent and I had to I admire the work he put into it, but in the rush of a working day, with a bunch of customers waiting to be served I often wished he would just drop the lawyer talk and spit it out, already.

"Rick," he would say, "it would appear that my original estimate of the amount of both ginger ale and tonic water needed for this group was somewhat amiss. Indeed, we are running dangerously low on both. Perhaps you wouldn't mind taking the dolly down to the basement and bringing up a few bottles of each, just in case the consumption exceeds the available supply."

By the time he got all that out, I could have been downstairs and back twice. On my way to the elevator I'd be wondering what would've been wrong with "go get more mix."

Mr. Graves stood to make a good buck on the catering end of the banquet business, but he had to keep a short rein on the overhead. He was apparently in charge of the running of the banquet rooms, from the bookings through to actually tending the bar himself.

Anytime a call came in about reserving one of the meeting rooms or the banquet room itself, we were instructed to take a number so that Mr. Graves could make all reservations himself. After that, he would pay the hotel for the use of the room and purchase liquor and mix from the management at discount prices.

He tried to explain the whole thing to me the first time I helped him set up for a meeting but I got so confused just trying to unravel his verbal acrobatics that I lost the thread. It was like riding some crazy oratory roller coaster, holding on to the meanings of his words as he plunged down one thought only to take a wild curve and end up on a steep climb to some new peak, with no idea where we were going until we reached the end.

"The poignant central concept behind any profit making enterprise is that of minimizing risk while simultaneously maximizing potentiality for profit inducing parameters, thereby ensuring that the enterprise remains on a firm foundation."

Translation; he didn't want me to drop any more bottles of pop on the way upstairs, because he had to pay for them.

Gary took me down to the basement to show me where all the booze and mix was stored in wire mesh cages with padlocks on the doors. The keys to the locks were all on the big ring that we kept at the desk, including the one to the cage where all the master keys were kept in a cabinet above the key cutting machine.

"Never, ever remove a master key from the cabinet." Gary told me, "If a key gets lost and the spare isn't on the ring, you get Eddy or Mike to cut a new one."

"So, we aren't supposed to cut keys ourselves?"

"No, no; you just go right ahead and cut yourself some keys, man. Cut all you want! Cut yourself a complete set and make sure you cut one for the office up on four where they keep all the cash boxes."

"All right, I get it. No key cutting."

"Spoken like a gentleman, sir. Now, here is the long-term storage locker. Lots of far-out shit in here, man." Gary opened the door to the caged room. "There's stuff in here from 'way back. Dig this."

He crossed the floor to a gigantic wooden crate in the corner. Reaching around the side, he flipped a switch.

Instantly, the dank cavern was transformed with light. A thousand rainbow-hued reflections danced about the walls and ceiling as light cascaded from inside the crate.

"Far out!" I exclaimed, squinting to see what the source of it might be. It looked like a Christmas tree made of diamonds had been hung upside down inside the wooden enclosure.

"What is it?"

"It's a chandelier. It used to hang in the lobby. Took it down for renovations and stored it like this so they wouldn't have to take it apart. Never got put up again."

"Who hooked it up?"

"I don't know, but somebody keeps replacing the burnt out bulbs." He indicated an opened box of oddly shaped light bulbs sitting on another crate nearby.

"Check this out."

Gary led the way over to another corner where a huge chest of some rich, dark wood stood brooding in the shadows. He grasped two of the ornate brass handles and pulled out a drawer. As he did, more reflections sprang from the interior to join the prismatic lights of the chandelier. Gary moved aside so I could see the inside of the drawer.

Row after row of cutlery; carving knives, ladles of various sizes, knife, fork and spoon sets with five different types of fork. The drawer was about six feet wide by half that deep, stuffed to the brim with hundreds of pieces of silver ware all nestled into shaped niches in ancient red velvet. There were four more drawers.

Gary picked up one of the larger ladles. Turned in his hand, it cast new reflections, like a flock of fireflies flitting around my head.

"Sterling silver. Not plate either, man; this is the solid stuff. Must be a thousand pounds of it in here."

"Why so many forks?"

"This stuff is, like, a hundred years old, man. Victorian shit. Back then they had a fork for each course, right? You got your salad fork, your meat fork, dessert fork, whatever. They probably had one fork that wasn't good for anything, just to see who's ignorant. There are even finger bowls and little things to hold salt. This set is for three hundred place settings, and it's all still here. Must be worth a fortune."

"It sure is shiny for being so old."

"That's another weird thing. Look at this."

He reached up to the top of the chest and brought down a white cotton cloth smudged with a rust color. Wrapped up in the folds of it was a worn brick of hard stuff, the same color.

"Jeweler's rouge. Silver polish. Somebody's been keeping this stuff shined up."

"Huh." I tried to imagine coming down here, alone in the dark and polishing silver by the light of the chandelier. I had to admit it was a bit weird.

"It's like Ali Baba's cave with that thing on."

"I thought you'd come with something like that. C'mon, we'd better get back upstairs."

Gary closed up the silver and switched off the light, plunging the basement into its former gloom. We took the service stairs in the back up to the kitchen where Gary introduced me to the chef.

The kitchen was an enormous L-shaped room, with the long side dominated by a single huge table. There were various work stations placed around the edge of it, each with its own set of tools and supplies. This was where the preparation work took place.

On the short leg of the L were all the machines used for processing the prepared stuff; huge cauldrons for boiling a hundred potatoes at a time, mixers, grinders, and ovens, all on an industrial scale.

There were a few people working there as we entered from the stairwell, all too busy to acknowledge us except for one nice-looking girl about twenty who looked up with tears in her eyes.

"Hey, Gary, how you doin'?" she asked, wiping her eyes with her sleeve.

"Hi, Patty. Meet the new man. Rick, this is Patty."

I took a step towards her and the smell of onion hit me in the face like a wet, acidic towel. I stepped back again. There was a pile of chopped onions about a foot high in front of her and sack of uncut ones at her elbow.

"Whoa...uh, hi, Patty."

"Hi."

"Looks like you got your work cut out for you, there."

"You wanna take over? I could use a break."

"No thanks. Not my job. Right, Gary?"

"That is correct. It's my job to teach Rick his job today, Pat."

"Yeah? Well, welcome to the nuthouse."

"Thanks. See you around."

"I'll be around."

There was an office tucked into a corner by the stairs. Glass panels showed a desk piled high with papers and bric-a-brac. The big man seated at the desk looked up.

"Gary! How's it hanging? Who's your pal?"

"Hi, Rick. Meet Rick, new bellhop."

Rick stood up to offer me his hand, which I took, looking up into his face. He must have been close to seven feet tall. His hand was the size of a catchers' mitt but his grip was mercifully restrained.

"Pleased to meet you, Rick new bellhop." His smile was open and genuine.

"Likewise," I replied.

"Taking in the grand tour, are you?"

"Yeah. Gary's showing me around."

"OK, well, let's see; what do you need to know about the kitchen... mainly room service, I guess, hey, Gary?"

"It's OK, Rick. I can show him, if you're busy."

"Nah, shit, I'm just fuckin' the dog, anyways. I'm looking for an excuse to get away from the paperwork. C'mon out front, here and we'll go over it for you."

We followed Rick out through the busy prep area. I gave Patty a smile and she stuck her tongue out at me, her eyes full of onion tears. We passed thru a swinging door into the short order kitchen where things were being cooked on a big flat top grill by two harried-looking Chinese guys.

"Kam, Tony; meet Rick-new-bellhop." Rick intoned as we swept through the room. The cooks looked up and nodded. I waved.

'Out front' turned out to be a smaller room between there and the café itself, where orders were placed on a window from the kitchen side and picked up by serving staff.

"This is the pass," Rick told me, "This is where all the action is. The trick is to get your stuff ready about the same time the hot stuff comes through here."

There were coffee urns and hotplates with steaming pots of water for tea, toasters and rows of squeeze-able bottles of every condiment you could think of.

Little white bowls were lined up along the counter, full of different garnishes for the various items on the menu, with a dog-eared list of what goes where taped to the wall.

Rick showed me where to find everything and then we went back into the pantry to see where to find more if anything ran out. He told me how to handle the bills and to post orders on the revolving tree for the cooks.

It all seemed pretty straightforward. Rick wished me well and Gary and I headed back to the front desk through the lobby doors. The lobby was quiet as we approached the desk.

"Betty's day off," Gary said, "I'll introduce you to Lenny."

He addressed the person behind the desk before I could see who he was talking to.

"Lenny, meet Rick, the new hop."

Draped bonelessly across the stool that Betty usually occupied, Lenny looked like he'd been poured there. His long, lanky frame was dressed in a suit jacket that clashed with his blue slacks and the uniform red tie did nothing to improve it. Lenny had a toothpick in the corner of his mouth, which made a quick journey to the other corner, apparently so that he could speak.

"Hey, how you doin?" he said with a smile, revealing a silver front tooth. He had a barely discernable mustache. There was something about the way Lenny smiled at me that made me want to check if my wallet was still in my pocket.

"Hi, Lenny."

"So, how's the first week on the job goin'?"

"So far, so good. Everything seems pretty easy."

"Yeah? Great. Or maybe you're just not appreciating the finer points of the thing."

"Don't listen to him, man. You are so full of shit, Lenny."

"Real nice." Lenny started to defend himself.

Just then the switchboard lit up, buzzing. Gary took the call.

"308 is checking out. You want to get the room tab ready?"

"Why should I? What's in it for me?"

Gary ignored him.

"I'll be right down with his bags." And he was gone, up to the third floor. I sat down at the switchboard and watched as Lenny totaled up the various bills and added up the total on the big adding machine.

"Watch and learn, my boy."

"Was if just me, or did Gary seem a bit eager to take this check out?"

"308 is Angus Goodstriker. He's the chief of the Stony tribe. Always stays here when the rodeo's in town. Always asks for 308. Says he likes the view. Big tipper."

"Ah."

"Tips are what it's all about, man. You gotta know who the big tippers are, and make sure they know you. By the way, did Gary explain the arrangement regarding tips?"

"Arrangement? What do you mean?"

"Well, you guys give me twenty percent of your tips, in return for which I point out the good prospects to you."

"Gary said we keep all our tips."

"He said that? Must have forgotten. Come to think of it, it's been a while since I collected off Gary."

"Nice try, turkey. You won't get any tips from me, man"

"Fine. Forget it then. Find your own high rollers. But listen..."

Lenny's voice dropped to a whisper. Looking around suspiciously he rolled his stool over closer to the switchboard.

"If any of the guests are looking to score, I'll pay *you* twenty percent."

"Score dope, you mean?"

"Shhh! Not so loud, ya moron—you wanna get me busted? Yeah, dope. What do think? Also hookers. I got an understanding with a couple of the girls. They pay twenty bucks for a date. We split it, dig?"

"You have got to be kidding. You want me to sell pot to hotel guests, fix them up with hookers?"

"Only if they enquire. What, you don't believe in free enterprise?"

"Take a hike, man."

"Is that any way to talk, after I offer to cut you in on a business deal?"

"Dope and hookers aren't business, Lenny. That's called *crime*."

"Holy shit—what are you; a nark, now?"

Before I could think of a snappy comeback, the door to the lounge opened and Carol came out. She was carrying her serving tray and had a handful of room tabs in her hand, which she brought to the desk and handed over to Lenny.

"Room charges. Tips, please."

She noticed me sitting there behind the board.

"Hiya, cutie! How's it goin'?"

"Hi, Carol. Fine, thanks."

Lenny rolled himself back over to the adding machine and started to tally the tips off the tab forms.

"I was just explaining the tips policy to the new guy."

"Oh yeah? What policy is that?"

"You know; the one where you pay me twenty percent."

Carol snorted.

"Hee-hee. Yeah, right. Good one, Lenny. You get twenty percent of nothin'. Don't let this guy bullshit you, Rick. He don't get nothin'. He don't deserve nothin', sittin' around on his ass all day."

Lenny handed her some bills and change. Carol counted it and put it into the brandy snifter on her tray.

"Who sits around on their ass all day?"

"You do. Thank you."

"You're welcome. You wanna sit on my face?"

"In your dreams, buddy. Bye-bye, new guy."

Carol walked back across the lobby to the lounge door as Lenny and I watched in silent appreciation. As the door closed behind her I turned to him.

"Is that how you talk to all the women that work here?"

"What? Hey, you don't ask, you don't know. Don't tell me you're in love with her."

"She's just seems nice, that's all."

"Sure, well—just don't get any ideas about Carol. Good way to lose your job."

"What do you mean?"

"What do you think? She's taken, man. She's the bosses property, dig?"

"Carol and Eddy? You must be kidding." The idea made me feel a bit sick.

"No, stupid. Nick. She may be a pig, but she's got some taste, anyways."

"Who's Nick?"

"Man, didn't anybody fill you in about the place? Who's Nick? He's just the owner's son, that's who."

"Eddy's brother? I didn't know he had one. Older or younger?"

"I dunno. Younger, I guess. Gets more action, anyways."

"Like Carol."

"Yup, and any other babe he wants. Guy gets around, man." Lenny lowered his voice and glanced towards the door to the manager's office. "Not like Eddy. Best he can do is old Betty. Yuch."

"Wait a minute, you mean Eddy's sleeping with Betty?"

"Shhh! Not so *loud*, man! What's *with* you?"

"I thought Eddy was married."

"Sure he is. So what?"

"I don't know, I just thought..."

"You don't know nothin'. Listen-here's something you need to know, and don't forget it; if Nick is upstairs with Carol, in 402, you don't let anyone get close to the fourth floor. Capeesh? It's only the executive suites up there and 402 is Nick's private boars den."

"Ok, nobody admitted to four when Nick's entertaining in 402."

"Entertaining. I like that. Where did Gary find you, anyway?"

"We play in a band together. It's kind of a rock band, but not hard rock, you know? We get into some older stuff, some Motown sounds..."

Lenny had gone over to the switchboard and put the headphones on. He picked a line up at random and plugged it into the nearest handy socket. Thumbing back the switch to ring the line, he pretended to answer a call.

"Hello? Yes. Yes, he's here...oh. OK, I'll give him that message." He pretended to hang up, then quickly scribbled a line on the message pad. "It's for you."

Puzzled, I took the paper from him and unfolded it. "Don't give a Shit." The message read. I must have looked confused or something, because Lenny started laughing hysterically.

"Well, you asked, man," I said.

"I didn't ask for your freakin' autobiography, man. Just remember; nobody goes up to four if the man is in. Especially Mrs. Nick."

"Mrs. Nick? You mean he's married too?"

"Sure. What's it to you?"

"Nothing, I guess. How will I know her if she comes in?"

"Easy, man. She'll be the tall, beautiful blonde who's spitting nails. Hard to miss, believe me. Got a rock on her finger the size of a fuckin' Buick."

"And we're expected to lie to her and say that Nick's not here. What if it's some kind of emergency?"

"Not even if the place is burning down. His words. Now fuck off and stop buggin' me, I got work to do."

Lenny picked up the receipts that Carol had dropped off and went back over to drape himself across the stool. Just then a line lit up on the switchboard. It was room 206.

"Front desk."

"I'll be checking out now. Will you send somebody up for my things?"

"Certainly, ma'am I'll sent someone right up."

"206 is checking out."

"Whoopee shit." Lenny grumbled, but he was already reaching for the room file.

"Just do the bill up, huh? I'll be back."

I met Gary on my across the lobby.

"Come and get me when you're done," he said, "I'll show you the roof."

I went upstairs and took care of 206 to the tune of a nice five-buck tip, and then headed back to the lobby to find Gary. On the way through the little hall from the side entrance I noticed this guy who seemed to be watching me.

He was an older man; late fifties, maybe, well dressed in a sport jacket and slacks, with close-cropped hair and a heavy five o'clock shadow.

There was something about his face. He had been handsome once, before too many scars had given him that curiously homogeneous look you see on old prizefighters. He was of average height and well built with uncommonly large hands with no rings.

His eyes locked on me as I came in from the hallway and followed me as I passed him into the lobby. I could feel his gaze on my back as I approached the desk. When I got there I turned around and sure enough he was still watching me from the entrance. It felt a little creepy.

"Lenny?"

"Whattaya want?"

"Do we have a security guy, or something, in case there's-you know-trouble?"

"Oh, yeah," Lenny replies without looking up from the section of the journal he's reading, "We got a security guy, all right. The only problem is, the only security he's interested in is his own. Tiger's real good at disappearing when any real trouble starts. Why?"

"Probably nothing, I guess. Just, this guy over there has been looking at me funny and he won't stop staring."

"What guy?" Lenny folded the paper and laid it aside.

I nodded discreetly in the direction I'd come from, where the man could still be seen, just standing there gazing in my direction.

"That guy? The one in the green blazer? He's been staring at you?"

"Ever since I came in from the parking lot. He won't stop."

"Gee whiz, we better do something about this. Tell you what; I'll page Tiger on the p.a."

"No, no, don't bother, it's probably nothing..." I began, but Lenny had already grabbed the mike. Thumbing a switch, he announced the call.

"Security to the front desk please. Security to the desk." His voice reverberated from the speakers all over the hotel.

"Really. Lenny. You don't have to do that. It's probably just a case of bad manners."

As I spoke, the man pushed himself off the wall he'd been leaning on and started walking across the lobby towards the desk. He seemed to be almost stumbling, weaving a bit, having a hard time keeping his balance.

"Shit, here he comes!" Lenny observed, "Man, he looks like he's had a few. I wonder what he wants?"

Something in his voice made me look over at Lenny. He was grinning like the Cheshire Cat. I looked back at the approaching figure, now almost to the desk. It was obvious he was drunk by his shambling walk. Panic gripped me as I instinctively stood up and backed away from him. Lenny continued to grin inexplicably at me. Where was this security man?

The man in the green jacket arrived at the front desk and looked at Lenny.

"Yeah, what's the problem?" he asked.

"Oh, no problem, Tiger," Lenny said, "I just wanted to introduce you to the new bellman."

Lenny turned to me and his grin became a cynical sneer.

"Rick, I'd like you to meet Tiger, our chief of security."

"Pleased to meet ya," Tiger said, offering his hand. He frowned at my hesitation.

"Nice to meet you," I finally got out. My hand disappeared completely inside his as we shook. He had a grip like iron.

"First day on the job?" Tiger asked.

"No, sir. I've been here since Monday."

"Well, just keep your nose clean and everything'll be jake."

"Jake? Oh, right. Thanks."

"Don't mention it. See you around."

As Tiger returned to his post in the hallway, I turned to Lenny.

"You bastard."

Lenny collapsed in laughter.

"You should have seen your face!" He managed to get out between hoots of hilarity.

"Fuck you, man."

"Fuck you, yourself, turkey."

I couldn't think of any way to answer that, so I split. Later on I told Gary about Lenny's little joke.

"Aww, that's just Lenny. Getting people mad just makes him happy. Ignore him, man."

I told him about the way Tiger walked.

"Do you think he was drunk?"

"Punch drunk, maybe." He took a hit off the joint we were smoking and passed it over. We were up on the roof. There was a sheltered spot at the back of the building where you couldn't be seen from any of the windows, accessed through a window in the maid's room. We stood behind a huge air conditioning unit that perched there among the old brick chimneys like a shiny sheet metal invader.

"Too many shots to the head, it screws up your sense of balance. Something to do with the inner ear, I guess."

"What, on the job, you mean?"

"Here? Naw, Tiger never mixes it up with any serious threat, not if he can help it. He was a prizefighter down south before he came up here. Somebody told me he came to Canada to get away from a murder charge. Killed some guy in the ring, they said."

Gary accepted the joint back and took another hit. He coughed and blew it out right away.

"Of course, that's what they say about every burned out boxer that comes from somewhere else. Tiger probably started the story to give himself a rep. Who knows? Anyways, he walks like that all the time. He's not going to take the risk of getting caught drinking on the job. He's got it too cushy."

"Bouncing in a place like this? Cushy?"

"It is, if you know how to avoid trouble like Tiger does. He's real good at making a big thing out of giving some bum the toss, but try and find him if there's anything serious going on. All he does is stand around all day. Cushy."

"I guess so."

If that was Tiger's job, ours was different. There was always something that needed doing. And if we couldn't find a way to at least look busy, we could find ourselves having to empty the ashtrays.

There were about twenty public ashtrays scattered about the hotel; five in the lobby, one inside the elevator and four on each floor. They consisted of a three-foot high aluminum cylinder capped by a metal bowl that held about two cups of sand. They were handy and convenient for extinguishing a cigarette but sooner or later they got full and had to be emptied.

It was a relatively simple thing to empty the bowl. After you used a little kitchen strainer to get all the stuff out of the sand, you just took the whole bowl off the thing and dumped the butts into the cylinder.

The nasty job was emptying the cylinder itself. We're talking about three or four pounds of cigarette butts mixed with chewing gum and God knows what other kinds of detritus people threw in, and the moist, mildewed ash-dust at the bottom was sometimes months old.

The procedure was in three steps; first you took the bowl off as before but without bothering to strain the contents. Changing the sand was part of the job at this point, so you just dumped everything, sand and all, into the cylinder. Then you took a green garbage bag and arranged it to receive the contents. This was trickier than it sounds and if you didn't get this step right, then step three could be a nightmare.

The idea was to up-end the cylinder in one smooth motion, tipping the rubbish into the bag and closing it before the cloud of smoke-like ash could rise and cover you.

This evil smelling powder was so fine it could find its way into the most intimate crevices on the human body. If step three didn't go well, you could spend the next week cleaning ash colored deposits from unexpected places on your person. And it smelled just like what it was; old cigarette butts.

Gary accomplished this task with typical aplomb and natural grace, never getting a spot on him. When you could do it right it wasn't so bad but it never went that way for me. It was the most disgusting, filthy and downright demeaning job I could imagine. I hated the duty but I always seemed to be the one doing it.

The bell hop who failed to look busy enough when Nick or Eddy came through the lobby ran the risk of being told to take care of the ashtrays. This usually happened in the lull between the morning rushes or the one after lunch. I ran myself ragged in the mornings but after the early room service was through, I had a habit of hanging around the desk, indulging in one of my favourite hobbies; people watching.

Tiger's walk continued to intrigue me. It reminded me of something but I just couldn't quite put my finger on it. I found myself watching him to see if I could nail it down.

He would come into the lobby from one of the various entrances and stop. This made sense for the security guy to do; scoping the room out, but I couldn't shake the feeling that there was something more to it. The way he stood there looking, for all the world, like a big lost kid trying to decide where to go next.

The choices were limited but it always seemed to take Tiger a while to run through them. The decision almost seemed too much for him. Sometimes he would stand for five minutes or more before some impulse moved him to shove off in one direction or another, and even then he would often change direction in mid stride. Sometimes I would see him do this several times in one trip across the room, weaving this way and that until something exerted enough attraction on him to take him to a destination.

One day, I noticed that I wasn't the only one watching Tiger. I saw Mrs. Russell doing the same thing from her perch on the big chair across the lobby. She put down her magazine and turned in her chair as soon as she saw Tiger enter the room. Only when he'd found his way into the smoke shop did she go back to her reading.

I caught Mel doing it too; not watching, of course, but every time Tiger came into the lobby I noticed Mel would stop what he was doing and stand motionless with his head turned towards him, listening until Tiger left the room.

I could tell that, like me, they weren't interested in where Tiger was going. He wasn't going anywhere. The thing that had them watching and listening was Tiger's walk.

I remember reading somewhere that, from an engineering standpoint, walking was nothing more than the continuous process of not falling down. The idea had made sense to me at the time, but watching Tiger proceed across the floor I felt that it had never been depicted so well. He lurched from one step to the next, each one a potential disaster, avoided at the last second only by committing himself to the next.

It continued to remind me of something but I was darned if I could say what it was. Mel finally gave me the key.

I was standing in the smoke shop, leafing through a magazine when Tiger came down the stairs and, as usual, paused before launching himself off towards the lounge. I wasn't aware of Mel standing just behind me until he spoke.

"The sailor comes home from the sea," he said.

He startled me a little, so I didn't make the connection for a few seconds. When I did, and my focus returned to Tiger tacking his way across the lobby, it was a revelation. Of course that's what it was-the perfect description. He looked like a sailor who's fresh off the boat, trying to get his land legs back.

As I turned to Mel with a grin of discovery on my face and saw his upturned face and blank eyes, I came up short. He'd done it again. How the hell would a blind man know, just from *listening* to a man's walk, what it *looked* like well enough to describe it so eloquently?

"It's all about the rhythm. You ought to know that." he said, "That and memory."

"Now he's reading my mind," I thought.

"Not really." Mel said, "Just making good guesses."

"OK," I thought, "now this is getting spooky. I'd better get back to work."

"OK, see you later, then." Mel said.

I flee the smoke shop in the direction of the front desk, where a well-dressed woman is checking in. I get about halfway there when the door to Eddy's office opens and a tall man in a nice navy suit steps out. Noticing the guest (an attractive redhead), he approaches her.

"Good afternoon," he says with a wide smile that reveals a mouthful of perfect teeth, "Welcome to the Ritz."

He extends a manicured hand with a couple of tasty rings and a Rolex on it. The woman is a bit surprised but game enough to give him her hand, which he actually leans over to graze with his lips. He straightens up looking her right in the eye with a steady gaze, which she meets unflinchingly.

"Nick Cymboluk, general manager. And you are?"

"Evelyn Pierce."

Nick is everything his brother is not. Where Eddy is short and a little dumpy, Nick is at least five nine, slim and fit with a full head of wavy blond hair worn just long enough to make a statement. About the only thing I can see that the two men have in common are the light blue eyes, which in Nick's case are set off nicely by a deep tan.

He looks every inch the playboy he's acting like and this gal has seen it all before. She has a tiny smile of amusement on her face but still she continues to meet Nick's eyes. He hasn't yet let go of her hand.

"Well, Evelyn. It's a pleasure to have met you and if there's anything I can do to make your stay more comfortable, will you let me know? Anything at all."

"Why thank you. I will."

After I get her settled in her room I return to the desk where Betty is applying lipstick to the filter of a Rothmans King.

"So that's Nick, eh?"

"What, you never ran into boss number two before, kid? Hyup, that's him in living color. Man could keep ice cubes in his mouth all day and then sell them unmelted to Eskimos, as long as they were female Eskimos."

"Is he always that way with the guests?"

"Only the good looking female ones. But everybody loves Nick, except maybe his brother." She stubs out her cigarette, closing one eye against the smoke. "That's not grist for the mill, though, all right?"

"I get it. I think."

Just then a girl came out of the lounge, carrying a tray. I thought she was Carol at first, walking across the lobby, partly because she was wearing the same uniform, with the short shorts and halter top, but as she came closer I saw that it was a different girl.

As she approached the desk Betty saw me looking and made introductions. Her name was June. She wasn't quite as hot as Carol but close, and as she left she gave me a look that was half quizzical, like she thought she might know me from somewhere.

Something bugged me about her, too. I felt like we'd met before. It occurred to me that if we had, she might be fooled by the short haired wig. I decided to reveal myself to her. I don't mean... well, you know what I mean.

I bided my time and before long an opportunity presented itself. She was in the café having an after-work snack just when I got off an afternoon shift. I went upstairs and changed into my civvies, doffing the wig, and joined her at the booth with Lenny and Patty.

She reacted immediately.

"Oh, my God," she said, "That's who you are."

I couldn't wait for her to enlighten me.

"You're that guy."

"Yeah?"

"Yeah. You're that guy from Jasper."

A cold draft blew through my memory. Jasper?

"Patty, this is that guy I told you about; from Jasper."

"You're kidding me. Rick?"

"Yeah."

"Rick is the guy from Jasper?"

Looking at June's face I suddenly made the connection. It was the uniform and all the makeup that had thrown me.

The summer before, on leave from my job at the Wasic café, I'd gone camping with my buddy Bill. He'd quit his job on a landscaping crew and I'd just got paid, so we decided to stick out our thumbs and head for the coast.

Things had gone pretty well until we hit the mountains. The weather was fine and the rides were good all the way to Hinton, where we made camp for the night. We should have known things were about to go sour, just by the chili incident.

My mom had sent a big tub of frozen chili along and it tasted good for supper around the fire. We saved enough out to make sandwiches for our lunch the next day, planning to be in Jasper by then.

Next morning we had a slow start but finally an old black guy in a pickup stopped about 10:00 and took us into the park. We jumped out just outside of town and started walking up a hill that overlooked the highway. We'd talked about it the night before and figured it would be the perfect spot for an al fresco luncheon.

The thought of those chili sandwiches made my mouth water all the way to the top of the climb, but when I went to get them out, I realized that the surplus army side pack I'd put them in had been left in the back of the old guy's truck.

We ended up walking into town and buying some day-old bread and baloney from the grocery. We ate in the little park at the centre of town. The food was a sad disappointment, compared to what we had imagined our lost sandwiches could have been like.

Our trip went steadily downhill from there. We stood on the highway with our thumbs out for most of the rest of that day and into the evening without luck. Finally we trudged down the road to the campground at Whistlers and took a site for twelve bucks.

It had begun to rain as we set up camp, and just as we finished up it started really coming down. We headed for the tent and were huddled in the semi-darkness watching our fire get drowned by the downpour when Bill said;

"I bet those chicks in the next site are getting soaked. Maybe we should invite them over to share the tent."

I hadn't noticed any girls so I stuck my head out of the tent door to see what he was talking about.

"The other way, man. I can't believe you missed them."

I looked through the thin screen of brush at the campsite on the other side of ours and sure enough, there were two young ladies cowering under their picnic table, looking pretty miserable.

"They sure look like they wouldn't mind getting out of the rain."

"OK, you stay here and I'll go invite them over."

Bill put up the hood of his jacket and ran over to the girls' site. I could hear the tone of the quick conversation he had with them before they all came sprinting back to the tent.

It was pretty crowded in that little two-man pup tent but we all managed to find room to get in. The possibilities of the situation were rapidly presenting themselves to me when, as suddenly as it had started, the rain stopped.

It was bit embarrassing, having been thrown together by the downpour and now having no practical reason to keep the party going. Bill decided to mention how wet the girls had gotten. This was no great feat of observation on his part. It was pretty obvious, owing to the fact that they were both cold and braless.

Bill built the fire back up. He suggested the girls stay and warm up, in such nonchalant tones that the young ladies acquiesced and arranged themselves on the picnic table. Bill and I broke the record for finding dry firewood in a rain-drenched forest and soon the fire was blazing.

I retrieved the mickey of rum we'd procured in town from my pack and Bill brought out the last of our hash. It was a good, black, gooey Afghan product that Bill had been saving for the trip. The stuff was top quality and had been known to make grown men break down and think creatively for hours. Dope like that was not easily replaced once gone but, unspoken between us was the agreement that tonight, it was no holds barred, all hands on deck and the devil take the hindmost.

Half an hour later I breathed out a great sigh with a lungful of miraculous smoke and passed the pipe over to June. It was one of those situations where no one says anything for a long time, and everyone there is completely comfortable with that.

We sat close to each other in the dark and stared like children into the crimson embers, allowing ourselves to be lulled by the mood and letting our other mind take over.

Watching the sparks from the fire shoot upwards to varying heights before winking out, I was struck with an inspiration. It wasn't anything important, just a thought that I felt moved to share.

"The fire is like life." I said.

"He gets like this." Bill said to the girls.

"No, no-really. The fire is, like all of us, together, you know? Like the mass of humanity; the human condition, maybe. And the sparks—the sparks are like the ones that *do* something, you know? Like Van Gogh, or Einstein, or John Lennon. They aren't content to just stay down in the accepted parameters. They explode with creativity and ascend to heights far above the norm, before they wink out. And who's to say they don't burn out faster for having chosen the creative life?"

I looked to my side where June had been listening in rapt attention, studying my face as I spoke. Our eyes met and lingered for a second. And then she spoke.

"You are so fucking weird. What are you, nuts or something?"

Bill, who had been ardently kissing the other girl, interrupted himself to say; "It's OK-he gets that way." And then resumed his dental inspection.

" Right. Well, it's starting to rain again," said June, "so I'm going to go get my pack and get into the tent, OK?"

We all said OK and she disappeared into the night, returning a few moments later with both their packs. She went to the tent and in through the flap, then stuck her head out and said she needed a few minutes alone.

I went and found the outhouse and got lost on the way back, imagining every garbage can to be a black bear until I stumbled breathlessly into our site. The fire was burning low and there was no one to be seen. I heard someone giggle inside the tent.

Unsure as to how to proceed in light of June's comments, I sat on the picnic table to ponder if there was any hope of kindling some kind of attraction. A little patter of rain began.

Then, as can only happen either up in the mountains or on the ocean, the heavens opened and a billion gallons of water hit the ground at the same time. It was the kind of rain that instantly forms puddles and then, in seconds, blasts them into froth until they blend into an inch of water covering the ground. The fire was snuffed out in the first barrage. I dove for the tent but I was soaked to the skin before I even got to the door.

Once inside the flap I stopped to take stock of the sleeping arrangements. It was pitch black. I turned a bit, listening for a clue as to where everyone was.

"Hey man, you're on my foot," said Bill.

"Hee-hee-hee...mine too," said the other girl.

I moved and my hand fell on something familiar; my sleeping bag. I remembered putting it inside the tent after we set it up. I also remembered thinking at the time that the tent had been placed badly, with one side in a little gully where it would be in the path of any water in the case of rain, but that was Bill; never mind doing stuff right, just get 'er done. I had put my sleeping bag on the uphill half of the tent.

Bill and his girl were in the middle of the space, sharing Bill's bag. There was a space of maybe nine inches between them and the wall of the tent, a cheap Army & Navy nylon thing. Anyone who's owned one knows they will turn into a shower enclosure the instant anyone touches the inside wall when it's wet out.

My eyes were adjusting to the gloom and I could just make out another lump on the floor, over on the other side of the two lovers. There were faint snoring sounds emanating from it.

Already a small rivulet had formed on that side of the tent. The nylon floor had sunk below the inch-high stream as it sought the lowest path. The deluge outside sounded as strong as when it started. I could see plainly that if June stays where she is, she'll be laying in four inches of water in about a minute. I reached over Bill and shake her arm.

"June."

"Fuck off, man. I mean it—I got a knife."

I guess she'd only been pretending to be asleep. Her tone was enough to snuff out any hopes of romance. I'd have to settle for not having her drown in my tent.

"Relax. Only, you have to move. You'll drown in your sleep."

"You come near me, psycho, and I'll slice your balls off."

"No, I mean it. The tent is set up in a creek bed, man."

"Leave me alone, man!"

I was in agony. My out-dated sense of chivalry was not going to stand for me allowing her to sleep in the water, which was now visibly rising over the tent floor.

There was only one alternative. I got my sleeping bag and a spare ground-sheet and left. I dragged the picnic table a few feet to high ground and made camp the best I could with the table over my head and the ground sheet under me.

A couple of minutes later I heard June moving her sleeping bag over to the dry side of the tent. At last I could get some sleep.

In the morning I was up long before the rest and got the fire going. Once I had a bed of coals to cook over, I boiled water for tea and by the time the smell had woken everyone I had hot porridge ready. June and I put a lot of effort into not looking at each other.

After breakfast we lost no time breaking camp and then Bill and I walked the girls out to the highway. They were going back to the city. Our plan to hitch all the way to the coast seemed pretty ambitious in the light of day but that was the plan, so we parted ways.

The girls were picked up right away by a guy in a holiday camper.

Bill didn't bring up the events of the night before. We sat on the side of the road all day and into the evening, finally giving up the idea of making to the coast by thumb. I was pretty sure I had a cold coming on and somehow the trip had lost a lot of its appeal. Besides, we were out of hash.

We crossed the highway in the waning light of dusk and almost immediately got a ride all the way back to Edmonton with a long haul trucker. I had never seen June again and hadn't expected that I ever would.

Sitting across from her now, with Patty looking at me in shock and surprise I wished I never had.

"You're the guy from Jasper, eh?" Patty said.

"I guess so." I replied miserably.

"You're the weird guy."

"Yup."

She reached over and patted my arm as she got up to go back to work.

"That's the way I like 'em." She said with a wink.

I watched her walk away with some interest before I noticed June was watching me watch. She got up to leave as well.

"I think you look better with the wig on," she said.

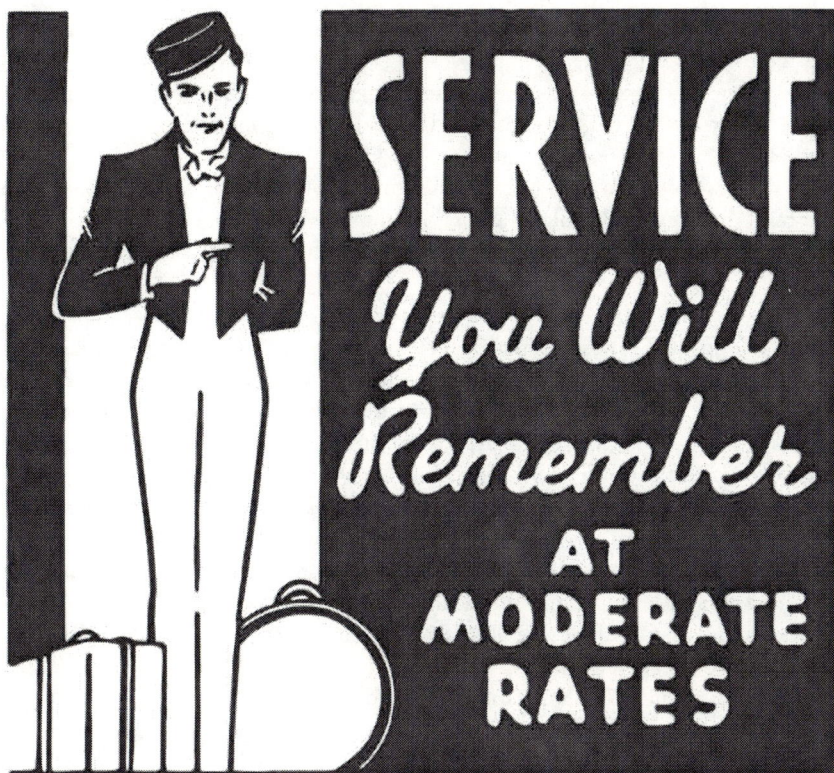

SERVICE
You Will Remember
AT MODERATE RATES

THE SADIST

The Burger Stop was our favorite downtown lunch spot. It had been there for decades, right across the alley from the Ritz, serving up all the standard diner fare but specializing in breakfast for the early riser office crowd.

I ordered a clubhouse and Gary got a burger. We both had a chocolate shake. We always had a chocolate shake. They made them so thick, it was all you could do to drink them through the straw.

"Have you heard the new Fleetwood Mac album yet? No? Come on over to my place and we'll give it a listen. There's a couple of songs on it that I bet we could do."

After lunch the two of us walked down the avenue to work. The banquet was scheduled for later in the afternoon, so we knew Mr. Graves would be pushing to get everything in place early. I expected to be sent straight to the banquet room to help him.

Eddy was at the desk when we came in together. He was talking to Betty but when he saw us coming through the glass walls of the entrance he motioned us over to him.

"I need someone to clear out the public restroom on two," he said. "Gary, you can take your new buddy along and show him how it's done."

"Sure thing, Mr. Cymboluk." There was something odd in Gary's voice when he said it.

We took the stairs up to two and Gary led the way to the left, where the Men's was located. These public washrooms were left over from the time that the hotel had been remodeled after the fire. In those days there had been a "smoking lounge" on every floor, long since divided up into revenue-producing rooms in later renovations, but the washrooms had stayed. I had been aware of their existence but up to now I hadn't known what a problem they were.

We entered the Men's and found it empty. Gary opened each of the toilet cubicles to make sure. He wasn't talking and his mood had me reluctant to ask any questions, so we proceeded in silence over to the other wing, to the Ladies'.

There was a flurry of movement inside when Gary opened the door. There seemed to be about six people all trying to get into the same toilet stall at the same time. Gary sighed heavily.

"All right, girls, let's go. C'mon, time to go."

I stayed back, holding the door open as a procession of Indian ladies emerged from the cubicle and made their way past me into the hall. One rheumy-eyed woman of an indeterminate age paused when she caught sight of me.

"Who's this? You got a new helper, Mac? 'Fraid you can't handle us by yourself anymore?"

"Yeah, yeah. Just keep it moving, please girls-you know the way. Same way you came in."

We escorted them out into the main hall and back to the service stairs. Our footsteps echoing in the tiled stairwell made a chaotic clatter. Talk was put off until we saw our charges out the back door and into the alleyway behind the hotel.

Gary removed a plastic milk crate from where it had been blocking the door from closing. He gave the door a sturdy slam and checked that it had locked.

"Come on," he said, "we need to talk to Rick."

We followed the short hallway leading from the back door to the kitchen. Rick was in his office with a handful of invoices in one hand and the phone in the other.

"I don't care whose responsibility it is to sign the orders. If I get overcharged again I'll be getting my veg from Merco from now on. You see to it. Goodbye."

He hung up the phone and tossed the sheaf of papers on top of the pile on his desk.

"Fucking wholesalers, man. Look the other way for two seconds and they're charging you double. What can I do for you, gentlemen?"

"The back door was blocked open again, Rick. We had to go upstairs and evict unwanted guests."

"Ah, shit. Sorry about that, man. I tell them not to do it, but they do it anyways. It's really hard to hear the bell when the equipment is running, so they block it open for the delivery guys."

"Yeah, I know. It's just that…I really hate having to deal with this, Rick. Eddy always gives me the duty. You know."

"Yeah, sure. I know how it is. I'll talk to them again. Maybe if everybody just checks it whenever they go that way, you know? I can't guarantee that it won't happen again."

"I know, OK-that's a good idea, if we just remember to check. Thanks, Rick."

"You bet."

On the way back to the lobby I couldn't help but ask.

"Gary? How come that woman called you Mac?"

"That's their pet name for me. Mac, as in Macintosh."

I drew a blank.

"As in Macintosh apple? You don't know that one? It's what Indians call Indians that have gone too far over to the white ways-red on the outside, white on the inside. Apple, get it?"

"I get it. So how come Eddy only gives you the duty?"

"I don't want to talk about it."

"OK."

Over the next few weeks there were three more incidents with the upstairs washrooms needing to be cleared out. Eddy was always the one who noticed it and he never took care of it himself. He only let me do it once, and only then because I was alone on duty that day. The other times, he insisted on Gary going up.

He was upstairs the second time when Lenny came on shift and asked where Gary was. I told him.

"I think it really stinks that Eddy sends him up every time."

"Yeah? How does Gary feel about it?"

"He doesn't like to talk about it."

"Well," said Lenny, "there you go."

But I couldn't let it go. It felt so unfair for Gary to have to be the only one to deal with the problem. What possible reason could Eddy have for sending him up time after time, even when there were other hops available for the job? There was only one answer.

I thought about Gary's family. I remembered going over to his place at Christmas time; a house full of his mom's sisters and their kids, laughing and chatting in Cree while they prepared the feast and more coming up the sidewalk bearing big roasters and Corning ware pots and shopping bags full of presents.

Gary and I got put to work decorating the living room. Every so often an auntie would come smiling to us with a little plate of something to try, nameless little treats made of bannock and berries drowning in thick cream or bits of meat rolled up in dough. All the ladies would stop what they were doing and wait for us to try a bite, silent until we nodded our approval, then bursting out in laughter as if we were just the funniest things they'd ever seen.

I'd come away with a memory of round smiling faces amid warmth and laughter, just as Christmas should be. I'd never really thought of them as Indians.

I remembered a day, driving up to Jasper with Gary and Doug, the bass player for Joyband. It was mid winter, the mountains and valleys covered with snow as we wound our way through the valley towards the town.

One of our band vehicles had broken down on a recent road trip and had to be left for repair at the local mechanics. We were to retrieve it and convoy back home.

As we rode through the icy majesty on all sides of us, the mood was light. We chatted and joked, enjoying the excuse for a road trip as we always did. The miles rolled under the wheels and we found ourselves on the last leg of our journey, passing a huge granite cliff topped with pines. I'd been through this way a dozen times or more and the imagery always suggested the same thing to me.

"Every time I look at this cliff, it reminds me of those scenes in the Westerns, where the Indian war party suddenly appears on the top of the rise, lining the cliff with their war bonnets silhouetted against the sky."

There is an uncomfortable silence in the car and I'm suddenly afraid I might have insulted Gary, referencing such a stereotype. Too late, I try to assuage the situation, digging myself deeper.

"I always wonder; what are those guys saying, you know?"

The silence goes on a few seconds longer. If no one says anything now, I'll know I stuck my foot in it for sure. It'll always be there, between us. I feel awful.

Then Gary says;

"Hey, you guys—quit 'em pushin'!"

It's perfect. The image is hilarious. We all crack up, me especially, with relief as much as anything. The spell is broken and the moment passes, just another joke on the road, soon to be forgotten. That's Gary, always with the right thing at the right time.

That's why I can't just let him be singled out for the duty on the second floor.

I start making a habit of going up to check the washrooms myself before every shift. Anytime I go by the back stairs, I check to make sure the back door is locked.

Twice I have to escort the ladies out the back way, ignoring their insults and comments about the "new sheriff in town."

After a couple of weeks of this, Gary invites me for coffee one day. He is uncharacteristically dour as we stir our cups. I wait for him to start.

"I know you've been doing the duty up on two, man," he says. He lays his spoon down and picks up his cup, blows on the hot brew.

"Yeah, I just thought..."

"Don't."

"Wha..."

"If *you* do it, that son of a bitch wins." He speaks into his coffee cup, then looks up into my eyes. "So, thanks, but don't. All right?"

"All right, Gary. I didn't... I see. All right."

Just then Betty hollers "FRONT!" from the desk.

"I got it," says Gary. He puts a buck on the table for the coffees and splits through the lobby door.

We don't talk about the second floor washrooms again.

Later on my shift, Mr. Whelan is on the phone, talking to his friend about music. He is excited about a classical recording that he's just heard for the first time. Standing behind the desk with the telephone receiver cradled on his shoulder, he's simultaneously filing check-in forms and describing the music.

"It has power," he says, "majesty, even. There is contrapuntal harmony throughout the opening movement, which develops later into these imaginative modal sections. At some points, the theme is carried by the entire string section in *unison*. It's huge and glacial-ponderous, even, but not pedantic. You simply have to hear it."

I'm sitting at the switchboard, trying to look like I'm not overhearing. The passion in Mr. Whelan's voice is so uncharacteristic of him that I can hardly conceal my surprise.

Mr. Whelan is an older man in his sixties, clean cut and as well dressed as someone on his salary can be. He's normally gruff to the point of surly with staff and guests alike. I guess that'll happen if you stay behind the front desk for thirty years, like he has.

I'm finding this exuberant tone a refreshing surprise. I'm eager for him to get off the phone, so I can engage him in conversation, reveal that we have this love of music in common and begin a dialogue that might turn into a friendship.

I don't see the man approaching the desk until he's there. He's come out of the lounge where he appears to have spent a bit too much time and money. He stands across the desk from Mr. Whelan, weaving unsteadily on his feet and peering nearsightedly at the figure before him.

"I want a room," the man slurs drunkenly.

Mr. Whelan regards him over the top of his horn-rimmed glasses, as a person might regard a cockroach he's just noticed in the room.

"Listen, I'm going to have to go," he says into the phone, "may I call on you later? I'd like that."

He hangs up, but he's taken too long for the man, who bangs his hand down on the desk.

"I WANNA ROOM!"

"WHO THE HELL DO YOU THINK YOU'RE YELLING AT!?" Mr. Whelan replies with surprising volume. "CAN YOU NOT SEE WHEN SOMEONE'S ON THE PHONE?!"

Shocked as I am at the forcefulness of his outburst, the drunk is not impressed.

"I WANNA ROOM!" he bellows belligerently, "I WANT ONE RIGHT NOW!"

He accents the last two words with a couple of solid whacks of his hand on the marble desktop.

'He's going to feel that tomorrow.' I'm thinking to myself, when, to my horror, Mr. Whelan produces a short, vicious looking billy club from under the desk.

"The only thing you're going to get here is a cracked skull if you don't clear out, savvy?" He brandishes the sap at the man. "Now get the hell out! Do you hear me? Get out!"

Everyone in the lobby has stopped to watch the drama unfold. Like me, they are all wondering if Mr. Whelan will really hit the guy with that lethal looking thing. Standing three feet away from him, with a clear view of his face, I'm betting he might, if it comes to that, but it doesn't.

Something has finally penetrated the fog in the man's brain and he focuses owlishly on the weapon, then on Mr. Whelan, who gives it a threatening wag for effect. The drunk executes a sloppy left face and exits through the front door.

I let out a breath that I'd not been aware of holding. Mr. Whelan turns to me.

"What the hell are you looking at?" he says. He still has the bat in his hand. "Don't you have some duties to perform, or something?"

I don't need to be told twice. I grab the master key ring and hightail it up to the roof, thinking maybe fifteen minutes and a smoke might help me to put some kind of perspective on what I'd seen. It doesn't.

I'm as confused on my way back down to the lobby as I was when I left it. I'm just hoping I can find something to keep busy with, preferably away from the desk. I'm even considering doing the ashtrays when my thoughts are cut short by a sound from one of the rooms.

"You Bastard!" says a female voice. There is fear and pain in it.

"Shut up, you *slut!*" answers the voice of a man. The last word is almost drowned out by the sound of flesh hitting flesh. By now, I'm becoming some-what of an expert on the sound of people getting hit. This has more of a slap cadence than that of a punch but, judging by the crash that follows, it must have been a good one.

Somebody just got knocked across the room.

"Did that make you feel good? Huh? That get you off?" the girl's voice rises with scorn. She's trying to turn it into disdain, hoping to ruin it for her tormenter and she comes close but right at the end it modulates up into raw terror.

I've got my hand on the doorknob and the master key in the lock. The only reason I can hear what the man says next is that I've got my ear pressed right up against the door. It's barely audible, even then—a low animal growl.

"Not quite yet, bitch. But hey, we got all night."

BANG! BANG! BANG! My fist hits the door. I can't believe I'm doing this.

"Open up, please! Hotel Management!" I'm just about to use the key when the door opens and I find myself face to face with a large man. He is all red in the face and looks quite upset at the interruption.

"What the hell do you want?" he demands. He looks past me into the hall, both ways, and seems surprised to find that I'm alone.

His jowly face is sweaty and his hair is out of place. He's in his sock feet and trousers, his shirt unbuttoned to reveal a sweat-stained undershirt. I notice that his belt is undone.

Behind him I can see a young woman crouched in the corner. I recognize her as one of the street girls who sometimes pick up guys in the tavern. There is a trickle of blood on her chin from a split lip.

"We had a complaint about a disturbance in your room, sir. The manager sent me up to make sure everything is all right."

"Is that right. The manager sent you up, did he? Well, you can tell him for me that everything here is just hunky-dory. OK?'

He starts to close the door. I put out a foot and stop it.

"Is that right, miss?" I call over his shoulder, "Is everything all right? Are you all right?"

"Get the fuck out of here, kid and mind your own business. I told you, everything is just fine."

He pushes on the door. I push back. He looks down at my foot, back up at me. He can't believe this skinny little twerp is going up against *him*. I can sympathize. I can hardly believe it, myself.

"Is that right, Miss? Is everything just fine?"

She hesitates, unsure if she should take the chance. I'm guessing that, from her point of view, I don't exactly instill a lot of confidence. Then the fear wins out.

"No." she says, "No, it's not all right. I want to leave and he won't let me."

"Shut up, you!" he yells over his shoulder. "Who the fuck do you think you are, huh?" he punctuates the question with a hard finger jabbed into my chest. It *hurts*.

"I represent the management, sir. I have to inform you that it is hotel policy to call the police if we suspect any crimes are being committed on the premises, such as unlawful confinement, for example. Or assault."

We look each other in the eye. I become aware that I'm sweating more than he is, now. I can feel my short haired wig starting to slip upward and I issue a silent prayer that it doesn't do the sideburn thing *now*.

I'm lying through my teeth, of course. The last thing Eddy would ever do is call the cops on a paying customer. Not for a hooker, anyway, unless maybe she was already dead.

We stare each other down for a few seconds; the big angry man and the frightened kid in the funny outfit, and then a crack appears in the armor of his face. A frown creases his forehead. Maybe there's a wife at home, or he has a record. Something brings him to his senses.

"All right hotshot, you win," he says, "Get her out of here and make it quick."

He steps back and opens the door a few inches. The girl, clutching her things to her chest, has to squeeze past him. He doesn't move an inch to let her by. In fact, he acts exactly as if she doesn't even exist. He keeps his dead eyes on mine.

"Don't be thinking you changed anything here, kid. I know what I like and I know how to find it. There's always another hotel, you know?"

I don't know how to respond to that safely, so I just stay in 'polite' mode.

"Yes sir. Have a nice day." It slips out automatically.

"Don't push your luck, asshole." He replies. He waits one second to see if I respond, then steps back and slams the door shut.

The girl is already half way down the hallway. No 'thank you,' no acknowledgement that I just risked a thorough ass kicking for her. So, why did I bother?

I turn around and head back upstairs for another smoke. I need it, after that. So what if I might be needed at the desk.

And somebody else can do the fucking ashtrays, too.

THE PUSHER

Early afternoon on a hot August day that shows every sign of getting hotter, I'm at the front desk. I have nothing to do. I'm trying to look busy re-arranging check-in cards so I won't have to go clean out ashtrays.

Eddy comes out of his office.

"Rick, I've got a something I need you to do for me," he says, briskly. Eddy says everything briskly. He's a brisk sort of guy.

I'm thinking 'Oh, no; not the ashtrays, please...'

"I need you to evict the people in 203."

"Sir?"

"I want you to evict the people in 203," he repeats, in exactly the same tone of voice.

Unlike most people, who might re-phrase their words or offer some more information to clear up any misunderstanding, Eddy just repeats himself. It's like he can't imagine a communication problem more complex than that. You just didn't hear him the first time.

"Umm...evict, sir?"

"That's right. When they come in, tell them they're out."

Just like that. Like it's some everyday thing.

Eddy heads back into his office.

"Sir, what if they want a reason?"

He stops, looks up at the ceiling and heaves a long-suffering sigh of exasperation before turning back.

"Look; it's simple. When the people from room 203 return and ask for their key, you tell them they are no longer guests here and ask them to leave the premises. They already gave us a credit card imprint when they checked in. We just want them out. If they ask why, tell them there were complaints about the noise from the room and we want them to go somewhere else to party. OK?"

"I understand. I just wondered if I should have Tiger standing by just in case there's any trouble."

"You can have the Keystone Cops standing by if you want. They'd probably be easier to find. Just get them out. Today."

Looking at his retreating back I'm thinking; 'Man, this stinks. It's not a job for a sixteen-year-old bellhop. It's his job and he knows it, he's just too chicken-shit to do it himself.'

It will certainly be unpleasant, possibly dangerous. I mean; what kind of people party that loud in hotel rooms? Are they bikers? Suddenly I'm a bit scared. No one else is scheduled in for the evening shift. It'll just be me, armed with my short haired wig, facing whatever goes down alone.

Then Eddy comes out of his office again.

"Maybe it would be better if you go up and clean the room out first."

"Sir?"

I'd think he was joking, except that Eddy never jokes. He doesn't understand the concept.

"I said you'd better go up and clear their stuff out of the room before they get back," he's speaking slowly, as if to a child or an idiot. "Make sure you get it all. Bring the bags down to the desk. Do it now."

"Yes, sir."

I grab the master key ring off the wall and make for the elevator. This is truly amazing. Eddy is worried that if these guys are allowed back up to the room they'll trash the place. So I get to go up and mess with their stuff and risk them walking in on me doing it, setting the scene for a really ugly confrontation either way.

The doorknob has the 'Do Not Disturb' sign hanging on it. I leave it there as I open the door with the passkey and slip inside. What a mess.

It looks like at least twenty people got seriously bent in here last night. Beer bottles are everywhere, some only two-thirds empty with cigarette butts floating in the dregs. One of the beds has been torn apart and the mattress relocated to the floor in front of the TV. Pizza delivery boxes cover most of the horizontal surfaces in the room, with the odd twenty-six of Sauza Gold scattered about for effect. Modern Hangover décor.

I despair for a moment but then I remember that I'm not here to clean up. That's not my job. All I need to do is remove anything that doesn't belong to the hotel. Where to begin?

Something is keeping me from focusing on the job as I survey the wreckage. It's been teasing the edges of my notice since I entered the room. I realize that it's the unmistakable pong of pot hanging heavy in the room. I've smoked enough weed to know that this was some quality cannabis, too.

OK, systematic search of the room by quarters, piling all non-hotel items in the middle of the mattress. There's a big duffel bag under the bed and an old yellow backpack in the closet. I work my way across the back wall and find a pair of men's briefs wedged between the bed and the wall and a nice lacey bra as well. The matching panties are across the room, behind the TV. Must have been quite a party.

Stripping back the covers on one mattress reveals more clothing but as I pull back the blanket on the other one my breath catches in my throat. Laid out neatly across the sheet are six large cellophane bags, each containing what must be a pound of marijuana. Oh, my goodness.

A seventh bag is filled with a similar quantity, but this is divided into ten or twelve smaller bags. Ounces, I guess. I have never seen anywhere near this much pot in my life. The dime and nickel bags that guys sell out of their high school lockers are one thing, but this—this is serious. This kind of weight can get you fifteen years for trafficking.

Now I'm really frightened. People who deal in this kind of quantity are not generally nice folk. Even I know that. The newspapers are full of stories about what happens when these people get feeling threatened.

My mind is racing as I rush to get the rest of the room cleared away. I'm trying to figure out where I stand. This is a whole different ballgame, now. Eddy can't be a part of this. All he'll do is call the cops. That won't do.

All I need is for these guys to bet busted here, on my shift. I would have to testify in court, making me the target of who-knows-what kind of intimidation or retribution. At the very least, my job would be history.

I'm still trying to work out a strategy when I open the drawer on the bedside table and find—you guessed it—more pot. This little baggie is almost empty. Inside it are half a dozen joints, tiny little things no more than a quarter of an inch in diameter, indicating that I was right about the quality of the stuff.

Seeing them gives me an idea. Maybe there is a way I can come away from this in one piece. It all depends on timing, now. I can't risk them getting back before I get downstairs. I need to be alone when they do. Just the way Eddy wanted it.

Everything that won't fit into the backpack goes into the duffel bag. I put the dope near the top of the duffel, covered by only one layer of clothing. I spread it out, so it's easy to count.

When everything is packed I stand still for a few seconds, listening for the elevator and going over my plan in head. Then I make one last sweep of the room, slip the joints in my pocket and head for the back stairs with the luggage.

Eddy is on the phone when I return to the desk. I put the bags just inside the little door to the desk. He doesn't even look at them.

"I've got to go out. Don't know when I'll be back."

"Sure, no problem Mr. Cymboluk," I say, thinking ; 'You'll be back when the coast is clear, you spineless bastard.'

After he leaves I check the clock. 3:17. I'm on my own until seven. Those guys are bound to be back before then, if only to freshen up before dinner. This is the hardest part; just waiting and trying not to think about all the ways my little plan could go wrong.

Mel is on duty at the smoke shop. Mrs. Russell comes down for her tea. The hands on the clock move too slowly, as the afternoon fulfills its promise of getting hotter. A couple of times, customers come to get their keys or check for messages. It all goes by in a fog as I wait for the inevitable.

And then they are here. A laugh and a shout from the hall, followed by two youngish men emerging into the lobby, giving the place energy where there was none. They saunter and gambol over to the smoke shop first, where one of them buys a pack of Export 'A's while the other one thumbs through a Playboy. He finds something of interest and they both stop to admire it before erupting into laughter again. The magazine is left back on the rack as they make their way across the lobby to the desk.

One of them drums a short tattoo on the desk with his knuckles and thumbs, exuding confidence, insolence and the odors of pot smoke and beer. He's taller than me by half a foot even discounting his shag haircut. He's wearing white hip-hugger bell-bottoms and a coral colored muscle shirt two sizes too small. There are tattoos on his arms but I can't make them out because he never stops moving.

His body is constantly in motion, turning this way and that, twisting at the waist and glancing around the room through rose colored aviator glasses, his jaw working athletically at a wad of gum, moving non-stop, like he can't.

"Hey buddy; key to 203."

"203?" As if I don't know. "There's a note from the manager in your mailbox."

I hand him the note I'd typed up while I was waiting. He takes it with one hand while the other one reaches up and puts his shades up over his forehead. Before he starts to read he gives me a hard look right in the eyes.

As he reads the note his body slows and stops its constant motion. When he's done he looks up at me. He hands the paper over to his friend without taking his eyes from mine. We wait for his buddy's reaction.

It takes a while for him to get through the contents of the note. In my peripheral vision, I can see his lips moving as he reads.

"What the fuck?" he exclaims finally, "This is bullshit, man!"

"Are you fucking serious?" asks the first guy.

"The manager is the one who wrote the note. Yes, I think he is serious."

I drop the 'sir'. With guys like this it'll probably just piss them off more.

"What a crock of shit, man!" Yells the second one. He wads up the paper and throws it at me, narrowly missing my face.

The first guy is just standing there regarding me calmly. As animated as the other one is, it's this one that's making me nervous. He reminds me of a snake, coiling up in preparation for a strike. Number two is still going on.

"What a great fuckin' city, man. You people get a big hard on about what a great place this is but when a couple of people try to have a good time, you kick 'em out. What a crock of shit!"

"Look, guys, I don't make the rules. It's the manager who left the orders. I just work here, all right?"

Mr. Cool takes the shades off his forehead and folds them up, hanging them from the hem of his shirt. He leans across the desk to put his face close to mine and when he speaks it's almost a whisper.

"Well, if the manager is the who's kicking us out, maybe he's the one we should be talking to about it."

"Yeah! Where is this turkey-fuck manager anyways-huh?"

"I'm afraid Mr. Cymboluk has stepped out for the afternoon. I don't know when he'll be back."

"You gotta be kiddin'. You mean this prick orders you to kick us out and then he fucks off and leaves a kid like you to do his dirty work for him?"

"That's about the size of it."

"Well that's just too bad for you, pal. 'Cause, I don't appreciate being treated like some second rate bum, OK? So, what if I don't feel like leaving my room, huh? What if I come over this counter and take my key whether you like it or not? What do you think you're gonna do about it, pal?"

As a survivor of ten and a half years of public school, it has been my observation that tough guys share certain behaviors. You can see them come out if you're watching for them. This was one of the more common ones; every bully in the world has a name he uses to address his next victim. They start using the name with you and the next thing is the fists and the boots.

The magic word with this guy was "pal." Now that I was his "pal", the fists and boots would not be long in coming. I had to derail that train before he reached the point of no return.

"I don't think you want to do that." I said.

"Oh, yeah? Is that right? Why is that, pal? You gonna call a cop? You think they're gonna get here in time to stop me? Just who the fuck do you think you are, pal?"

He has started moving again, twitching and shifting his feet like a boxer in the ring. It's the prelude to the explosion he's working himself up to. He's not expecting an answer to his rhetorical question, but I give him one anyway.

"I'm the guy who cleaned out your room."

He stops moving again. That got his attention. The two of them exchange looks.

"You said what?"

"I said; I'm the guy who cleaned your room out. The manager told me to."

"Fuck, man, let's just kill this fuckin' twerp." Offers number two. Number one puts up a restraining hand.

"I did a very thorough job. I'm pretty sure I got all of your...*possessions* out of the room. It's all here. You might want to check and see if I missed anything."

I open the gate and push the two bags out with my foot, keeping my eyes on Mr. Cool. He keeps his on me, too. We study each other, a regular little mutual admiration society.

"Check it out." He instructs number two, who kneels down, temporarily out of sight. There is the sound of clasps un-clasping and zippers un-zipping. Number two stands up and moves over close to Number One. Pitching his voice low, he reports.

"It's all there, except for the doobies I rolled this morning."

Mr. Cool's only reaction is his right eyebrow raising an inch. The question is plain.

"I assumed the items your friend mentions were left as a tip." This is the tricky bit. He has to be smart enough to realize I can just as well use the joints as evidence in case he doesn't back off.

Then, the potentially fatal error in my plan occurs to me even as I'm saying it. I left the damn things in my pocket. There's nothing stopping him from just stomping me into the ground and taking them. Stupid!

I struggle to keep my panic from showing.

"I've put them away in a safe place, in case I might need them later," I add, praying that nothing in my voice or my face has revealed the lie.

A long moment of remarkable stillness ensues. In my peripheral vision I can see Mel over in the smoke shop. He has the phone to his ear and his finger poised in the rotary dial. I dare not take my eyes away from Mr. Cool's calculating gaze. After what seems like whole minutes, his fingers start to drum on the countertop.

"Just like that." he says.

"Just like that." I agree.

He starts chewing his gum again as he reaches down to pick up the backpack. Number two takes his cue and retrieves the duffel bag. Mr. Cool puts his sunglasses on again, pulls them down to the end of his nose so he can regard me over the rim of them. There is something akin to admiration in his face, just under the insolent sneer.

"Pretty slick for a..."

"Bellhop."

"Whatever. Just don't get too slick. See ya around."

Relief washes over me as I watch them leaving. Across the lobby Mel lets out a long breath and hangs up the phone. I pat the pocket of my pants, feeling the baggie and its contents there. What a dummy. I'd almost blown the whole thing.

Beads of perspiration are dripping down from my wig. I'm starting to appreciate its usefulness as a sweatband.

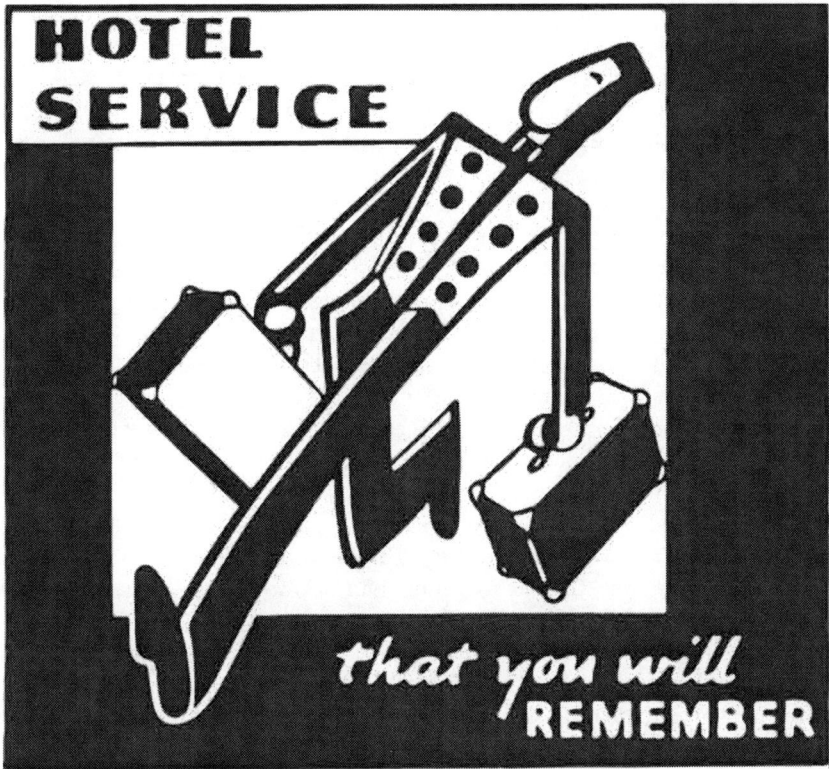
HOTEL SERVICE *that you will* REMEMBER

INTERLUDE

I stand behind the front desk, surveying my domain. It's three o'clock in the morning in the middle of the week and the place is all mine, or almost. I share it with a select few.

Manny the poet, also night janitor, is down in the tavern mopping floors with his nostrils full of that unmistakable mixture of spilled draught beer and ashes that says 'tavern' but what he's really doing is composing dark free-form verse to the denizens of the alleys and the boarding houses that he knows.

Dapper, be-spectacled Mr. Vona is up in 412 auditing the days' receipts. In the summer he will pretend to take a month-long vacation in Venice as he has done every year for twenty-eight years in a row. What he will actually do is take a Greyhound to Penticton and spend two weeks in a cheap motel near the beach. He can't go to Europe, as much as he wants to, because he is afraid to cross the ocean.

Mr. Vona is afraid of a lot of things. He does everything on a rigid schedule, right down to the minute. He's never late, never early and he never varies his routine. It's like he believes that this tireless devotion to consistency will keep him safe.

Eddy will take over the night audit when Mr. Vona goes on vacation and will be grumpy and out of sorts until Mr. Vona gets back.

In the kitchen, Danny Noisy Cook is facing down a mountain of dirty dishes, one eye shut against the smoke that drifts up from the smoldering roll-your-own he always has in the corner of his mouth, trying to get through the easy stuff and on to the pots before the grease has had time to congeal and seal itself onto the porous surfaces like contact cement.

Danny isn't sure how old he is, only that he's worked at the Ritz for twenty-six years, and he only knows that because Mr. Vona remembers when he was put on the payroll.

Danny started as a short order cook but now that he's gone so deaf that he can't hear the orders he's taken over the dishwashing station.

He came over from China as a young man to work on the railroad, only to find that the flyer advertising the jobs was ten years out of date and the railroad had already been built. He'd gotten work as a cook in the oil patch and that's where he got the nickname. When asked what his real name is, Danny just waves his hand, to dismiss such nonsense to the past where it belongs. Maybe he can't remember his real name.

The ticking of the big old clock over the mantle is clear and constant in the silence as the Ritz sleeps.

Nick is not here, but I know better. About two-thirty, Carol finishes locking up the lounge and comes across the lobby to the desk looking tired and sexy in her mini-skirted uniform and hairstyle straight off the cover of a 'Ventures' album. She has a bottle of the good stuff in one hand and reaches across the desk to get the key to 402 with the other.

"Hey, Carol."

"Hey, kiddo. How's it goin'?"

The only other person in the world that calls me that is my older sister. I guess that's how Carol thinks of me, as a little brother. It's not the way I think of her, although I think I've managed to hide my infatuation well enough.

"Slow." I answer.

Carol stops to light a smoke. One wispy lock of her hair has escaped from her beehive. She tosses her head to get it out of her eyes, blowing smoke out her nose. Why is that so damned attractive? All the movies-all the chicks do that-light a cigarette, blow smoke out their nose. It should be repulsive but it's not.

"Yeah, well, that's how it goes, eh?"

She turns toward the elevator. I can see her squaring her shoulders, fighting off the fatigue as she walks across and punches the 'up' button.

"See you later, kiddo." She tosses over her shoulder. "And, listen..."

"I know. You're not here."

"Not if the place is on fire."

"You got it."

The elevator door opens and Carol gets in. Taking a long drag from her cigarette, she hits the 'close door' button and she's gone. Lovely, sad, sexy Carol.

It was mainly her that kept me company on those long, lonely night shifts. Imagining her upstairs with her hair finally released from its confinement. Thinking about how she would be afterwards; tired and sleepy. Imagining the weight of her head on my arm as she slept.

Thinking, inevitably, about him. Envying his casual success but hating the way he takes her up there like a late night snack and leaves instructions to deny it ever happened. Hating him for the hopeless sadness he'd put in her eyes, in her smile. In the dark hours of the night, just sitting there, hating him.

LIZ LYONS

Mid morning on a quiet day, I'm sneaking a sandwich while minding the desk. Technically, I should be sitting *at* the desk but I still haven't gotten used to being up in the clerks' chair where everybody can see me. I've found that if I stay behind the switchboard I can monitor the calls and still be handy for desk duty should the need arise.

It does.

The sound of footsteps stopping in front of the desk is followed by the clunk of a suitcase hitting the floor. The bell rings for service. Time to go to work. I grab a swallow of coke to wash down the bite I'm chewing and stand up to greet the guest.

"May I help y..."

The words die in my throat at the sight before me. Across the desk stands a man—or, at least I think it's a man.

There are lots of things to support the theory. He looks about forty, big and heavy. His face is wide and jowly with a low brow and a hint of five o'clock shadow on his strong, masculine jaw line. And then there is the nose.

It's a nose that's been around the block a few times and not without a few adventures on the way. It's a fighters' nose—a boxers' nose, and therefore, logically, a mans' nose, but it's sitting in the middle of a face with more makeup on it than a forty-dollar whore.

The dirty blond hair, styled into a bouncy bob, is obviously a wig.

Long false eyelashes trim the brown eyes, under eyebrows that have been plucked almost to extinction and then penciled into arches. Pale, pinkish rouge covers the cheeks, each of which sports a mouse of some size. The lips are thin but have been given the impression of fullness by a liberal application of glossy lipstick.

The perfectly plucked eyebrows spring upwards in surprise at my sudden appearance from behind the switchboard. A hand, tipped with crimson false nails, flies to the throat of the low cut polka-dot blouse he's wearing.

"Good Lord," exclaims a rich contralto voice, "What are you doing, hiding back there?"

I open my mouth to reply, only to find that my last bite of sandwich has stuck in my throat, cutting off my air. I gag and choke and, grabbing for the can of coke, I knock it over. The sticky stuff splashes across the counter and onto the polka-dot blouse.

"JESUS CHRIST ON A BICYCLE!" The contralto is gone, replaced by a rumbling bass. A handkerchief somehow appears and a futile attempt to remove the stain meets with little success.

"Oh, I'm sorry..." I grab a tissue from the box on the desk and reach across the desk to help. A massive hand swats mine aside.

"Get away, you!"

"Sorry, uh..." I realize that I don't know whether to address my guest as sir, or madam.

Just then Eddy comes out of his office, takes one look and advances to the aid of our stricken guest.

"Miss Lyons!" he exclaims, "Whatever is the matter?"

Miss Lyons? Well, at least now I've got *that* straightened out.

"Can't you see? This *boy* is *regurgitating* all over my new blouse!" Turning to show Eddy the front of her, she's making little shooing motions with her hands. "I mean, *really*, Eddy."

"Oh, dear. Here, let me..." Eddy begins, as he takes his handkerchief out of his pocket. He moves towards 'Miss' Lyon's chest, reaching for the sodden mess, which by now has started to spread.

"*HOW DARE YOU!*" cries Miss Lyons. Again the huge hand lashes out, dashing Eddy's hand away with respectable force.

Others are now becoming aware of the altercation. I can see Mel peering around the corner of the smoke shop, moving his head in little circles as if a fresh perspective might improve his vision. Across the lobby Mrs. Russell has put down her magazine and twisted around in the wing-backed chair by the fireplace.

I check the floor behind the desk for any newly opened holes that I might crawl into, but no such luck.

"Please forgive me," says Eddy, offering his hanky.

"Thank you." Miss Lyons turns 'her' back modestly as she dabs the front of her blouse. She then hands the crumpled handkerchief back to Eddy, who wordlessly replaces it in the pocket of his suit jacket.

This accomplished, 'Miss Lyon's' demeanor is transformed.

"Honestly, Eddy," she scolds playfully, "where do find these people you hire? He doesn't look a day over twelve. He can't even keep his food down! Are there not standards?"

"My most sincere apologies, Miss Lyons, and my assurances that such a thing will never occur again..."

"Yes, yes. Just forget it." But Eddy has already turned to me.

"Rick, this is Miss Liz Lyons; one of our best and dearest customers."

Behind him, Miss Lyons is practically swooning at the praise, batting her hefty eyelashes demurely and plumping her coif. I notice for the first time that she's wearing a pair of skin-tight leotards and pink pumps. I suppress a shudder.

"Miss Lyons is accustomed to only the best we have to offer. You will apologize and take steps to see that she receives only the best service from now on."

"Of course, sir. It's just that she kind of took me by surprise, there..."

"Enough! I didn't say make excuses. I said *apologize*."

"Yes sir. I'm very sorry, ma'am."

"All right, just as long as it doesn't happen again. I will be sending my blouse down to be cleaned and I don't expect to find the charge on my bill."

"Of course, of course. Now, is there anything else, before I see you up to your room? I think that, under the circumstances, we might dispense with the usual formalities."

"Oh, I just want to get out of these *shoes!* It's such a long ride from the airport, here. I had to take the milk run up from L.A. I've been *days* in these clothes..."

She takes Eddy's arm as they proceed to the elevator. Mrs. Russell takes up her magazine. Mel busies himself behind the glass. I watch them go, trying to remember when my break is due.

One thing about working the front desk, you got to know people.

The front desk of a hotel is like the nerve center of the place. Sooner or later, everyone who worked there showed up at the desk needing something. Sometimes they would stay for a chat if they had time.

Tiger was the most frequent visitor and he always had time to "chew the fat," as he put it, because his job consisted of little more than wandering around the hotel. He didn't seem very comfortable in his role. I got the impression that he was expecting at any moment to get caught goofing off. His visits were rarely about anything. He would usually just be looking for a place to kill a few minutes.

He would come ambling over on one of his aimless tours of the lobby, looking everywhere except where he was going. His eyes were constantly roving about, watching out for "trouble," I guess, and never focusing on the person he was talking to. When he talked, his vocabulary was like something out of a Dick Tracey comic strip. Come to think of it, Tiger looked like Dick Tracey, with the heavy five o'clock shadow, the hawk nose and the square jaw. He talked to you out of the corner of his mouth, which gave the impression he was passing on secrets, betting tips perhaps, but it was actually always the same routine. He'd slap his hand on the marble.

"So. Whaddaya know?"

"Not much, I guess, Tiger. How about you?"

"Aw, you know-same shit, different day. How about you-everything copacetic?"

"Oh, yeah, same as ever."

All this time his eyes would be flitting feverishly around the room, never lighting on any particular thing.

"OK, well, better be goin'. Don't take any wooden nickels, eh?"

"Not me, Tiger."

"There you go. Bob's yer uncle"

And off he'd go, this way and that, like a big ungainly butterfly looking for another momentary resting place before once again commencing his aimless wandering. That's the way it went most days but not always. Sometimes Tiger would be on a Case.

Tiger had reduced the world of people into two categories; you were either OK, or you were Trouble. Tiger knew how to deal with people who were Trouble, but he was careful who he put into that category because you never knew who might be Connected. A person who would ordinarily be considered Trouble might not be designated as such if they turned out to be Connected. So if Tiger suspected you might be Trouble, you would become the subject of an investigation to see if you were Connected. You became a Case.

"Say, kid-what can you tell me about this long drink'a water moved into 212?"

"212? Geez, I don't know, Tiger. He seems OK to me."

"I don't know. I think this palooka might be trouble."

"What makes you think that, Tiger?"

"I dunno, kid. Sometimes it's just a hunch, ya know. This guy just feels pale."

"Really?"

Tiger was probably telling the truth. He likely had no idea what made him start to suspect someone of being a candidate for the Trouble file, but over time I started to notice certain similarities in the people he "investigated."

Long hair was one indicator, as was flashy dressing. Anyone who came in late and especially those who ordered booze up to their room, as well as anybody who was in any way affiliated with the entertainment industry would attract Tiger's vigilance.

Liz Lyon's presence in the hotel drove Tiger crazy. Being both an entertainer and a transvestite, she was undoubtedly Trouble in his eyes but she was so obviously Connected, what with Eddy fawning over her at every opportunity, he knew she was beyond his reach. He didn't dare to even start an investigation.

Of course, Tiger's investigative powers were severely limited. About the only source of information he had was the front desk. He could ask to look at a guests' check-in card, and from there get their address and "reason for visit," which he would duly note in his pad, but I doubt if it ever went further than that. He might hang around the lobby a bit more and take note of a Subject's comings and goings. He might have a look at their room service bills to see what they had been having sent up to the room. I think mostly it was just something to do and maybe an attempt on Tiger's part to look like he was, in fact, doing something.

It all seemed like just a silly game to me until one day I got a first hand view of how Tiger dealt with Trouble when he knew you were it.

It was a rainy mid-week afternoon when I noticed Tiger coming across the lobby. He was walking with a completely different manner about him, with no trace of the clumsy meandering I'd grown used to. His eyes were fixed on a man standing inside the main entrance.

I'd seen this man a few times, coming and going from the lounge. A couple of times he'd had too much to drink and been asked to leave. He was well dressed in suit and raincoat and appeared to be doing nothing more than waiting for a taxi, or for the rain to lessen before venturing out onto the street.

As Tiger approached him from behind, his eyes never left the man's back. For once Tiger's eyes were focused with a chilling concentration. As he came within a couple of feet of him, Tiger addressed the man.

"Hey, you," he said, "Get the hell outta here."

The man turned, surprised and a little unsteady on his feet. Seeing Tiger, he raised his finger to begin answering with some lofty prose. He never got the chance.

The old boxer had gone into a crouch, balanced on the balls of his feet. He executed a series of little steps, like dance steps, lining himself up and presenting his left side to his opponent. At the same time his hands had come up-no fists yet, just relaxed hands moving into position and then...

"Pop!...Pop POP!

It sounded like someone hitting a ham with a hammer. The man's head snapped back with the first punch, rebounded back just in time for the second to straighten it out and put it at the perfect angle for the third and final blow of the combination-a solid uppercut that lifted the guy clean off his feet and sent him flying backwards, out the door. Through the glass I saw him land, out cold, on the sidewalk, his head smacking the cement with sickening force.

Tiger looked at the inert body for a few seconds and then turned to leave, dusting his hands off, like he'd just thrown a sack of potatoes out the door and not a man. He caught my eye.

"Call the cops, wouldja, kid? This cream puff don't hold his liquor real good. Better get him off the sidewalk before some honest folk trip over his sorry keester."

His eyes were lit with an unusual feral look. He turned to go, but something in my face made him turn back.

"You OK, kid?"

"Sure. I'm OK." I lied. It seemed to satisfy him. He was off, walking with his usual broken gait. I called an ambulance instead of the police, and they took the still unconscious man to the hospital. I told Gary about it later.

"He looked like he was high, or something."

"He was hearing the bell ring. Everybody's got their triggers, man."

"I guess. It's just...Christ, I don't know."

"Tell you what you do about Tiger, buddy," Gary took a big hit off the joint we were sharing, "You stay the fuck out of his way. He's been here, doing what he does for longer than you and me have been on the planet and he ain't gonna stop just because it offends your middle-class sensibilities."

How he managed to say sentences that long while holding in a big toke was one of the things about Gary that I never knew. I had to admit he was right. I decided to stay out of Tiger's way.

Mornings at the Ritz were a blur of activity from the time the kitchen started up at six thirty until about ten. The cooks came in at five thirty to prep for the breakfast rush, standing around slurping coffee and slowly sliding into the routines that would see them through their day.

It was my favourite time of day. After the long silent night, the sounds and smells and all the activity combining and rising into the hubbub that meant business as usual. The Ritz was waking up, stretching and yawning and ready to start a new day.

Room service ran from seven a.m. until nine o'clock at night Monday through Saturday, during which times it was the bellhop's responsibility to take the orders over the switchboard and get them up to the rooms.

It was a hectic time for the kitchen staff without having to deal with our orders. There was little sympathy and less cooperation to be had from the staff, if we wanted to get our trays upstairs with any chance of a tip, we ended up doing most of the orders ourselves.

The kitchen would do the hot food in the order we got the bills in, but the rest was our problem. We prepared the tray while we waited for the order to appear on the pass, making sure all the proper condiments were included; salt & pepper, cream & sugar, ketchup and pats of butter, along with jam and/or honey in their handy little single serving packages. These were stored in the prep area in bins that were constantly being raided by the staff to take home with them, leaving them low or empty almost daily. I soon learned to come a little early and top them all up, saving precious minutes later as the eggs lay cooling on the plate.

The other thing we had to take care of at breakfast was the toast. In the café, this was the waitresses' duty so we had to compete with them for the use of the single, four-slice toaster in the station. There was always a wait and it was clear to all that the lack of adequate toaster capability was a major bottleneck in the system, but the management was just too cheap to buy another one. We did the best we could but the inevitable result of our inefficiency in the toast department was the occasional cold breakfast, or worse yet in my opinion-cold toast.

I developed a system. After setting up a tray I'd go check my order with the cook. Once the eggs went on the grill, I'd put my toast on. If all went well, I'd be buttering the hot toast just as the eggs and bacon came over the pass. A quick application of plastic wrap over the plates and I was off upstairs to deliver a piping hot brekky, for a nice fat tip.

It got to be one of my favorite parts of the job. I liked the busy clatter of the kitchen and the no-nonsense way the people who worked there got things done. I found that I was good at this kind of thing and I did well at it.

That is, until the morning after my first meeting with Liz Lyons.

It was a typically busy weekday morning, the breakfast shift in full stride. The incident with "Miss Lyons" the day before was the furthest thing from my mind as I struggled to keep up with the workload.

I had just finished taking two orders upstairs and returned to the desk for a break. Betty had just gotten finished with some check-outs and assured me that the switchboard had been quiet while I was gone.

I no sooner sat down than it lit up. Room #302. I automatically plugged the jack in and thumbed the switch.

"Front desk."

"Room service, please." It was a gruff, gravelly voice that I didn't recognize.

"I can take your room service order here, sir."

There was a pause. When the voice continued, it was changed. Pitched higher with a note of annoyance. Anger, even.

"*Fine.* I'd like two eggs over easy on brown toast and a side of bacon, black coffee and a large orange juice. Have you got that?"

A chill went down my spine as I realized who was on the line. It was *her; Liz Lyons.*

"Hello?"

"Two eggs over easy on brown, coffee black and a side of bacon. Got it."

"And a large orange juice."

"Large juice. Right-will there be anything else, ma'am?"

"Yes, I'd like a copy of the morning paper, please."

"Globe and Mail, New York Times, Toronto Daily Star or Edmonton Journal?"

"The Journal will be fine. And soon."

"It's on its way, ma'am."

My hand was shaking as I unplugged the jack. Betty must have noticed.

"Something wrong, kid?"

"No, just...that was 302. Miss Lyons."

"Oh, yeah. I heard about your introduction to our Miss Lyons. Guess you kind of got off on the wrong foot."

"I'll say. And I just called her 'sir', so she's mad at me again. I didn't know who was in 302—Eddy checked her in. She sounded like a man, at first."

"OK, don't blow a gasket. This is your chance to make it up. By the way, just so you know, she always takes 302. The bathroom's bigger. She's really not so bad if you get to know her. Maybe you want to do something special, just to let her know you didn't mean it."

"Like what?"

"How should I know? Put a little something extra on her breakfast tray-some fruit, or something. No, wait. Not fruit, she might take it wrong. Use your imagination, kid."

"OK, I'll think of something."

"And kid..."

"Yes?"

"Hadn't you better call her order in?"

"Oh, cripes. I forgot."

I rang the kitchen line. After a moment it was picked up.

"Kitchen." It was Patty, the nice young girl chef.

"Hi, Patty. It's Rick. I've got a room service order I need done in a hurry."

"Really? How novel. I'll alert the press."

"No, really; I messed up and forgot to call it in. Could you do me a favor?"

"For you? Sure. What do you need?"

"Eggs over easy and a side of bacon."

"You got it. Three minutes OK?"

"Thanks, Patty. You're the greatest."

"I know it. Now that you know it too, when are you going to ask me out?"

"Uh..."

"Never mind. See you in two minutes and forty five seconds."

"On my way."

I jumped up to go get the tray prepped and banged my shin on the corner of desk. Betty didn't even look up.

"Slow down, kid, and get it right."

"Right."

I ran through to the prep station and started the toast-no! *Brown toast.* No need for cream and sugar, but I'll include a selection of jams. OJ...large, she said. I don't want to screw up anything on this order.

I'm waiting for the toast, looking around, trying to think of something to add, like Betty suggested. My eyes fall on one of the tables in the café. Someone has put little cut-glass vases on each table and in each vase, a flower. A daisy. Perfect. I grab one and put it on the tray just as the toast pops up and Patty puts my eggs through the pass.

"Order up!" She looks at the tray quizzically.

"So, who's in 302, someone special? Don't tell me I have competition?"

"Liz Lyons. You know her?"

"The transvestite comedian? I caught her show at the Club one time. She's hilarious. I didn't know you had leanings that way. Does this mean it's over between us?"

She has this wicked little crooked smile.

"It's a long story. I gotta go."

I'm rushing past the desk on the way to the elevator when Betty, without taking her eyes from her magazine, taps an ash from her smoke and says:

"Newspaper."

"Oh, Jeez-thanks." My only answer is a plume of cigarette smoke from behind the cover of 'Chatelaine.' I hurry over to the smoke shop, where Mel is casually sorting change. As I snatch up a copy of the day's Journal, he stops counting.

"Twenty-five cents, please, Rick."

I plop a quarter down on the counter, wondering only fleetingly how he knew it was me and what I'd picked up.

On the way up the elevator I'm talking to myself, trying to calm down.

"She's just like any other guest," I tell myself, "just treat her like you would anyone else."

I take a deep breath at the door to 302 and knock.

"Room service."

"Just a minute!" comes a muffled reply. There is the sound of heavy foot-steps. The chain rattles and the door opens.

Jesus Christ.

Liz Lyons stands there looking like some deeply cynical caricaturist's idea of a woman in the morning. She's wearing a fucia teddy that must be size twenty. Through the shear material I can plainly see a bra, about a 52C, I would guess. It's trimmed with pretty little pink flowers along the strap—daisies.

The carefully applied makeup of the day before is a shambles. Mascara has dripped and pooled in the deep crevasses of her face while the dark red lipstick is smeared freely around her mouth. One of her false eyelashes is missing, giving her face a slightly demented look, which is augmented by the fact that there is nothing covering her head except a nylon stocking with a little bit stick-ing up comically at the top.

Liz Lyons is as bald as a billiard ball.

I find myself once again speechless in her presence but, remembering my earlier resolve, I try to treat the situation as routine.

"Your breakfast, ma'am."

"Well, that was quick," she says and turns around to motion towards the desk. She takes a step away and I follow. If she has recognized me from the pre-ceding day, she makes no sign.

"You can put it down over..."

I guess she must have caught sight of herself in the mirror over the desk, or spied her glorious wig resting on its Styrofoam roost on top of the vanity, and realized how she looked. It's the only explanation for what she did next, which was to whirl suddenly around and throw her hands up to cover her naked pate. Needless to say, I wasn't expecting her to do that, or I wouldn't have been following so closely behind her.

Her hands caught the bottom of the tray with such force that it and its contents were launched a surprising distance into the air. Things went flying in all directions but most of it seemed to go straight up and then came more or less straight back down again.

Eggs (over easy), toast (brown) and a side of bacon were about evenly distributed over Miss Lyons and myself, although I think it's fair to say that she got most of the orange juice (the Lyon's share, one might say) while I had the coffee (black). The tray itself missed us both and clattered noisily to the floor between us.

Just for a frozen instant we stood looking at each other while an egg that had landed on her shoulder slid down her now orange-stained teddy and fell to the floor. I noticed that the daisy I had so thoughtfully added to the tray had come to rest on her other shoulder.

I felt a mad compulsion to start laughing. I think I might have, had Miss Lyons not shaken off her shock and reacted first.

She shrieked. Gathering up pinches of ruined fucia fabric between thumb and forefinger of each hand, she let loose a sound like the whistle on a steam locomotive.

I'm a bit embarrassed to say what I did then, but I'm not exactly sure why. In retrospect, it seems like a reasonable thing to do, given the circumstances.

I took to my heels and ran like a thief.

I ended up in the basement, where I hid for a couple of hours. Petrified to face the consequences, I seriously considered leaving my vest and wig down there and just leaving the hotel forever. I couldn't. I needed the job, if I wasn't already fired. If I could just put off facing Eddy until I'd pulled myself together. I knew I couldn't avoid it for long.

I went up to the maids' room and killed some time sorting through some laundry to give myself a legitimate reason to leave the hotel, taking it to the dry cleaners' down the street.

When I got back to the desk, everything seemed normal, so I knew she hadn't called down to complain. Yet.

I asked Betty if she wanted to take an extra break so I could look at the account for the room. Ms. Lyons was booked for three weeks. No way I was going to be able to avoid her for that long. I knew that if I stayed working on the morning shift I would inevitably have to take another order up to 302.

I phoned one of the bellhops that normally worked afternoons and asked him if he wanted to trade shifts for a week or two. He was surprised but delighted to get in on some of the morning tip action. This meant I wouldn't go to work the next day until noon. I congratulated myself, thinking this would somehow save me having to deal with the fallout. It didn't work.

The next morning I slept in, dreaming nightmares that involved winged eggs and toast. When I arrived for the afternoon shift Gary was waiting for me at the desk.

"Eddy wants to see you in the coffee shop."

I froze in my tracks.

"He's been having lunch with Liz. I guess she wants to talk to you too, something about laundry. You screw up again?"

A cold, clammy hand clutched at my heart. Her laundry?

"Oh, man." I said, "She's there, too?"

"Big as life. Bigger, actually and not looking too pleased. You'd better go. Eddy said to send you in the minute you showed up."

The last thing in the world I wanted to do was walk through those doors to the café. The thought of fleeing and not coming back returned, but only for a second. I knew I was screwed. Maybe there was a chance that he wouldn't fire me. Maybe I could keep my job; keep my drums.

I went into the restaurant. I saw them immediately, sitting in a booth at the other end of the room. Eddy saw me come in and motioned me over with an impatient gesture. Liz was sitting with her back to me but, seeing Eddy's wave, turned to watch me approach them.

She was wearing some kind of one-piece body suit in a stretchy fabric, which looked to be stretched to the limit. The spots of what might have been intended to be leopard skin looked more like tiger stripes on her.

Standing before the two of them I felt like I'd been called into the principals' office. My knees were weak and I could feel a flop sweat starting to accumulate under my wig. I knew I couldn't trust my voice.

"You wanted to see me, sir?" I managed to croak out.

"Yes, I do." Eddy began. He folded his hands together and placed them judiciously on the table in front of him. "Miss Lyons has come to me with a problem related to our dry cleaning service."

"Dry cleaning, sir?" I couldn't stop my eyes from flicking to her face. Surely this was about the breakfast debacle, but something nagged at the corner of my mind-something about dry cleaning.

"It seems that yesterday morning Miss Lyons entrusted some items of her apparel into our hands, for dry cleaning. You were on morning shift yesterday, were you not?"

The thing that had been hiding at the edge of my mind crept into the spotlight and took shape. It was the memory of taking refuge in the maids' room, keeping out of sight after the breakfast disaster and sorting some laundry. Had there been a polka-dot blouse in there? The corners of my vision began to cloud in. My knees were trembling. All I could do was nod.

"So you would have been responsible for sorting any laundry that came down from the rooms yesterday."

I nodded again. I knew my voice had packed it in altogether. I noticed Liz Lyons studying my face with some intensity. There was a plastic bag beside her on the seat, the kind that the dry cleaner used to return orders to the hotel.

"So anything that Miss Lyons sent down would have been sorted by you."

"Yes, sir." It was no more than a whisper but Eddy caught it.

"Yes, well-Miss Lyons has shown me a garment that she sent down to be dry-cleaned. It was apparently laundered, instead."

Liz opened the bag and produced the garment in question. It was the polka-dot blouse she had been wearing when she had checked in, or what was left of it. The bright pink dots had faded and run, bleeding into the white background. There was a tear under one arm where it had likely got caught in the machine. It also seemed to have shrunk, but not evenly. Parts of it looked sizes smaller than other parts, giving it a twisted appearance, like an old dishrag.

"It's completely ruined," Liz said, unnecessarily. "Do you have any idea how much a blouse like this costs?"

I did not.

"Miss Lyons has insisted that I not fire you, provided she is reimbursed, which I've already done. The sum will be deducted from your pay at the rate of fifty dollars each week. Understood?"

It was almost half my pay. I nodded.

"Now, Miss Lyons has asked to have a word in private with you. You will excuse me." As he got up to leave, he gave me a look that said 'I don't know what this could be about, but you'd better not screw it up.'

When we were alone, Liz picked up her coffee with both hands and spoke over the rim before sipping.

"We don't seem to have much luck with things, do we?"

"No, ma'am, we don't."

"That *is* all it is, isn't it? I mean, you don't have a problem with the way I dress, or anything like that, do you?"

"No, ma'am, I don't." I looked her in the eye. "You kind of took me by surprise, that first time, and this was just an accident. I was still shook up after the thing with the breakfast tray..."

"Oh, yes—the breakfast tray. I neglected to tell Eddy about that."

As the significance of that sank in, I noticed her shoulders started to shake. She took a napkin from the little stainless steel dispenser and held it in front of her mouth. Then she put it to her forehead as she lowered her head a bit.

I realized that she was laughing.

"Thanks for not telling Eddy."

She cleared her throat and dabbed at the corners of her eyes.

"Oh, you're welcome. After all, I think that was probably as much my fault as it was yours, don't you agree?"

"I don't know, ma'am. If I'd had a better grip on the tray..." I began, but she waved my words away with her hand, the napkin going back up to her face as a new set of spasms rocked her frame.

"Honestly, the look on your face...and when you took off like that. I couldn't believe it. I almost died laughing." The shoulders were going again. She took another napkin and made some repairs to her mascara.

"Well, I just wanted to see your face when you said it." She heaved a great sigh, apparently gaining control of her laughter at last. "You see...it's Rick-right? You see, Rick, there are a lot of people who do disapprove of me, you know? And some of them will go out of their way to make things difficult for me, in lots of ways. I just needed to be sure you weren't one of those."

"No, ma'am, I'm not."

"No, I can see that. It's too bad about the blouse, though. I rather liked that one."

"Maybe I could find you another one like it."

She seemed surprised at the offer.

"That's very kind of you, Rick, but maybe we could just concentrate on not having any more of these...incidents, OK?"

"Yes ma'am."

"OK. So, I promise not to open the door half dressed if you promise not to throw any more eggs at me. Deal?"

"It's a deal."

"After all, a lady should never appear in public without her wig on." she smiled.

"I'll let you get back to work. Oh, and Rick..."

"Ma'am?"

"The flowers were a nice touch."

"Yes ma'am."

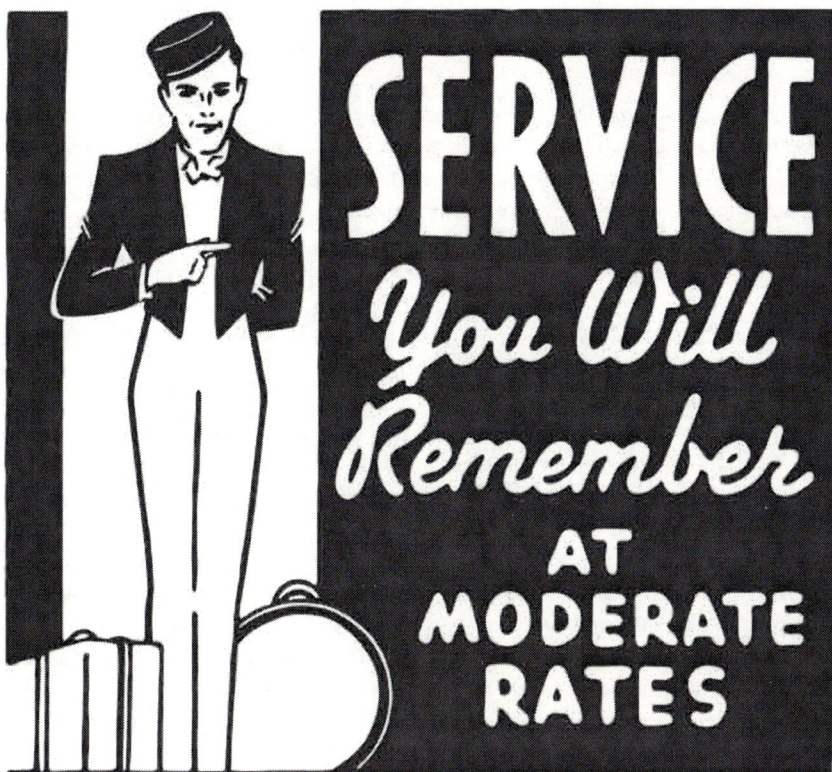

MRS. RUSSELL

"I'll be right up, Mrs. Russell." I unplug the jack and take off the phones.

Lenny leers at me from the desk chair, where he's been industriously linking paper clips together into a chain. The chain is about three feet long.

"Going up to see your girlfriend?" he asks.

"Room service." I answer curtly.

"Oh, I bet." Lenny drawls as I head off to the kitchen, "I bet you give her *real* good service."

"Fuck off, Lenny."

He's noticed that Mrs. Russell always waits until I'm on shift before ordering something, usually tea and cookies, up to her room. It bugs him because he thinks I must be getting tipped well.

If he only knew.

109

Mrs. Russell is one of the Ritz' two permanent residents. She and Mr. Moss in 304 have both been living in the hotel for longer than anyone could remember.

Mr. Moss was a recluse. A health nurse came to look in on him once every two weeks. Other than her, no one in the hotel had seen him in years. His meals were left outside his room and the empty trays collected from the same spot.

His suite had two rooms on either side of an adjoining bathroom and he was always in the locked one while the maids made up the other.

My first visit to Mrs. Russell's rooms I was surprised, when she opened the door, to see that it was furnished differently than the other rooms in the hotel. The bed was a huge old Victorian four-poster with burgundy bed curtains. There must have been thirty pillows piled artfully up on it, no two alike.

Across from the bed was a massive chest of drawers, made of some dark wood with big, heavy looking brass handles on the drawers. A matching vanity with an oval cut-glass mirror stood on one side of the door leading into the other room, which appeared at a glance to be similarly stuffed with vintage pieces.

The whole idea of somebody *living* in a hotel full-time seemed odd to me. It was something out of an old movie with Mae West or somebody like that, conjuring up scenes where everyone stood around in tuxedos with glasses of champagne in their hands, talking in clipped upper class accents.

The surface of the vanity was covered with period feminine hardware, including a brush the size of a paperback, made out of real tortoise shell. Perfume bottles with squeeze balls kept company with silver compacts and in one corner stood a big jewelry box overflowing with expensive-looking baubles.

Being in Mrs. Russell's rooms was like entering a movie set made up for that bygone era, accurate down to the last detail.

When I mentioned it to Betty she said it *was* from another age.

"This place ain't always been a dump, you know. Time was, this joint had real class. That old dame has been here since before it turned into the shithole it is now."

I tried to imagine the Ritz back then, with the cream of prairie society wandering through the halls dressed like Fred and Ginger, smoking through long cigarette holders and chatting oh-so-cleverly about nothing in particular.

"Room service, ma'am," I said in my best professional tone.

"You're new," she said, in an accusatory tone, "Where's David?"

David was the guy I had replaced. Mrs. Russell had apparently been unwell and had just returned from a stay in the hospital. She'd missed David's leaving and had expected to see him at the door. He hadn't been around for weeks, I told her.

"I see. We shall have to break you in, then."

"Ma'am?" I noticed for the first time how tall Mrs. Russell was. Even stooped with age, she had a couple of inches on me. She must have been near six feet in her younger days.

"You will find that I like certain things done in very specific ways," she said, motioning me in. "When one gets to be my age, one no longer appreciates surprises."

I put the tray down on the little side table by the door.

"What kinds of things, ma'am?"

"Well, for example, I notice that you've neglected to pour the water over the tea. In order to make proper tea, it is necessary to pour the water over the tea while the water is still hot—preferably boiling. You will kindly do so in the future."

"Oh. I didn't know that. OK, I can handle that, ma'am. Anything else?"

"Many things, but let's not get ahead of ourselves. There will be plenty of time to...what is the phrase? 'Bring you up to speed.' I think that's it."

"I understand, ma'am. Will there be anything else today?"

"No, I think that will be all, for now. We will resume the lesson tomorrow."

She reaches out and I cup my hand to receive the tip. I try to mask my surprise when she puts, not a bill, but a *coin* into my hand. I wait until I'm out in the hall to look. She's given me a dime.

On my way downstairs I have time to reflect on just how out of touch you'd have to be, to think that a *dime* was a good tip.

Over the next few days I found myself going up to Mrs. Russell's room often, almost always with a tray of tea and 'biscuits'. She almost always had something new to teach me about how she liked things done. I found that she shared my horror for cold-buttered toast.

One day, she ordered two teas. I assumed that she had a guest, but when I got up to her rooms there was no one.

"I thought you might like to join me," she said in the same aloof tone as ever, "Or don't you like tea?"

I said I liked tea just fine and thus began our friendship.

We spent a few minutes together almost every day after that. She was always careful to time her room service order towards the end of the morning rush and she didn't mind waiting if I had a few other customers to take care of first. She knew I would be there when I had time to stay for a cup of tea and a visit.

For my part, I welcomed a little break at that time of day and Mrs. Russell's rooms were a safe haven from other duties, complete with a perfect alibi. I began to look forward to our time together. Mrs. Russell was an amiable enough person in her way, although she never left any doubt that, as far as she was concerned, I was still "the help."

When I joined her for tea (always Earl Grey), Mrs. Russell would invite me into the second of her two rooms, which she referred to as "the sitting room." It was furnished with a large overstuffed sofa and matching chair in a dark burgundy fabric that had a leaf design work into the surface. A coffee table and two end tables were of a very dark wood, possibly cherry, with incredibly detailed carving on the legs. There was a stained glass lamp on each of the end tables and a hinged room divider with the same peacock pattern in the stained glass panels. Behind it I could glimpse a beautiful satin covered chaise lounge with an afghan throw across it.

On the back of the chair and lounge were draped big cloths, like doilies. Three more of them adorned the back of the couch. I'd seen them at my grandmothers' house when I visited there as a child and I'd always wondered what they were, so I asked Mrs. Russell one day.

"Those are called antimacassars," she said, "so named because the men would slick down their hair with something called 'Macassar Oil', which ruined the backs of your chairs. They've outlived their function. I suppose, over time, they just became a fashion. Why would such a thing interest someone your age?"

I told her about my grandma's house.

"I don't know, I guess I've just always been into stuff like that."

"You've got an inquiring mind, Rick. Tell me, what do you do with 'stuff like that', once you find it? Do you keep some kind of record?"

"Naw, I just like to find stuff out, you know? It's cool."

"It's more than that. It's research. You should write it down, Rick. You should keep a diary, or a journal. If a thing is worth finding out, it's worth preserving. The human memory is not a reliable thing."

She was curious about my life out in the world and grilled me about it endlessly. I tried to be forthcoming about things and, oddly enough, I found myself opening up to her in ways I never had with anyone, except maybe Joe Wasic. She never hesitated to give me advice when she felt I needed some but she always stopped short of patronizing me. Like Joe, she treated me like an adult.

When it was my turn to ask questions I was rewarded with wonderful stories from her life, and what a life it had been. She was old. How old, I never knew, but she remembered her father allowing her a glass of champagne at the party for the turn of the century, so that gave me some idea.

She was the granddaughter of early settlers in the area, who'd done well enough in the fur trade and various other enterprises to purchase a lot of land along the river and hang onto it until the real estate boom around the turn of the century had made them rich. They'd sold off all of their property except a modest farm overlooking the river valley.

Mrs. Russell remembered going to visit the next-door neighbors at Christmas, a journey of half a day, by horse drawn sleigh.

"We would heat up stones in the oven until they were red hot and then father would have our man carry them out with the ice tongs and lay them into a sort of iron cage under the seat. Then we'd all wrap up in a buffalo robe and be comfy and warm the whole way there."

She had gone to school in a one-room schoolhouse somewhere near the downtown area, and then at the brand new school across the river for high school.

As a young woman, she went to Paris to study art for a couple of years but had to return after an "affair of the heart" had left her broken-hearted and depressed. She never told me the name of the guy, but it could have been any one of the major artists of the time. She knew them all; Picasso, Monet, Degas. She hung around with these guys in the cafes and modeled for them.

"Picasso was a boar of a man with no manners whatsoever. He used the women in his life as models and whatever else suited his fancy and when he was done with them he discarded them like stale bread," she told me.

When the First World War started she and a couple of friends volunteered for the Red Cross and she ended up at a forward aid station near the front. She was close enough to see the artillery flashes on the horizon and hear the bombardments as they fell. Then the casualties would come in.

"It was terrible to see what they'd done to those boys. That's what most of them were, just boys, not much older than you. It was impossible to see them come in torn apart, missing limbs or eyes and to go on functioning, but there was no choice. They needed us. So we did it anyways, binding them up and stitching them up and holding them while they died anyways...we put our feelings away and did what we had to do for those beautiful boys. We did our crying later. I cried for years for those boys."

I'd had the feeling she had forgotten I was in the room but suddenly she focused back on me and she reached across to grab my hand in hers as her eyes burned into mine with a desperate ferocity.

"Never let them tell you there is anything noble or heroic about war, Rick. There isn't. War is nothing but blood and slaughter. It is the worst that we can be. Don't let them tell you otherwise, so they can get you to put on a uniform and fight for them. Promise me you'll never go to war."

I promised. And I meant it. The way she'd described the things she'd seen made me understand the true nature of war in a way that all the theatrical realism of the TV shows had not. I was suddenly aware of the awful reality of the contract I'd been ready to sign with the Military; sure, they'd teach me how to play in a marching band and a lot of other stuff, too. All I had to do was be ready to get called up and with a few weeks advanced training, get shipped off to the next place they needed young men to be shot at.

My experience in the basement of Girard's house had taught me just how quickly death could come and how final it really was. Looking down the barrel of that shotgun as Girard's finger tightened on the trigger, I knew that it wasn't like the games we'd played as boys with our toys. I wasn't going to fall down in the grass and count to ten before I got up again. I knew that when I fell down this time, there would be no getting up and that all the things I'd always thought would come to me through my life would be irretrievably lost forever.

I vowed to quit the cadets and I meant it. Mrs. Russell seemed to accept me at my word. She relaxed a bit and went on.

"Once back in Canada, I just became bored and decided to 'do the tour' with my sister. That's what they called going around the world in those days, only we didn't make it even half way around the world, really. 'The Tour' consisted of cruising down the coast of Europe in a luxury liner. If you wanted something to look at besides ocean, you travelled POSH. Port out, starboard home. That way you could see the coast from your stateroom. We sailed down the coast, stopping in at various ports of call along the way, and through the Mediteranean. The furthest south we got was Gibralter, which apparently was considered almost Africa."

She met a Spaniard in Malta and followed him home against her fathers' wishes, shacking up in a villa near Madrid. When the Revolution came, she found herself siding with the communists and against her fascist boyfriend.

She joined the International Brigade and fought in the streets of Barcelona. Her face lit up as she described the victory there and the feeling of solidarity among the fighters.

"I met a young Catalan officer and fell in love, followed him into battle and spent several months living in a trench while the snipers tried to end the tryst prematurely. They need not have bothered. The family fortune had been wiped out in the depression at home and he lost interest when the checks stopped coming."

The future Mrs. Russell returned home to help the family recoup and found herself resorting to desperate measures just to keep body and soul together.

She told me how she and her brother would hitch up the old horse and take their buckboard wagon down to the train yards, where the cattle were unloaded at the stockyards.

"The cattle cars all had straw laid down on the floor for the manure, you see—so that the floors wouldn't get so slippery that the cattle would fall and injure themselves. An eleven-hundred-pound Hereford with a broken leg is no easy thing to move.

After they unloaded, the men would just sweep it all out between the tracks and leave it to rot. It was the best fertilizer in the world."

They would shovel it into the wagon until they had a full load and take it to the rich part of town to sell to the gardeners. It wasn't strictly legal, because technically the fertilizer belonged to the railroad, but apparently the supervisors in the yard had a thing for watching the tall girl shoveling cow shit.

"I'd be lying if I said I didn't give the meaner ones a little smile now and then," she said candidly.

The family made the most of what they had and somehow got through the thirties with the remaining quarter section of the original estate intact. After WWll, the city was growing like crazy and they found themselves in the middle of a new land boom.

Their land, once located a couple of miles outside of town, was now surrounded by sub-divisions and much in demand. They wisely held on and divided it up themselves instead of selling it outright. One of her brothers went into the construction business and developed the lots at a huge profit.

It was around this time that Mrs. Russell got involved with a married man. He was rich and powerful and apparently swept her off her feet before she learned of his marital status. It did not end well. She told me that he was in politics and was planning on running for high office, so the affair had to end before the press got wind of it.

Once again she mentioned no names and I've wondered ever since who it could have been. I had to admire her discretion, though, when, after all, the cad had taken advantage of her.

The obvious thing to do after that, of course, was to go around the world again, only this time, with modern aircraft to help out, she really went around the world. She visited every major city in every country on the globe. It took three years and when it was over she was in Australia, where she met Mr. Russell.

He was the kind of man you read about in biographies—the kind that we don't see anymore because of the way that the world has changed so much. He grew up on a cattle station in the outback, already well-off from his fathers' labors, and became one of the first people to realize that the center of Australia held more than murderous deserts and poisonous snakes. It also held wealth in the form of mineral deposits the like of which the world had never known.

The story was that he'd become a flier and spent a lot of his time flitting about the outback in his small plane, looking for adventure and new horizons. One day, tooling around over the edge of the Nullarbor Plain, he'd developed engine trouble and had been forced to put down on a rocky outcrop. When he stepped down from the cockpit he noticed that the rock he was standing on had a strange ringing resonance to it when walked on.

Long story short, he'd discovered the biggest load of almost pure iron ore ever found. Almost overnight he was the richest man in Australia. A few years and several more well staked claims later he was the richest man in the southern hemisphere.

James Russell was one of that breed of men who never found anything that he couldn't become good at. His life was a constant search for new contests, almost as if he hungered for one that he couldn't win.

As a pilot he set records that stood for decades. He discovered several new species of wildlife in Australia and had an island named after him in the South Pacific. A consummate sailor, he led an expedition to Antarctica that came near to being lost in the pack ice but for his skill as a navigator. Mrs. Russell had a photograph of him standing in front of a tent with several other men, all dressed in some kind of military uniform.

"That's Earnest Shacklton-lovely man. Next to him is Arthur Conan Doyle, monumental fool and writer of foolish drivel, and this one is Jan Smitts, who later became the Prime Minister of South Africa. That pasty-faced little man in the foreground is Roger Pocock, who wasn't anything in particular except a very poor writer and the one who started this little group of theirs. They all liked to think of themselves as soldiers, you see—ready to go to the rescue of the Dominion at a moments' notice. Called themselves the 'League of Frontiersmen,' or something."

They met at some high society do in Sydney; she fresh from her world tour and brimming with stories, he looking distinctly uncomfortable in his tux and tails. The chemistry was instant and obvious between them but for some reason he had failed to pursue it and she flew home the next day, feeling that something important had been missed.

She needn't have worried, though, because he followed her there a few weeks later. Russell had heard about the oil discoveries in the Canadian west and decided to come north to seek the black gold, or at least that's what he told everyone.

"His arrival in town was reported with great rhetoric in the society pages of the local press. He and a small entourage of business types and secretaries set up shop in the hotel, taking the entire third floor, including these two rooms."

A fancy dress ball was thrown in his honor, where he was delighted to see the tall Canadian woman who'd so impressed him. He wasted no time pledging his troth and in the shortest possible time, they were wed.

"We were soul-mates," she told me, "there was no doubt about it, right from the first moment our eyes met."

Russell was an expert shot and a keen hunter who had returned again and again to Africa where his adventures on safari alone would have made for a lively novel. They had their honeymoon on safari in Kenya, where James was delighted to find his new wife to be an eager student to the mysteries of the hunt. She took to the bush like she'd been born there and learned to shoot large bore guns with unnatural ease.

Together they bagged an impressive array of the world's most dangerous prey by day and in the evening he would entertain her around the campfire with stories of hunts he'd had in the past. By the time their scheduled hunt had neared its end, they had shot every beast known to the white hunter's trade save for one; the white rhino.

"Our guide had been forced to leave us in the hands of a second in order to keep prior engagements, and knowing the new man had not actually led a rhino hunt before, James rashly decided to carry on and try to cap the hunt with the one trophy still outstanding."

It was to be his last mistake.

"The wind shifted and the beast caught our scent. The two men assigned to cover our flanks lost their nerve and ran. We could have called off the hunt even then and backed away from the animal, but James wouldn't have it. You could see it in him, the blood lust. He smelled a kill.

It was never like that for me. I hunted for the skill of it; the pitting of ones' abilities as a tracker, a hunter and finally a shooter, against the wild instincts and the senses of the prey. To outwit the beast—that was the hunt for me. Not James. For him it was a visceral thing. Sensual. Sinful, I suppose but in Africa those lines become blurred.

He pressed on and when the rhino charged, it was only yards away. That's something you never forget, once you see it—the charge of a full-grown rhino. It's like having a mountain suddenly decide to fall on you. There seems to be nothing you could do to stop it. You can lose your nerve in the face of that kind of power and if you lose your nerve, you will die.

Not that James lost his nerve. That man had no nerves on the hunt. No, he didn't lose his nerve. He missed his shot."

She turned to me, then, angry and indignant at an unfair fate. It was like she'd never gotten a chance to give Russell hell about it, so she was giving me hell instead, all these years later. I didn't mind. I was riveted by the story.

"How the hell can you miss something that big at such a close range? A child could have made that shot! I could have made that shot with my eyes closed! My God!" she cried, banging her fist down on the arm of her chair.

Then the anger went out of her and she sank back in her seat.

"He missed." She said simply, shrugging her boney shoulders, her palms turned up helplessly. She paused, staring at the floor.

"I had no shot. The big lummox was standing in the way. I couldn't kill the damned thing until it was already done with him..."

Mrs. Russell shook herself and came back to the present.

"So he died there in Africa and I became a widow. I came home and found that we still had the rooms booked for the rest of the year. I've never left."

So that's how Mrs. Russell ended up living in the Ritz. It was nice and central, had all the amenities and she was able to do a bit of travelling without having to worry about someone to look after her place.

"I always loved meeting new people and as I got on a bit and travel became more difficult and less enjoyable, I found it was perfect for me, living here. The new people came to me, you see?"

I asked her why she'd never married again.

"Oh, I had a few proposals, over the years. Of course, one could never be sure if they were attracted to me or to Mr. Russell's money, but I don't think that was the reason I never took another husband. They were all fine gentlemen, each in his own way, but I suppose I always measured them against James. Not fair to them, really. They just don't make them like that anymore."

So we passed the time each day, telling each other stories and somewhere along the way we became friends. At the end of each visit, Mrs. Russell would always tell me to hold out my hand and give me my tip. It was always the same—a dime. I started saving them one day, just to see how many I ended up with.

On my way up to her rooms now, I have no idea what she might want and no way of knowing that this would be the visit that would change our friendship forever. I arrive at her door and knock as usual but this time there is no reply. I wait a respectful minute before knocking again. Still nothing.

I'm getting worried and thinking about using the master key when the chain on the door slides loose.

"Mrs. Russell? Everything OK?"

The door opens just a sliver.

"Sssh-you must be quiet."

"OK," I answer in a whisper, "are you all right?"

"Yes, yes. I'm going to open the door but you must be quiet and move very slowly."

"All right, I promise." What the heck is this? Does she have mice in her room?

The door swings open slowly. Mrs. Russell is behind it, beckoning with one hand as she holds the door with the other. I take a step. She holds up her hand.

"There." She whispers. "You should be able to see them from there."

The room is empty, as always. Mrs. Russell is pointing to the mirror on the door to the other room, looking at me expectantly. There is nothing out of the ordinary in the reflection of the next room, either.

"What is it I'm looking for, Mrs. Russell?"

"Shhh! You'll frighten them away. Didn't I tell you to be quiet? Well, they're gone, now."

"What is it, mice?"

"No no no, it's not mice. You might as well go. You can't do any good if you can't keep your voice down. I'll call you when they come out again but this time you must *be quiet*."

I have to move fast to keep from having the door closed on my feet. It slams in my face and I'm left standing in the hallway, bewildered. If it's not mice, what is it? A shiver runs down my spine.

Several times over the next few days this scene is repeated. When I go up for tea, Mrs. Russell is distracted, on edge. Her eyes dart about the room, looking for something that I can't see. When I press her to tell me what it is, her answers are vague.

"You'll see. They can't hide forever from you. You'll see them and then you'll know."

By now I realize that Mrs. Russell is losing touch with reality. I wonder if I'm the only person who knows. I take it up with Gary.

"Sounds like she's losing it, all right. Bummer, man. I like the old girl. Everybody does. I guess it was inevitable, rattling around in those two rooms for so long. One thing for sure—you don't want Eddy to find out."

"Why not?"

"He's been looking for an excuse to kick her out for years. She has a lease agreement on those rooms that goes back to when she first moved in. Iron clad. Can you imagine how cheap rooms must have been then? And she probably got a special price by paying in advance for who-knows-how-long. They lose money on those rooms but there's nothing they can do about it."

"Wow. You're right. Well, he won't hear it from me."

"Yeah, me neither."

It was about this time that Mrs. Russell sprained her ankle when she missed a step on the stairs. She never used the elevator. She thought it was for lazy people. For a couple of weeks she had to take all her meals in her room. Of course, I was only there for breakfast and lunch, so the other bellhops were taking her dinner to her. It wasn't long before the stories got around.

One morning as I'm getting ready to take tea up to her, I notice Lenny watching me with a sardonic grin on his face.

"Ain't you gonna take your butterfly net up with you?"

"Fuck off, Lenny."

"Who's gonna make me—you?"

"Just keep it to yourself, all right? She doesn't need everyone knowing her business."

"Yes *sir*."

I head upstairs with the tea tray, my feet heavy with dread. On the way past the smoke shop I notice Mel 'watching' me pass by. He shakes his head sadly and makes a little 'tut-tut' sound.

Upstairs, I pause and take a deep breath before I knock on Mrs. Russell's door. She opens the door right away and stands back to let me in.

"I think this has gone on long enough," she says. Her voice sounds strong, in control like the old Mrs. Russell, but she looks awful. Her hair is a mess and her makeup looks like a five-year-old had put it on.

"What is the problem, Mrs. Russell?"

"You know perfectly well what the problem is. I want them out!"

"You want...*who* out, ma'am?"

"Don't you be impertinent with *me*, young man. I have been calling and calling...well, no more! I want them out, and I want them out today, do you hear?"

"Mrs. Russell, I hear you. I just don't know what you are talking about."

She turns and takes a step towards the chest of drawers. She turns back and poses dramatically before indicating the space under the chest with a theatrical sweep of her arm.

"There!" she cries. "Them!"

"I'm afraid I just don't see anything, ma'am."

"Do you mean you are going to *stand there* and deny their presence to my face, when we can both see them, plain as day!?"

"Mrs. Russell," I say, as calmly as I can, "there's *nothing there*."

"Ahhh, I see how things are. It seems to me that *they* never came out until after *you* came."

"Please, Mrs. Russell..."

"Well, what are you after, eh?" she takes a step towards me. I retreat a step. "My jewels?" She takes another step. I take another one backwards. "I saw you looking at them. That's it, isn't it? Well, you won't get them, I tell you—you and your little *friends*."

By now, she's backed me right out the door into the hall. As I stand there gaping at her ferocity, she slams the door in my face. I can still hear her, though, ranting and raving through the door.

My hands are shaking. I feel sick to my stomach. I could easily leave, go back downstairs and let somebody else deal with this later. I can't. I can't run away and leave Mrs. Russell to fight the little imaginary men alone.

The maids' room is just around the corner. I use my passkey to get in. It only takes me a minute to find what I need. Returning to Mrs. Russell's room, I don't hear anything at the door. I knock softly.

"Mrs. Russell, it's me," I say through the wooden door, "I'm here to help. Will you let me in?"

After a short pause, she opens up, looking at me curiously.

"I think we've fooled them, ma'am," I whisper, "have they come back out yet?"

"Just now, but what…"

"Shh…" I show her what I've brought; a big bristle broom. "This is what we need to get them out but we have to take them by surprise."

"Oh!" her hand flies to cover her mouth. She looks at me with a mixture of excitement and trepidation, like a little girl on a prank with her older brother.

"Here's what we'll do," I continue in a whisper, "You invite me in as usual and then stand back, by the door."

She nods, warming to the whole idea.

"Oh, it's you again. Come on in." she says out loud. If she'd been auditioning for a role in a play just then, Mrs. Russell would have gotten the part. I try to do as well.

Holding the broom out in front of me, I advance menacingly to the chest of drawers.

"All right, you little creeps—the games up! You've over-stayed your welcome!" I take a swipe at the empty space under the bureau. "Go on, get!"

I do my best to mime chasing the little men out of there and into the hallway, where I pretend to pursue them to the end of the corridor. When I return to the room, Mrs. Russell is looking under the bed.

"Did we get them all, Mrs. Russell?"

"Yes, I think so," she says. She looks at me with her eyes shining with relief and gratitude. "Thank you so much! You don't know what it's been like, living here with them under there, chattering away in that language of theirs. I haven't been able to sleep. But I shall sleep tonight, thanks to you."

"That's great, Mrs. Russell. Well, I'd better be getting back to work, now."

Suddenly she seizes my hand in both of hers. They feel like cold lizard hands, dry and papery. Her nails are digging into my skin. She peers into my eyes with fright in hers.

"You don't suppose they'll come back, do you?"

"Oh, I don't think so, ma'am. I really put the fear into them, you know? They won't dare come around tonight. But if they do, you call me and we'll chase them away together, OK?"

"Oh, that's wonderful. But—wait. I almost forgot, what with all the excitement."

She goes over a retrieves something from the clutter on the bureau. I know what it is even before she presses it into my hand. It's a dime, to add to my collection.

That's the way it went for a while. Mrs. Russell would call down when she knew I was on shift and whisper over the phone for help. Upstairs I would go, brandishing my trusty broom and chase them away so she could sleep.

At first, the little men would stay away for a week or so after each exorcism but, as time progressed, they would return sooner and sooner until I was going up to her rooms every day.

"They are growing bolder, you know." she confided.

Still, at least we were friends again and I was helping her the only way I could. I didn't mind, most days. I suppose I knew that it couldn't go on forever. I just couldn't think of anything else to do.

The trouble was, I wasn't the only one she told about her little visitors. Some of the maids started to complain. It wasn't long before her behavior took a turn for the worse.

She began to accuse people of taking things from her room. Several times, Tiger was called upon to investigate thefts that turned out not to have occurred. Finally Eddy insisted on taking an inventory and putting all her really expensive stuff in the safe downstairs.

Tiger talked about her like she'd come down with the plague.

"Crazy old bat, she's headed for the looney bin, sure as hell."

It wasn't hard to see that the time was coming when the trouble she was causing would finally give Eddy the excuse he needed to get rid of her and free up her rooms. When it did come, I was surprised how it affected me.

I came to work on the afternoon shift to find an ambulance parked out front. Fearing another altercation between Tiger and some hapless drunk, I entered the lobby unprepared.

Betty saw the look on my face and filled me in.

"It's old Mrs. Russell," she said, "They've come to take her away."

As I turned to the elevator, the door opened and there she was, trussed up in blankets on a gurney with restraints across her chest and legs. Two cheerful looking, burly young fellows wheeled her straight for the front entrance. I moved to intercept them and one guy made a sweeping motion with his hand.

I stood aside to let them pass. My fists kept clenching and un-clenching. The closer they came, the more clearly I could see Mrs. Russell's face.

She looked like someone who needed to go to the hospital. In the harsh light of the lobby it was easy to see how far she'd slid. There seemed to be no trace left of the dignified lady from another time. Her wild hair and glaring eyes made her look completely like the madwoman she'd become.

Then, just as the gurney came abreast of me, she turned her face to me. Her eyes cleared as she recognized me.

"There you are, Rick," she said, "I didn't want to go without saying goodbye. We seem to be leaving in a bit of a hurry. Would you mind sending my things along?"

I had to swallow a big lump in my throat so I could answer her.

"No problem, Mrs. Russell, I'll see that they are sent off as soon as possible, ma'am."

"Thank you," she said, then she turned to one of the attendants. "This is the one."

"You Rick?" he asked, coming around the end of the gurney as his partner continued out the door with it. "I got something for you. She said she'd come along quietly if we promised to deliver this to you."

I looked down at the object he placed in my hand. It was a roll of dimes.

"Must mean something special, I guess, eh?" the guy asked, curious.

I looked outside to see that the other attendant had already closed the back of the ambulance and gone around to the driver's side.

"Something special. Yeah, that's right. Thanks."

That week I resigned from the cadets as I had promised her I would. I gave back all the government owned loaners and gave the rest to Miles. It was all I could think of to do honor to her. It hardly seemed enough.

THE BIKERS

RRRNNNGGG goes the front desk bell.

It's midday on a Friday afternoon. Hot, stuffy July air hangs like a sentence over our heads in the lobby. Everybody's got that little edge to them that you get when the hot weather just won't let up.

A morning spent cleaning up after a Shriners convention in the ballroom hasn't improved my mood, although I do have a new appreciation for human ingenuity. I counted thirty condoms hanging down from the light fixtures, filled with something that looked suspiciously like whipped cream. The light fixtures were about thirty feet up, so the obvious question was how they got them up there.

I'd find it more amusing if the other question wasn't "who's going to have to get the ladder out of the basement and get them down from there?" because I know the answer to that one.

"Could be worse," I'm thinking, as I get up to answer the bell, "I could be working tonight."

If the weather didn't let up, and it was showing no sign of doing so, the hotel was going to be a dangerous place tonight.

"May I help you?" I ask of the bell ringer. He is a smallish gent in his mid thirties, a bit thin on top and rumpled elsewhere. He has a brief case but no other luggage with him.

"Salesman." I think to myself.

"You have a room, um reserved, ah...'"

"Under what name?"

"Oh! Ah, um-it would be under Lakeland Sales, er...Wynn...is the name."

I can spot 'em a mile away, by now.

"Ah yes, here it is. Mr. Wynn, a single bed. Three nights, is that correct?"

"Oh. Ah, yes—that's right, except that I might want to stay through to Tuesday if, uh that is depending on um..."

"Depending on how the sales calls go?"

"Yes! Er, yes, if the requirement comes up for me to meet with a client on Monday, um."

"So, would you like me to reserve the room for one more night, with the option to cancel, if it turns out you don't need it, sir?"

"Oh! Yes. That would be fine, that is, um-if there would be no charge...er."

"No extra charge, sir. You pay for the room only if you use it. OK?"

"Y-Yes, that will be fine, then."

"Great. Just let the desk know on Monday whether or not you'll be staying over, say, by noon or so."

"Noon? But check out time is eleven, isn't it...ah?"

"Usually it is, sir, but on a Monday it's really not that crucial. The place is generally about half empty on Monday."

"Oh! Well, is the restaurant open...eh?"

"Yes, sir. You can get room service from seven a.m. until nine."

I slide the registration card across to him, thinking 'How did a nervous Nelly like this guy get into sales? He must be one heck of a closer.'

Just then another guest comes up and asks for his room key. Mr. Jessop, room 222. I don't have to look, I checked him in myself this morning. There are no messages in his slot, so I just hand him his key.

When he reaches for it, Mr. Wynn suddenly becomes aware of him and jumps about a foot to the side, startled.

"Sorry, pal-didn't mean to surprise you."

"Yes, yes—no...um, excuse me." Says Mr. Wynn.

"OK." Says Mr. Jessup, heading for the elevator, and gives me a look that says 'Hoo, boy!'

Mr. Wynn has finished filling out his registration card. I can tell by the way he places all the fingertips of both hands on the very edge of it and pushes it towards me.

"I have some luggage, uh, er, in my car...ah, in the parking lot—that's free for guests, is it, um... not?"

"Yes, sir. Here is your parking pass. You'll want to put that in the front window of your car. I'll just get someone to cover for me while I get your bags. Where are you?"

"Umm, well, right here—I don't..."

"I'm sorry, I meant to ask where your car is."

"Oh! Yes, of course. It's just at the side door, there in the little alley...I hope that's all right."

"In the breezeway? That's fine. Save us a walk. I'll follow you out, just let me get the desk clerk."

I give the bell a smack and yell 'FRONT!' to let Betty know she's needed. Mr. Wynn jumps another foot to the side. Too many more loud noises and he'll be out the front door.

"Sorry." I say. Now he's got me doing it.

As Mr. Wynn precedes me across the lobby, I see Betty coming through the café doors, balancing a cup of coffee and a piece of pie. Hurrying through the short hall that leads out to the breezeway doors, I step out into dazzling sunlight.

I can just make out the shadowy outline of a battered Valiant parked by the curb. A fuzzy shape about the size of Mr. Wynn stands beside it.

"Is this your car?" I open my mouth to say, just as another voice says the exact same words.

"Is this your car?"

I turn, confused, toward the sound of the voice but I still can't make out any detail, just a large form haloed by the brilliant sunlight. Mr. Wynn is just as confused by this turn of events as I am. Asked the right question by the wrong person, he answers automatically.

"Yes, um... this is it." He gets no further before the dark shape advances toward him, into the partial shade of the walkway above, resolving into an unexpected sight.

He is large, dirty man with long hair and a gritty black beard. His brawny arms are bare except for tattoos, of which they boast several. He has on a sleeveless shirt under a denim vest.

'Dirty' doesn't begin to describe the state of the jeans he wears over solid-looking black leather boots, which match the wide belt and the sheath of the big hunting knife suspended from it. He has a huge black leather wallet, as well. It sticks out of his back pocket, secured to the belt with a length of sturdy chain.

He walks over to Mr. Wynn, takes hold of the lapels of his suit and lifts him bodily into the air.

"You need to learn better driving manners, asshole," he growls.

"Urk," replies Mr. Wynn.

Mr. Wynn's assailant carries him over to his car and throws him down on the hood. The sound of his body landing on the metal hood echoes in the confined space.

For the first time, I notice the two chopped Harleys, leaning on their kick-stands behind the Valiant. On of them is occupied by a slightly smaller version of Mr. Wynn's attacker, who is grinning a big happy grin like he's really amused. His muscular forearms are folded on his chest, revealing an equal wealth of tattoos.

"*Smack!*" I know *that* sound. Turning back to the car, I notice the big guy's vest has a crest on the back. It says "Wild Boars" in ornate old English letters over a grotesque rendering of a pig with massive tusks. Underneath it says, "Seattle."

Mr. Wynn, glasses askew, peers at me from under one of the bikers' armpits. "Help! I'm being assaulted, here!"

I automatically take a tentative step forward but as I do, I notice the other guy, on the bike, looking at me. Grinning like it's all a big joke, he raises one hand, forefinger up and waggles it at me.

"Ah-ah-ahhh!" His voice rises in imitation of someone chastising a child. I get the message. What was I thinking, anyways? I look back at the door I just came through, weighing options.

"Smack!" another blow lands, knocking Mr. Wynn's glasses to the ground.

Adrenaline is surging through me, screaming at me to *do* something, but what?

Call Tiger? He's the security man. This is what he gets paid for. How? The P.A. system at the desk, dummy—now *move*.

I'm off, through the doors and down the little hall toward the lobby. Rounding the corner, I nearly collide with one of the maids, a new girl. I can't remember her name.

Consuella? That's it.

"Consuella, have you seen Tiger?" I grab her shoulders, shouting into her face. Her eyes widen with fright.

"Que?"

"Do you know where Tiger is? You know, Tiger the bouncer? There are two big apes attacking Mr. Wynn in the breezeway! They're Wild Boars, from Seattle!"

The color drains from Consuella's face. Her voice comes out in a tiny mouse-like squeek.

"No comprende, senor."

I abandon the girl and run for the front desk, where Betty is simultaneously eating pie, reading a magazine, smoking a cigarette and drinking coffee. She puts her coffee cup down when she sees me coming.

"Betty, quick! Page Tiger! Two bikers are assaulting Mr. Wynn, out in the breezeway!"

Betty closes her magazine and eyes me suspiciously.

"Mr. Wynn, did you say?" For all the excitement in her voice, I might have just told her that he'd called down for an extra pillow.

"Wynn, right—new guest, just checked him in—went out to get his bags and these two guys jumped him. Where's Tiger?"

She puts her cigarette in the ashtray and takes her glasses off, studying my face for a second, then moves over to the switchboard. Picking up the headset, she dials for an outside line all without taking her eyes from me.

"Outside in the breezeway, you said? And this is happening now?"

I nod, too out of breath to speak. I'm literally hopping from one foot to the other.

"Dispatch?" she says into the phone, "this is Betty, front desk at the Ritz. We have an assault in progress. Can you get a car to the west entrance right away? That's right. Betty. West entrance, in the alleyway. Thank you."

She hangs up and picks up the big steel microphone for the hotels' public address system. Thumbing the switch, she speaks into it and we can hear her voice reverberating from speakers all over the building.

"Hotel Security, to the west entrance immediately, please. Security to the west entrance."

I've been standing there with my chest heaving, filled with the need to be doing something, anything.

"Maybe I'd better go back out there and see if I can help Mr. Wynn?" It comes out like a question.

"No, don't do that," Betty tells me. "You know, I think Tiger might just be on the fourth floor and I'm not sure the P.A. is working up on four. Why don't you just run up and see if you can find him?"

I start off toward the elevator.

"No time to wait for the elevator, kid. Better take the stairs. And if you don't see him up there, check the tavern."

By the time I get back from my fruitless search upstairs and down, I've burned all that adrenaline out of my system and missed all the excitement. The cops arrived to find a disheveled but otherwise unharmed Mr. Wynn locked inside his car, where apparently he'd bolted after the biker turned him loose.

The blows I heard were slaps, not punches or he probably would have been a lot worse off. I figured he was lucky to have come away from it all with nothing more than a broken pair of glasses but he was most indignant about the affair, insisting that he'd done nothing to provoke the attack.

There was still no sign of Tiger. Betty had called Eddy down from the accounting office to talk to the police and they'd requested that Consuella and me go to his office to give statements.

There were two officers on the case; a younger one with an impatient air about him and a thing about taking notes, and a world-weary corporal with lots of grey in his hair. They decided to take Consuella's statement first and that's how I ended up sitting behind the switchboard, waiting my turn.

The door to Eddy's office is a little ajar, so I can hear what they are saying. So can Betty and, unfortunately Lenny, who came on shift to find the fun all but over. We're all three crowded around the switchboard desk, straining to hear the maid's shy voice.

"Speak up, please, miss," says the young cop, "and please, English only, OK?"

"Si. I mean, jess, sir."

"Now, why don't you just take it from the beginning and tell us what happened. You were coming down the hall, and the bellboy came running in from outside, is that right?"

"Si-jess, sir. And he was jelling."

"Yelling."

"Si, jelling. He asked me did I see a Tiger in the hotel."

"A tiger."

"Si. And then he says there is Gorillas in the alley."

"Gorillas?"

"Jes, sir. He says there is two gorillas attacking Senor Weend in the alley. And then he says the Tiger...he is bouncing!"

"Bouncing?" this from the other cop-the young one.

"Tha's what he says. The beeg apes is attacking Senor Weend in the breeze, and the Tiger is bouncing in the Hotel. I theen' maybe he is smoking the marijuana, this boy."

"Whoa, hold on a second here." It's the older cop again. "Let's just back up a bit...was it Apes, or gorillas?"

"Beeg apes, he says. Is the same theen, jess? A couple' beeg apes, beating up Mr. Weend in the breeze. Then he says about the bouncing Tiger."

"Ah, excuse me, officer," Eddy interrupts, "If I might interrupt -"Tiger" is the name of our security man here."

"Security man. The bouncer."

"That's right."

"OK, so Tiger is the bouncer."

"I theen he was talkin' about Weenie the Poop."

"Say what, now?"

"Jou know, Weenie the Poop? He has a fren' called Tiger, who bounces on hees tail."

"What in the thundering Jesus..."

"Tigger, corporal."

"What?"

"I guess you'd have to have little kids, for that one. It's a kids' story called Winnie the Pooh. Winnie the Pooh is a bear who has a friend called Tigger, who bounces on his tail."

"Si! Si! Weenie the Poop! Jou know heem?"

"Not personally, miss. Was there anything else you can recall?"

"Oh, si senor. After he tell me about the Tiger bouncing, he says the beeg apes aren't apes...they are Wile' Peegs!"

"Wild Pigs?"

"Si. From Seattle."

"Wild Pigs from Seattle."

"Si."

"And what were they doing here?"

"Who?"

"The Wild Peegs, er...Pigs."

At this point I notice Lenny behind me. I look over to see his face convulsed in suppressed laughter. Betty is likewise incapacitated, fanning her face with her hand and shuddering with silent mirth.

"What were the Wild Pigs doing while the apes were beating up Mr. Wynn?"

"They was coming from Seattle."

Betty emits a little snort. She crams her knuckles into her mouth and turns away, her shoulders shaking. Lenny mouths the words 'Man, are you screwed' to me.

"I see, well, um...I don't see much point in detaining you any further, miss. I'm sure you have duties to get back to."

"Oh, si. Jou should talk to thees boy, senor. I theen he's a lil' bit crazy."

"Uh-huh, well, thanks for your time."

Consuella exits the office by the lobby door. We all scramble to look busy as the side door opens and Eddy looks out.

"OK, kid, you're up." He gives me a hard 'you'd better not mess this up' look as I move past him into the office. The two policemen are looking at me expectantly.

The older one is sitting by the side of the desk. The young guy looks down at his notebook and applies an eraser vigorously. Eddy motions me to the only free chair and perches himself on the corner of the desk.

"Well... Rick, is it?" the older cop starts, "Right. We were hoping you could shed some light on the events of this afternoon."

"Please," mumbles the younger cop, earning a sharp glance from his superior.

"I hope so, sir. It's not as complicated as you think."

"Sure, well, why don't you just take it from the top and tell us what happened with Mr. Wynn?"

"Yes sir. I was checking Mr. Wynn in. He had reservations for two nights but he wanted to have the option of staying over for a third, depending..."

"Sorry to interrupt, Rick," the older guy says, "suppose we just try to stick to the relevant information, all right?"

"Sure. Sorry. Well, we went out to the breezeway to get Mr. Wynn's bags from his car."

"You went out the side entrance."

"To the breezeway, like I said. It was really bright out, you know? I couldn't see anything, at first."

"So you didn't actually see this man approach Mr. Wynn?"

"Not at first, but when he stepped into the shade I saw him well enough."

"Well enough that you could recognize him if you saw him again?" the young cop interjects.

"Let's not get ahead of ourselves," says the older one, before I can answer. He turns to me.

"You said guy, singular. I thought there were two of them?"

"Yes sir, but only the one came up to us. I didn't see the other guy at first, 'cause he stayed on his bike."

"OK, so one guy steps into the shade to confront Mr. Wynn and the other one stays with the bikes, which are parked-where?"

"Right behind Mr. Wynn's car."

"That would be the Plymouth?" asks the corporal.

"1962 Plymouth Valiant," says the younger guy, consulting his notes.

"That's right, sir."

"So what happens then?"

"He asked Mr. Wynn if the Valiant was his. Mr. Wynn said yes, and the guy grabs him."

"Grabbed him how?"

"By the lapels. Picked him right up. Then he said something about teaching him a lesson."

"A lesson, you say? About what? Can you remember exactly what he said?"

"Let's see...I think it was-'You need to learn some better driving manners', and he called him a name."

"You don't remember what name, or are you being polite?"

"He called Mr. Wynn an asshole, sir."

"Good, fine-this is what we need, is the details. Don't leave anything out, if you think it's relevant to the case, OK?"

"Yes, sir."

"Driving manners, eh? So maybe this incident in the lane had something to do with something that had occurred earlier, in traffic. Or on the highway, perhaps."

"I can only tell you what he said, sir."

"Of course. Don't mind me, son. I'm just thinking out loud. Sure sounds to me, though, like these two had a beef with Mr. Wynn over something that happened
on the road."

"Maybe he cut one of 'em off, or something like that." offers the young guy.

"Well, it never pays to speculate. We'll want to have another word with Mr. Wynn about this, though. What happened next, Rick?"

"The guy threw Mr. Wynn down on the hood of his car, and then he smacked him."

"Hit him with his hand? Open or closed?"

"Well, from the sound of it, I thought closed. It sounded like he'd socked him one in the kisser. But I've been thinking; we were in that echo-y space there in the alley and sound tends to reverberate there. I didn't actually see him get hit because the big guy had his back to me. But it makes sense to me that it must have been an open hand, or he would probably have knocked Mr. Wynn out."

"Pretty big guy, eh?"

"Yes, sir and Mr. Wynn, well..."

"He's not."

"Yes sir. A guy that size with plenty of muscles, too-I think if he'd really connected with his fist, Mr. Wynn would have been out like a light."

"You're probably right. Still, it sounds like a pretty one-sided affair, with Mr. Wynn not offering much in the way of resistance."

"No question about it, sir. One-sided all the way, plus the other guy had backup."

"Right. We've almost forgotten about the other man. What was he doing, while the alleged assault took place?"

"He was just sitting on his bike, but he made it clear that I was not to get involved."

"How did he put that? What did he say?"

"He didn't *say* anything, sir. He just went..." I showed him.

"Seemed to think it was all a big joke, eh?"

"That was the feeling I got, sir."

"OK, so this guy more or less threatens you not to get involved and that's when you went looking for the bouncer?"

"That's right."

"And ran into the maid on the way."

"All right, Rick. You've been very helpful, so far. I just need you to describe these two men in as much detail as you can remember. Think you can do that?"

I tell them everything I can recall about the two bikers' clothes and appearance, giving as much detail as I can. A couple of times the young cop asks me to slow down so he can catch up in his notepad. He must have filled three pages by the time I get to describing the crest on the back of the big guys' vest.

"Wild Boars. Must be a new group. I don't remember hearing about them before, have you?" the corporal asks his partner.

"Nope. Rebels, Coffin Cheaters, Sons of Adam up here. Seattle? No idea."

"Well, it gives us something to go on, besides some pretty good descriptions. Is there anything else you can think of that might help us to collar these guys, Rick?"

"Yes, sir. Tattoos—they both had lots of tattoos."

"Great. No better way to identify someone, short of fingerprints. It would be very helpful if you can remember what these tattoos looked like, even just a couple of them. Can you think back?"

I take a deep breath and close my eyes. The scene unfolds in my mind's eye, like I'm looking at a photograph of it. The big guy standing over the car while his buddy sits there with his arms folded. I see everything, including the tattoos, as plain as day.

Again the young cop needs me to slow down as he records my descriptions of the tattoos. The older guy develops a thoughtful expression as I continue and when I'm finished he kind of shakes himself.

"Whew! Well, OK. Outstanding, in fact. You are a very observant young man, Rick. I think we've got a good chance of apprehending these two, based on these descriptions alone. And if we do get them, with descriptions like this, we probably won't even have to ask you to testify in court, which could put you in a tricky situation, otherwise."

"You know, I think we'll just get this information over the air ASAP, and then maybe we'll take a stroll through the tavern."

"You don't think they'd still be on the premises, do you?"

"You never know. I've got a hunch about these guys."

"They'd have to be crazy to stick around here after something like this!"

"Crazy, or just plain arrogant. Either way, if you want to catch a wild pig, the place to go is the nearest watering hole. Humor me."

He stands up and offers me his hand.

"Thank you, Rick, you've been more than helpful. You can go back to work, now."

"Actually, I think my shift ended a while ago, sir."

"Well, do yourself a favor. Don't hang around. Don't go near the tavern entrance, especially. These guys may not be smart enough to have left the hotel, but if they are still here and we arrest them, seeing you again might be all they need to put two and two together, understand?"

"I understand, sir. Thanks."

"Thank you."

The next day I learned that the corporal's hunch had paid off. They arrested the two bikers in the tavern fifteen minutes after I left for home. Mr. Wynn was so upset by his ordeal that he cancelled all his appointments and his reservation and went home the same day.

I never even got a tip from the guy.

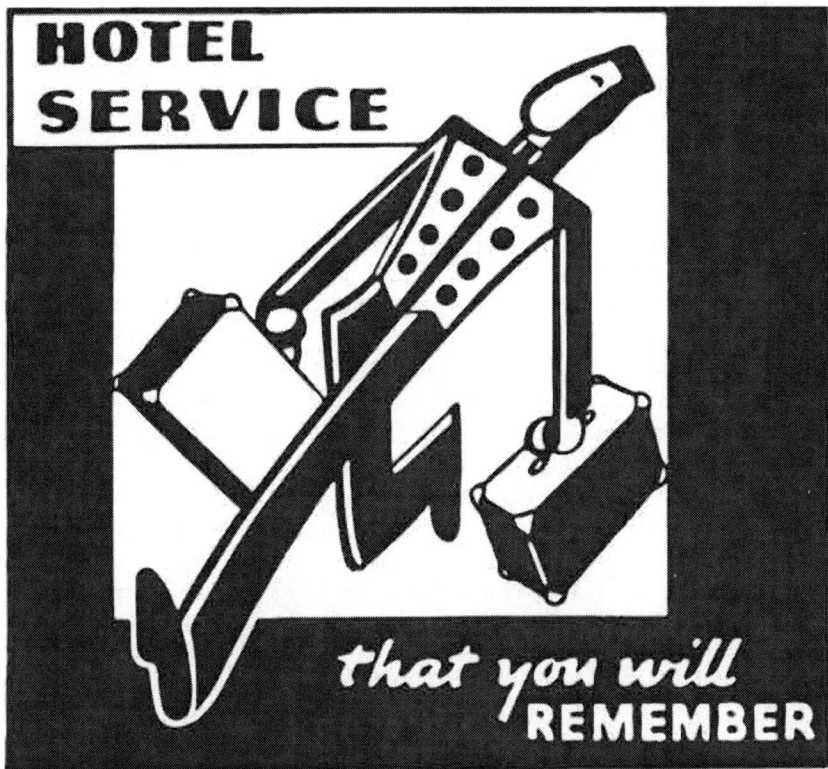

HOTEL SERVICE *that you will* REMEMBER

THE SHINE

The day I met Gus I was, as they say, fucking the dog. It was another muggy summer day and everyone in the hotel was on edge. I'd spent the morning fruit-lessly trying to find a single thing I could do, or even a place where I could do nothing without being yelled at.

When you are low man on the totem pole, it can be tough. As a bellhop, everybody else who worked there felt they had a right to treat me as an infe-rior, which can be digested in small doses, but on a hot day when all of them are looking for someone to unload on, a guy can start to feel like he's walking around with a bulls-eye painted on his back.

After several scorching encounters with various and sundry staff members, I retreated to the kitchen, where I could generally count on staying out of the way and being left unmolested. The kitchen staff were generally too busy to notice me, as long as I kept out of the way but after I got reamed out by the assistant cook for lounging in the way of a shipment that wasn't even due for another hour, I decided to resort to the last refuge; the basement.

It was always cool down there, and the chances of meeting up with someone were slim. I made myself comfortable on a crate of something heavy and checked my watch. I didn't want to stay too long and risk the ire of another over-heated superior. It wouldn't do if they were to come looking for me and discover the secret of my basement hideaway, so I marked the time and decided on a twenty-minute break.

I thought about having a smoke, but for some reason I never felt comfortable smoking down there, even though I knew the other hops did. The story Betty had told me about the old-timer who'd lit a match and blown up the natural gas had stayed with me and I could never bring myself to strike one there, myself.

It was enough just to sit in the cool air and be away from the hubbub, if only for a short time. I started to hum a little tune, sort of a jazzy sax thing that I'd heard somewhere; just a bit of melody, really. I had no idea what it was or why it might come to me now in the silence of the basement but there it was again; stuck in my head.

It was more of a rhythmic thing that kept repeating itself in a two-bar phrase and in the silence between phrases I realized that I wasn't just humming it to myself; I was *hearing it*.

I looked around me, trying to pinpoint the source. It was so soft and quiet I had to strain at times to reassure myself it was still there. It *was* rhythmic, just a soft thrum; a pitter-patter of sound.

I got up and walked around, trying not to make a sound with my feet, straining my ears for snatches of the sound. Then it seemed to disappear altogether. I stood stock-still, listening but nothing came for long minutes. It was gone, I thought, but just as I gave up listening, it started up again.

This time I had an idea of the direction it was coming from, and it seemed to be over by the fire doors, which led to the tavern. I went over and put my ear to the door. There it was; a soft pattering, like someone playing a beat on his knees with his hands.

I went through the door, knowing that I would find myself in a short utility corridor. At the end of it was another set of fire doors, which opened into the tavern through a little hallway by the wash rooms. As I approached the second pair of doors, the sound became louder and more distinct. By the time I got right up to it and put my ear to the crack, it was loud enough for me to pick up elements of the pattern that I'd not been able to hear before.

I put my eye to the crack between the doors and because it was so well lit on the other side, I could see the source of the mystery quite well.

It was the shoeshine man.

I'd known about him for a while. I think Gary told me about him when I first got hired but until now I'd never seen him. There was an alcove built into the wall across from the doors to the two washrooms in there and in it sat a shoeshine station.

It was a raised platform maybe six inches high by six feet long and on top of that were two old, leather-upholstered steel and chrome chairs with foot rests. On the side was a brass plaque that said "Collins Continental."

Drawers were built into the platform and one of them was pulled out to reveal a collection of tins and brushes, rags and chamois. A customer sat in the chair closest to me smoking an impressive looking cigar and examining a newspaper as his shoes were being done.

The shoeshine man was a black guy, dressed neatly in grey slacks and a white shirt and bowtie. It was hard to tell his age but his hair was all grey. He was all business as he applied himself to the task, wearing a serious expression and focusing entirely on what he was doing.

What he was doing was making the rhythm I'd heard with the rag as he snapped it back and forth over the surface of the man's expensive looking brogues.

Now that I could hear it clearly I was even more fascinated by it. The rhythms he produced with that rag were like a really good drum solo. They were subtle and multi-layered, dynamic and varied the way a good solo is. I couldn't quite believe he was able to do all that he was doing with nothing but a rag on a shoe, but he was. I listened, entranced until he stopped, then I opened the door and went in.

The customer was just getting up out of the chair as I opened the door. As he stepped down from the stand, the shoeshine man stood aside.

"That's a buck fifty, suh," he said.

"Here you go," the man said, producing a two-dollar bill, "Keep the change, boy."

He must have been twenty years younger, at least.

"Thank you kindly, suh."

I waited politely until the customer had gone. The shoeshine man looked at me quizzically.

"Hi." I offered.

"Hi yo'se'f. You los'?"

"Ah, no, I was just passing by when I heard you...um, shining."

"You ol' enough to be standin' in a licensed premises, boy?"

"Well, technically, no, but I work here, so..."

"You work here?"

I nodded.

"You work here. What you do?"

"I'm a bellman, upstairs in the hotel."

"A bell*man*. Well tha's a relief." He stepped up and took a seat on one of his chairs.

"The way you's dressed, I thought mebe you was a lion tamer, somethin'"

"Yeah, I know. It's the uniform. Have to wear it for the job."

"Well, you needs to be twenty-one to be in *here*. What you want?"

"Oh, well, like I said, I was just listening to you doing that man's shoes and I noticed how you make your rag sound like drums, sort of. I'm a drummer."

"You's a drummer. I thought you was a bellman."

"Well, I guess I'm both. I took the job here to pay for a new set of drums. I need them to go professional."

"Is that so? You gonna go *professional*, now, are you?" He took a pack of cigarillos out of his shirt pocket and lit one, settling back as he waved the match out and put it into the ashtray in the arm of the chair.

"Tell me, what kind of drums you playin'?"

"Mainly rock. We want to do some blues, too—maybe some R&B."

"You play mainly rock drums? Don't that hurt yo' hands?"

"Um, I use sticks."

"'Zat a fact. Well, then don't you break them sticks on them rocks?"

"I meant we play rock *music*. My drums are made of wood. The heads are plastic."

"I know, son. I was just funnin' whith y'all. You play wood drums—what's wrong with 'em?"

"Nothing, really, it's just, they're not really good drums, like the pro's play. You need to look good on stage, too."

"So you think havin' some shiny new drums goin' to make you a professional?"

"No, not really. But they'll sound a lot better. And it doesn't hurt that they'll look better, too."

"That's a big deal, lookin' good on stage, huh?"

"Sure. All the big bands dress neat for stage. You have to have lights, too."

"You ain't gonna wear that get-up, is you?"

"Ha! No way. I got some stage clothes."

"Seein' as how we got on the topic, I hope you don' mind my axin', but; what the hell is it you have on yo' head?"

I realized that my wig had somehow gotten a bit askew on my way downstairs. My secret was out.

"It's a wig."

"A wig. You mean a toupe, don' you?"

"Well, no. It's a wig, really. A short haired wig."

"Say what?"

"It's a short haired wig. I need to have short hair for the job."

"I hate to be the one to have to tell you, boy; there's a way you can get yo' hair to be short without a wig, you know?"

"Ha, ha. Yes, I know, but I need to have my hair long for the stage. It's the fashion, I guess."

He drew smoke in and held it while he inspected my face.

"So you wearing a wig to make it look like you got short hair when, in fac' you got long hair all up underneath there, is that right?"

"That's right."

"I'll be go to hell. Now I know I lived too long. How come you needs to have long hair on stage. Jus' to look like everybody else does?"

"No. Well, maybe, a bit. It's the style these days."

"Style? You know what style is? Style is the way everybody tells each other; 'It's OK, I'm just like you. Don't worry 'bout me, I ain't about to do anything unusual.' That sound like what a *professional* musician wants to be sayin' to folks? Seems to me, the fellas that do somethin' different are the true *professionals, son.*"

"Maybe, but the thing is, these days everybody wears long hair. You don't get taken seriously if you cut your hair short."

"By whom?"

"What?'

"Who don' take you serious if you cut yo' hair short?"

"Well, girls for starters. None of the girls I know want to be seen with a guy with short hair."

"Oh, I see. Now we getting' someplace. Why didn't you say that in the firs' place? I un'erstan' now. Only one reason in the worl' a young buck like you gonna walk aroun' wearin' somethin' as reediculous as that wig you got on. You want to get laid."

"No! Well, yes, but that's not why I wear my hair long..."

"Why you play drums?"

"Why? Well, I like it. I kind of always had a thing about rhythm, and I guess drums were the natural instrument..."

"No, no-I mean, look; all this getting' a job to buy new drums and wearin' a wig to get the job...it all seems like a lot of bother, boy. A lot of trouble to go to, just so's you can play drums in some smoky ol' place makin' diddley-squat. How come you go through all that? And don' you tell me it's for the love of it or I'll call that mean ol' bouncer, have yo' ass throwd outta here. What's the real reason, down at the bottom of it?"

I thought about it. He was right.

"You're right. I want to meet girls. I want to get laid. That's a lot of it, but that's not all."

"There you go. Sure it ain't all. But at leas' you bein' honest wit' youself, now. See, it don't matter if anybody else knows or un'erstands why you do what you do. It's just real important that *you* do, if you want it to come to anything. What's yo' name, son?"

"Rick, sir."

"Sir? Who you callin' sir? I'm just an ol' shoeshine man, boy. Don't you get caught callin' me sir, OK? My name is Gus."

He gave me his hand and I shook it.

"Nice to meet you, Gus."

"Nice meetin' you, too, Rick. Now why don't you jes' skedaddle on out of here before that mean ol' bouncer come sniffin' 'round?"

I took his advice and returned upstairs to deal with the rest of my shift. It didn't seem so hard to put up with everyone's bitchy attitudes, now. I felt like I'd made a new friend.

Visiting Gus at the shoeshine became one of my favorite things to do when I wasn't busy. I always checked through the crack in the door to make sure he wasn't tending to a customer and if he was, I stayed where I was and listened to him work. I loved it, the way he beat out time with the rag and then proceeded to jam. It never got old or repetitive.

When the customer left, I would go in and we'd talk. Usually we would just joke around. Sometimes he'd tell me stories about the things he'd seen and the cities in the south where he'd grown up.

Gus told me stuff I guess I'd never have known otherwise. One time we got to talking about pot. Some guys had gotten caught smoking a reefer in the can and kicked out of the bar. The sweet pungent odor of it filled the small space and masked the usual pong that emanated from the bathrooms.

"You smoke that shit?" asked Gus.

"Sometimes. I don't buy it, but it's always around, you know; at parties and gigs. Everybody wants to smoke up with the band."

"Yeah, it was like that back in Georgia, too. I'm talkin' way back, before the people in Washington ever got wind of it. Folks grew it and used the hemp for rope and cloth. The buds and leaves was just pig food 'till somebody noticed how mellow them pigs got from it. Horses like it, too. Some said the Indians used it in their peace pipes before we ever came over.

It was commonplace by the time I was comin' up. All the musicians used it, poor folk too. Lots of people used it when the prohibition come 'long. Tha's how Uncle Sam noticed it. When they gave up the prohibition, the gov'ment was mighty jealous 'bout who was makin' money from the sales of likker. They'd learned their lesson, watchin' the moonshiners and the mob get rich on it while it was illegal an' they didn't want nothing to compete with it, once they got control again. So that's when the "evil weed" come out in the papers and the movies an' such. They convinced every one that it was bad fo' you, as if booze wasn't. Then they passed laws to make it illegal. Man, in Georgia, you can go to hard labor for *life*, jus' for smokin' a reefer."

I learned more from Gus's stories than I had in ten and a half years of school, only the stuff I learned from him was about the real world.

Gus had been a shoeshine man for a long time. Sometimes he would talk about the places he'd worked—nightclubs and speak-easys and fancy hotels in all the great cities. He'd worked at the Hilton in New York and the Cotton Club, shining the shoes of famous people like Mayor LaGuardia and Duke Ellington.

"They don't call him Duke for nothin'," he said, "That man know how to dress. Never a hair out of place, nice fresh shine every day. And he wore *shoes*, man. Always tipped five dollars. The Duke bought me hot lunch everyday for two years."

He never explained what had led him up north, or how he ended up working at the Ritz, and I never got around to asking. I was eager to get him to reveal the secrets of the rhythms he played with his rag.

I would ask him where he had heard the rhythms he produced. I wanted to know names and see if I could find recordings so I could study them, learn them on the kit, but Gus was not forthcoming.

"That? Tha's jus' some old thang, ain't no song in particular, jus' a thang from the ol' days."

If he knew where the stuff he did could be found, he wasn't telling, so I had to try to learn it from him. When I asked him to help, he just became vague and distracted. When I pushed it one day, Gus got angry with me.

"Why won't you teach me?"

"You want me to teach you to shine shoes?"

"Well, no, not really. I just want to learn the rhythms you play."

"Oh, you jus' wanna learn the rhythms. Jus' like that."

"Of course, if learning to shine shoes is necessary, I'd be willing to do that, too."

"Oh, you'd be willin' to do that, too. Well, tha's mighty gracious of you, I'm sure."

"Did I say something wrong?"

Then he'd just go silent, or a customer would come. It was a bit frustrating, because I really wanted to know how to put what he did with the rag onto the drums. When I tried it, it didn't come out right, somehow. There was something I was missing and I knew Gus had the key. I would just have to keep working on it and wait for him to come around.

A couple of weeks after I began my visits with Gus, I had a visit from Tiger. I was at the desk alone, covering for Betty when he came out of the side entrance and, with a quick look around, made a beeline for me.

It was a curious enough sight to see Tiger travelling in a straight line but he seemed to moving with a purpose. There was a determined look in his eye as he fetched up at the desk.

"Hey, kid. Whaddaya know for sure?" he said, giving the desk a rap with his knuckles.

"Nothing much, Tiger. You?"

"Nyah, not so much as you'd notice." He turned sideways to me and scanned the room as usual, speaking out of the side of his mouth. I waited for him to get to the point.

"Listen, kid, I notice you been spending time downstairs lately."

"A bit. Why?"

"Well, you know that you're not supposed to be there, huh?"

"Sure, Tiger, I know. But it's not like I actually go into the bar. I'm not ordering drinks, or anything. I'm just visiting Gus."

"Gus. That'd be the old darky?"

"Yeah, Gus. We just talk. He tells me stories and stuff."

"Well, maybe that's not something you want to be doing, anymore, OK?"

"Why not? We're not doing any harm, just talking."

Tiger stopped his habitual surveillance of the room and turned to me. His rheumy, bloodshot eyes for once focused on me.

"Now, look; don't you give me any sass. It ain't right. A nice white kid like you hanging around with that old colored boy, it ain't right. Those people are different from us. There's no good to be had by mixing with 'em. You ain't supposed to be down there anyways, so you just stay up here where you belong and leave that old shoeshine man to his self, understand?"

"Tiger, this isn't Alabama, or someplace-this is Canada. Things are different, here. We don't have racial discrimination in this country."

"Is that what they taught you in school? Listen, facts is facts no matter where you are. Whites and blacks are different. That's a fact. It ain't right to mix with them. Even they know it."

"I think you're wrong."

"Fine. You go right ahead and think what you want. But if I catch you downstairs again, it'll have to go to Eddy. That'll be your job. I don't know what you get out of talkin' with that old colored but you better figure out if it's worth your job."

With that and a final slap on the desk, Tiger turned and walked away, meandering undecidedly across the lobby until the door to the lounge opened and sucked him inside.

It was a couple of days before I had a chance to go see Gus. When I did, I found him relaxing in one of his chairs. I took the other one. He seemed withdrawn and hardly acknowledged my arrival.

"I can't stay long. Got a busload of tourists coming in at two. Should be good tips." To my surprise, Gus got up out of his chair and addressed me. There was a hard edge in his voice I'd never heard before.

"Listen, bell *man*, it may surprise you to know it, but I works here, too. You are sittin' in my work, boy, an' I'm a busy man. You think you can jus' pop up here, where you ain't allowed anyhow and all of a sudden we gonna be buddies, on account of you being a *drummer*, or some shit. 'Bout to go *professional*, an' all.

Let me tell you 'bout bein' a professional, sonny. I gets up at six o'clock every mo'nin and I makes my way down here an' I takes care of my stand and takes care o' my customers for ten hours, *everyday* 'cept Sunday, which belong to the Lord.

Ain't no part time, ain't no shift work—it's ten hours a day *everyday*, for forty six years. *Tha's* bein' a professional."

"What you think, I'm gonna take time out o' my busy day to give you a *lesson*, or some shit, jus' 'cause you axe me to? Man, you better get yo'self out in the worl', find out how things is with folk.

What I do with that rag, I been doin' a *long* time. Don't come outta no book, ain't on some record somewhere an' it can't be taught in some *lesson*. An' even if it could, I ain't in the business of teachin' no imaginary drum shit to nobody. I'm in the business of shinin' shoes. If you wanna get yo' shoes shined, then you in the right place. 'Cost a buck fifty. If not, kindly stop crowding up my workplace."

He spoke fast, eyes down, angrily flicking imaginary bits of dirt from his chairs with his shoeshine rag. I don't think he meant to snap the rag on my arm but it stung anyway when he did. Gus showed no sign of noticing.

He took a newspaper from the rack beside the stand and sat back down in the chair, cracking the paper open with a snap and disappearing behind it. I couldn't think of anything to do but take my leave.

"Sorry, Gus." I said, as I went through the fire doors, holding the spot where the rag had snapped my flesh. It hurt all the way back upstairs.

THE ACCIDENT

I ran into Lenny on the stairs on my way back to the desk.

"Did you hear about old man Vona?" Lenny asked.

"What about him?"

"He cut his eye open. Some kind of accident. Blood all over the place. The ambulance came and got him last night. You should have seen the blood."

I had to wait until the next day to get the full story from Betty.

"Damnedest thing you ever heard of, kid. That man lived his whole life like a canary in a coal mine. He wouldn't cross the street without checking his insurance was paid up first.

So there he is, at his safe little desk upstairs in his safe little office, only the air conditioning is on the blink. He gets a bit sweaty and goes to wipe his brow with the back of his hand. But he just happens to be holding a memo card in his hand at the time.

What are the chances? One in how many millions that the paper would be turned in just exactly the right way, at just the perfect angle?

Anyways, ...eeyuw...I can hardly even say it without giving myself the willies. He cut his eyeball clean in half with the edge of the card. Talk about a paper cut! They took him down to the hospital but he's lost the eye. I went to see him last night. He'll be getting a glass eye in a month or so."

I tried to imagine something like that happening to me. It gave me the willies, too.

"Funny thing is, you'd think he'd be depressed, or something, but just the opposite. I never saw him look so chipper. He said he felt like this was the best thing that could have happened to him! Said he felt like he's been freed from fear, stuff like that. Of course, it could have been the painkillers, I suppose."

A couple of weeks later, Mr. Vona gave Eddy his notice. He had saved a tidy little nest egg over the years and, together with a severance package that Eddy had not apparently been aware of, he said he had enough to get himself a little apartment—in Venice.

The guy from the travel agency had helped him make all the arrangements. He had lunch with Mel in the café and told him all about it. It seems that, after all those years of hiding in his office upstairs and pretending to have a life, Mr. Vona was finally ready to go out and get one.

We didn't have a party or anything for him. It was generally agreed that he wouldn't enjoy being the center of attention. Instead we pooled our tips for a couple of days and bought him a set of luggage for the trip. I saw him when they gave it to him. He was grinning ear to ear.

Eddy wasn't happy, though. With Mr. Vona gone, the task of doing the daily audits fell to him until he found a replacement he could trust and he hated it. The rest of us weren't all that thrilled about it, either.

The audits had to wait until the business day was over, which in the hotel business could be almost anytime. In order to catch most of the day's receipts, the cut off was at six p.m. This allowed time for all the tills to be changed over to new floats and the tapes to get upstairs to the office. Correlating all that data could literally take all night, which was why it was referred to as the "night audit."

Where Mr. Vona would come in at seven o'clock sharp with his bag lunch and go straight up to the fourth floor, where he stayed until midnight or so, Eddy got bored and restless and took breaks, wandering the hotel at unpredictable times.

That's how he got wind of Lenny's sideline business with the working girls on the block. Lenny had been setting up dates for the male guests, travelling salesmen mostly, although, truth be told, there were a few middle-aged guys who came in on the weekends and always paid with cash, bringing nothing more than an overnight bag with them and putting bogus addresses on the check-in form. Whenever we mailed a forgotten receipt out to one of these guys the letter came back marked "return to sender."

These gentlemen would usually check in mid afternoon and then go out for dinner, after which they returned to the hotel for drinks in the lobby, hoping to score for free. When that didn't work out and they failed to work out terms with one of the regular pros that Eddy and Nick allowed to hang out in the lounge, they went to see Lenny.

Lenny worked the evening shift regularly in order to be there for his clients when happy hour ended, unless there was a good concert in town. He always seemed to have tickets to the best concerts. When he took a night off to attend one and one or other of us had to fill in for him, it wasn't unusual to have one of these individuals approach the desk around ten or eleven o'clock looking for him.

Most of us had been through the experience of trying to get across to these poor, generally well-lubricated, individuals the fact that the pimp service was closed down for the night. Occasionally things got ugly.

That's what happened one evening about three weeks after Mr. Vona left and I was filling in for Lenny on the night shift. A weekend regular came schoonering across the lobby from the lounge and made port at the desk.

"May I help you sir?"

"I wanna talk to Lenny."

"I'm afraid Lenny is not in tonight, sir. Is there something I can do for you?"

"Ah, jeez. I dunno...Lenny's not here?"

"That's right, sir. Lenny took the night off. What can I do for you?"

"Well, OK, so you're doing Lenny's job?"

"That's right, sir."

"I wantcha ta line me up with some company, OK?"

"Some company, sir?"

"Tha's right. You know what I mean, doncha?"

"I'm afraid not, sir."

"Aw, come on. You doin' Lenny's job, you gotta know about the girls, right?"

"Ah. The girls. The girls are strictly Lenny's concern, sir. I don't do that particular thing for Lenny. You'll have to try another time, when he's back, OK?"

"You don't...Whattaya mean you don't...Look, I paid good money for a room and I want to have the room service, too. Kapeesh?"

"Room service ends at nine. Sorry."

"Come on, pal. You know what kind of room service I'm talking about; get me a girl up to my room. I'll pay the usual amount. OK? I don't want anything special, just the usual. Like that girl last month—what was her name? Sheila? Sharon? Fuck, she'll do."

It was at that point that I happened to look over the guy's shoulder. There stood Eddy, about five feet away, listening intently to the exchange.

"I'm sorry, sir. I've already told you, that's not a service that the hotel offers guests. You must have us confused with another hotel."

"No, no—I always come here. Lenny always takes care of me. He knows all the girls. You give him a call—you got his number, you call Lenny-he'll tell you what's what. Alls I want is a girl up to my room. Lenny always takes care of me."

Eddy had heard all he needed to hear, by that time. He looked at me hard and mouthed the words; 'Call Tiger.' Then he turned around and went up to the fourth floor to finish the audit.

As much as I'd had enough of the drunk, I didn't want to sic Tiger on him, so I spent another twenty minutes convincing him that he wouldn't be getting what he wanted, and sent him out to the strip to fend for himself.

The rest of the night passed without incident and I went home at two, to grab a couple hours' sleep before returning to the hotel for my usual morning shift. When I entered the lobby again at six thirty in the morning, Betty was manning the desk. To my surprise, Gary was there, too, although he wasn't scheduled on until two in the afternoon.

"I just stopped in to get my pay cheque," Gary said, "and Betty told me what was going down. Eddy told her to call Lenny and tell him to get his ass down here at six thirty. He's inside with Eddy now. I don't want to miss a second of this."

Both office doors were closed, so we couldn't hear what was transpiring inside. We waited another five minutes or so before the lobby door to Eddy's office opened and the two of them came out. Eddy was first out the door and he made a beeline for the elevator with Lenny in hot pursuit.

"C'mon, Eddy—give me another chance, man. I didn't do nothin' you wouldn't do. I was just tryin' to make an honest buck."

Eddy reached the elevator and punched the 'up' button with vigor. He was studiously keeping his back to Lenny, who started circling him in an attempt to make eye contact.

"Eddy! For Christsakes, man—I've been here eight years. Haven't I taken care of business for you? What about that mess with the MP and the thirteen-year-old? Didn't I take care of your interests, then? Fuck, man—you can't fire me! You *owe me!*"

The elevator arrived and the door opened. Eddy got in and punched buttons. He'd obviously had his say in the office. Eddy didn't like to repeat himself.

Finally realizing that he wasn't about to re-open negotiations, Lenny decided he was going to have the last word.

As the elevator door started close, he reached down and grabbed up the cylindrical ashtray by the stairwell and flung it chest high into the elevator. His aim was just off and the elevator doors caught it on the way through, giving its trajectory an added spin.

The ashtrays hadn't been emptied for weeks. The loss of Mr. Vona had put that duty way down on the priority list. We caught a glimpse of Eddy cowering away from the spinning, twisting container as the lid came off and an explosion of fine grey ash erupted in the narrow confines of the elevator, an instant before the door closed.

"Fuck you, Eddy!" yelled Lenny. He turned and exited out the front door, giving us all the finger as he passed by.

The elevator went up to four, paused and began to descend. None of us expected Eddy to be still in it when the doors opened at the lobby, but he was. His usual crumpled brown suit was no longer brown. It had turned a uniform shade of grey, along with the rest of him. As he approached the desk, he left behind him a trail of ash on the floor and a vaporous fog of foul-smelling residue in the air.

He stopped in front of Betty and blew a small cloud of ash from his lips before speaking.

"Please have my wife send a spare suit by cab. When it gets here, I'd like it to be sent up to four. I will be in 412, having a shower."

Betty reached out and flicked a cigarette butt from his shoulder before wordlessly picking up the phone. Eddy went back to the elevator and upstairs. We waited until the light told us he'd left the lift on four, before we lost control. We laughed and laughed until I though I'd bust a gut.

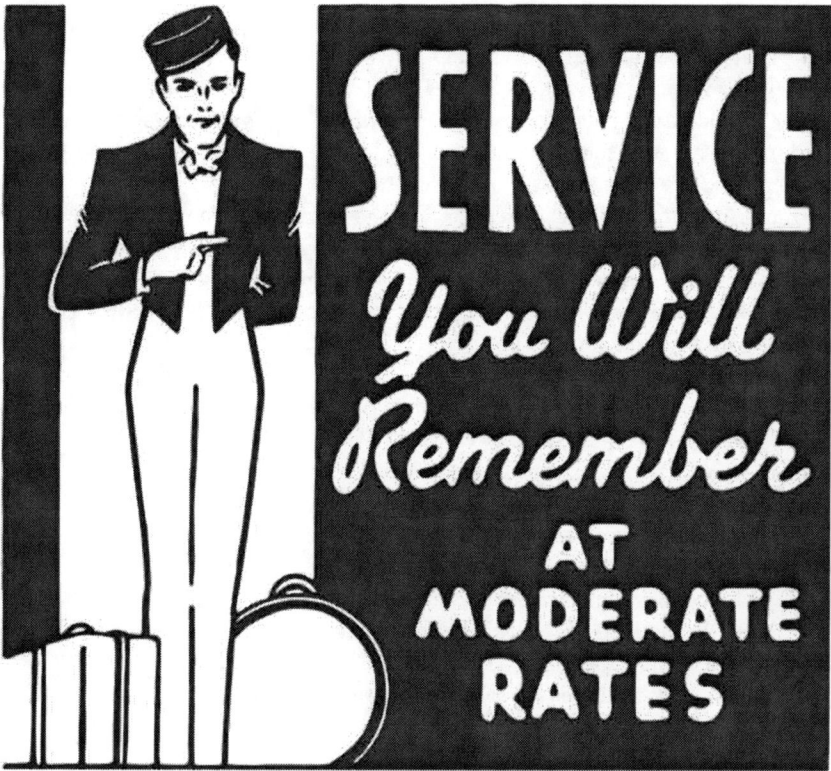

THE BABE

"OK, doll, I'll see you in a couple days, three tops, all right? Meanwhile, you behave and get to work on time, you hear me?"

I stand quietly by, waiting for him to finish, trying not to gawk at the object of his concerns. She is eminently gawk-able, though. I've been having a hard time keeping my eyes off her since the two of them showed up at the desk.

He's a black guy, tall and slim, sporting a huge afro and dressed to the nines in the style of the day, in a pair of pin-striped hip huggers with 24 inch flairs and a leather vest with blue and red stars and stripes over a gold satin shirt with ruffles on the front and sleeves.

All the way up in the elevator he's speaking in flowing, musical street-jive, calling her 'baby' and 'doll.' His hands are all over her, patting her on the butt and stuff but they don't really seem to like each other much.

She is a knockout, a gorgeous redhead maybe twenty-five, petite and with a body that, as they say, just won't quit.

"Why can't you stay with me, honey? You know I hate it, being alone in these places. Couldn't you stay with me just for a while?" She's squirming around him, rubbing herself up against him in ways that have me wondering how he can resist saying yes to her, whatever she wants.

Super-fly puts one ringed hand on her cheek. His other hand slips down and cups an equally shapely one below. She's rubbing his six-pack belly where his shirt is open to his belt. It's getting decidedly humid in the elevator. I'm glad to get out of there but now that we've reached the room I can't get past their little scene to unlock the door.

"You'll be fine, baby. I tol' you, I got to take care of bid'ness down south. You know I'll be talkin' to those record people 'bout a record deal for you while I'm there. You want me to do that for you, don't you? Jus' a couple days, den I come back to be wi' choo, OK, sweet cheeks? Jus' stay in yo' room, an' get down to that club in time to do yo' shows, a'right?"

"OH, all right," she says, pushing him away. She actually has her bottom lip stuck out petulantly. On her it looks adorable.

"You better bring me back somethin' nice, though."

"'Course I will. Don't I always?" he chucks her under the chin with one finger. She turns her head away.

He turns to go and sees me standing there feeling stupid.

"You still here, chump?"

"He's waiting for his tip, stupid."

"You want a tip, kid? I'll give you one—it's the best tip you'll get all week. Keep yo' han's off."

"Oh, Billy, don't be silly. He's just a kid."

I step past her and open the door. After I give her the nickel tour, she starts going through her purse, looking for tip money.

"That's all right, miss," I say and leave without giving her a chance to argue.

Heading back downstairs I pass 'Billy', still waiting for the elevator. He stops me.

"Listen, kid. I didn't mean nothin' back there, all right? I just want to make sure that little lady gets the best care, you know?" He takes a twenty-dollar bill out of his pocket. He holds it in both hands and snaps it like one of Gus's rags.

"Anything she wants, she gets, dig?"

"Sure. I can do that." I reply. He hands me the twenty, then holds onto it.

"Just one more thing," he says, "I want you to keep an eye out for me, too. All right?"

"Keep an eye out, sir?"

"Yeah, you know—if you see anything going on in that room, I want to know 'bout it, you dig?"

I'm not going to make this easy for him. This is just too charming.

"Something...going on, sir?"

"Man! What is this, stupidville? All right, I'll spell it out for you, chump. That girl is a dancer, OK? She's workin' down the street at Tito's. Sometimes the men in those places, they get the wrong idea about a girl like that, you know what I'm sayin'?"

The elevator comes and goes. Billy is still holding on to the twenty. Maybe the guy's just worried about her safety after all, I'm thinking.

"Some of these men, they follow a girl back to her room, proposition her, see?"

"I see, so..."

"So, she gets off at twelve. She comes in alone and she stays alone, or I want to hear about it, OK?"

It's like I thought. He's not worried about her. He's afraid she's going to pull a little action on the side and he wants a cut. Like I said—charming.

"I think I can handle that, sir."

He lets go the twenty. The elevator comes back and he gets in and punches 'lobby'. I'm taking the stairs. Just before the elevator door closes, Billy wags a finger at me.

"Remember what I said."

"Yes, sir," I reply, although I'm not sure what he means.

It isn't until he's gone that I realize he'd completely dropped the jive talk as soon as she wasn't around. I check the info on his credit card impression. Super fly is from Winnipeg.

Later that afternoon, I happen to have some stuff to do on the second floor that takes me past the door to Doll's room. As I near the door I can hear singing inside.

She's half singing/half humming, the way people do when they're alone. It's a song from "West Side Story," by Stephen Sondheim.

Her voice is good—strong and clear with a silky quality to it. It sounds as though she's just gotten out of the bath, the thought of which gives rise to a whole pile of other thoughts that I'd just as soon not entertain, standing alone in the hallway.

The second I start to walk away her voice stops. So do I, suddenly panicky. Did she hear my footsteps? Is she listening, waiting for them to start up again? I can't stay here. What if she opens the door and finds me lurking around her door like some kind of pervert?

She starts singing again as I tip-toe down the hall. This time it's Rogers and Hammerstein, from "South Pacific." I think it's called "Bali Hai."

Gary has tickets to the Deep Purple concert that night, so I'm pulling a double shift to cover for him. Betty is on the desk until midnight and I have nothing to do but wait for any room service calls that might come down. About seven o'clock, one does.

"Front desk," I intone into the mike. Then I look at the room number on the board. 212. It's her.

"Oh, hi. Can I get room service, please?"

"I can take your order, ma'am."

Ma'am? Doesn't sound right, somehow.

"Oh. OK, but...is there a menu, or something? I just can't think of what I want."

"There should be a menu in your room, miss. In the drawer, beside the TV. If it isn't there I can bring one up to you."

"Oh, no, here it is! I found it. Say, is this that cute bellhop that brought my bags up today?"

"This is me, miss."

"The one who doesn't take tips?"

"One and the same."

"Oh good. I want to do business with you. I'll save a bundle. Just kidding. Jeez, I don't see anything here that I really want. What would you suggest?"

"Me? Well, let's see. I'm kind of partial to the Monte Cristo, myself."

"Ooo, that does sound good but, you see, I can't eat anything fried like that. It isn't good for my skin. I've got really soft, delicate skin. My mom used to say that I never lost my baby skin."

"Well, if you don't mind my saying, miss, it certainly looked good to me."

"How nice of you to say so! Tell me, are all the bellhops so nice?"

"No, miss. I'm pretty much the nicest."

"I bet you are, too!" she giggles. It's a very nice giggle. It makes me feel like joining in but Betty is starting to take an interest in the call.

"How about this—the fruit and cottage cheese?"

"The dieter's special? Sure. Anything to drink with that?"

"Umm, let me see. Oh! Lemonade. Is it fresh squeezed?"

"I'm afraid not, miss. It's a mix."

"Oh, well, I can't have that, then. They put way too much sugar in those mixes."

"Tell you what; the chef is a friend of mine. I bet I could get him to give me some fresh lemons and I could make you some real lemonade, if you don't mind waiting."

"You'd do that for me? You are a sweetheart! Wow! That would be fantastic! Thanks."

"No problem. So that's one dieter's special and one fresh-squeezed lemonade. Will there be anything else?"

"You never know."

"Miss?"

"Oh, nothing. That's everything, I guess. Will you be bringing it up yourself?"

"Wild horses couldn't keep me away."

"Ha! You're funny, too. Say, what's your name?"

"My name? It's Rick, miss."

"Rick. Nice name. I'm Lori."

"Fifteen minutes..." I can't use her name with Betty's radar on alert. "Miss."

"OK, see you." Click.

"Just taking this room service order up." I tell Betty, ignoring her curious look.

I'm off to the kitchen, wondering how to make fresh squeezed lemonade. Patty comes to my rescue as usual, no questions asked, and it's not much more than fifteen minutes before I'm knocking on the door to 212.

"Who is it?" she sings.

"Room service."

"Just a second."

Then the door opens and it's all I can do not to drop the tray. She's wearing some kind of kimono thing that leaves nothing to the imagination. The room smells of flowery essences.

"Room service." I repeat stupidly.

"Come on in," she says, swinging the door wide. She turns and walks across the room to the desk. I manage to get my eyes back up to eye level just as she turns around again. The radio is set to a light pop station. Johnny Mathis is singing "Chances Are."

"Where would you like it?"

"Sorry?"

"The tray. Where would you like me to put it?"

"Oh, here is fine."

I have to brush past her to put the tray down. I wind up standing about eight inches away from her. She doesn't move.

"I hope I didn't keep you waiting too long."

"No, no—and look; you did make me fresh lemonade. That is so sweet of you to go to all that trouble."

"No trouble at all. I hope you like it. I brought some extra sugar in case I didn't make it sweet enough."

"I'm sure it'll be fine. If you made it, it'll be very sweet."

"Right, well I'll leave you to it, if there's nothing else you need."

"OK. I'm not going to tip you, you know."

"Oh, that's fine, miss."

"Because after you refused a tip today I had an idea. I'm going to save all your tips up and give them to you all at once. One big tip."

"That sounds great, miss. But honestly, you needn't bother."

"I thought we'd gotten past the 'miss' thing. I'm Lori, and you're Rick, right?"

"Right. Sorry, Lori. Hey, that rhymes!"

"Yes it does. How clever, Rick. I'll see you later. Thanks."

"See you later."

Outside I can feel my face burning. I let out a groan. 'Sorry Lori?!' I retreat back to the desk, mortified.

There is absolutely nothing going on in the hotel that Saturday evening. It's spooky, like the calm before the storm, or something. I'm so bored I'm reading a copy of "Stranger in a Strange Land" by Robert Heinlein, that someone left in one of the rooms. Struggling to keep my head from nodding off into a nap, I almost miss Lori heading out to work.

She's halfway across the lobby before I see her, wearing a snow-white halter top and micro skirt that's gotta be ten inches above the knee, with high laced boots that only leave a tantalizing three of them bare.

Lori sees me looking at her and wiggles her fingers at me.

"See you later," she sings on the way out the door.

Betty gets off at ten and Lenny's on desk overnight. He's late, as usual, which screws up the order of our coffee breaks. As it happens, that works perfectly for me because, though I miss her coming in a bit after twelve, I'm alone at the desk when Lori calls down from her room. I pitch my voice lower.

"Front Desk."

"Rick? Is that you?"

"One and the same."

"This is Lori, remember? In room...what room am I in, anyways?"

"212?"

"That's it. 212. How did you know that?"

"It's lit up on the switchboard, right in front of me."

"You are so smart. What would I do without you, Rick?" A giggle.

"I hope you never have to find out."

"Aren't you sweet."

"Yes, I am. Is there something I can do for you?"

"Oh, yes. I called because...isn't that funny; I can't remember why I called." Another giggle.

I get it. She's stoned. She probably had a couple of drinks at the club and smoked a joint on the way back to the hotel and now she's up there in her room, tripping all alone. Probably got the munchies by now.

"Something from the kitchen, perhaps?"

"Mmm, that's a good idea. There was something else, though....Oh, I know! The TV. It isn't working. Can you come up and fix the TV for me, Rick?"

"No problem. Would you like me to bring some food up, as well?"

"Yeah! Good idea—you could bring it up when you come to fix the TV."

"Good thinking. Listen, the kitchen is shut down, technically. About all I can bring you is some sandwiches, some chips, maybe. Is that all right or would you like me to order out for something hot?"

"No, no-that will be fine. As long as you're going to bring it."

"No problem. I'll just be a few minutes making the sandwiches."

"Ok, as long as you don't take too long. And Rick, do you think you could stay and visit for a while? I hate eating alone."

"Sure. I'll have to be there for a while, anyways."

"You will?"

"In order to fix the TV."

"Oh, right—the TV. You have to fix the TV, right?"

"Right."

"So you might as well stay and keep me company for a while."

"If that's what you want, Lori."

"That's what I want, Rick."

"Fifteen minutes."

"I'll be waiting."

I wait until Lenny's break is over and head to the kitchen through the empty café. Everything I need is in the little fridge reserved for staff and in ten minutes I've put together a nice selection of sandwiches, all wrapped in cellophane to keep them fresh. I drop some quarters into the machine in the back hall and select some bags of chips in various flavors. There is a bottle of red wine that the cooks use, open but with only an ounce or two gone, so I snag that and a wine glass, as well.

I make my way up to two by the back stairs. At the door to 212 I take a moment to make sure I'm presentable and knock lightly on the door.

"Room Service."

"Just a moment!" there is a special lilt in her voice.

The door opens and she's standing there wearing the same kimono thing. Her hair is wet from a shower and with no makeup she looks more radiant than ever.

"Hi."

"Hi."

I put the tray on the desk and go over to the TV. It's unplugged. I bend down and pick the cord up.

"I think I've found the problem with your TV."

"Really? So quickly? You are very clever, Rick," she's stoned, all right.

"Not really. It wasn't plugged in."

"No. Really? How silly of me not to have checked that. You must think I'm a complete idiot."

"Oh, no, I would never think that of someone who..."

Searching for a way to answer that, my eyes fall on an object on top of the TV. It's a wooden box, about a foot long and half that wide but hinged on one side to open into some kind of a playing board. Chess, maybe or...I pick it up and open it.

"Plays Backgammon."

"You know Backgammon? Do you play?" she asks, suddenly quite alert.

"Yeah, sure. My Dad taught me how when I was six or seven. We used to play all the time."

"Great. This is so cool. I can't ever find anybody who knows how to play. Want to play a game? Can you stay and play a game with me?"

"Sure, if you want. I'll play you."

"Oh, man," she says, grabbing the game and arranging things on the edge of the bed. I pull up a chair.

"You have no idea what it means to me, Rick, to have someone to play Backgammon with. I am so happy."

We played for hours, that first night. She was good; as good as I was but lacking a certain caution when it came to piling her stones up at the bar. I won three games to her two. We shared her sandwiches and chatted between games and by the time I left at about two thirty I knew I'd made a friend.

For the next week, I'd meet her outside the club at midnight and walk her back to the hotel, where we'd separate. She goes through the lobby and takes the elevator while I sidle around to the side entrance and cut through the ballroom to the back stairs. We meet at the door to 212, and I stay with her, playing Backgammon until I have to go home and get some sleep. A couple of nights we get so absorbed in the game we play until morning and I end up grabbing some zees on the chair, waking up early to have breakfast in the café and start my shift.

About ten o'clock I take a room service order up to 212—fresh fruit and muffins with fresh squeezed orange juice.

The night her engagement at Tito's is over, I go up to meet her as usual and we enter her room together. I can't find the Backgammon board.

"Lori?" I call into the bathroom, where she's freshening up, "where's the board?"

"I put it away for tonight." She giggles.

"Now why," I'm wondering, "would she do that?"

Behind me, she giggles again. When I turn around, she's already in the bed, the kimono lying on top of the covers.

"You remember when I checked in and you wouldn't take a tip?"

"Sure."

"And I said I was going to save up all your tips and give them to you all at once?"

"I remember." I say, although my throat was so dry I had a difficult time of it.

"Well, come and get it," she says, and giggled once more. She has such a nice giggle. It makes me want to join right in.

She is twenty-five and very experienced in the ways of men. I am sixteen and all but a virgin, which she finds endlessly fascinating. She doesn't work on Sunday and I have the day off, too.

And, there's always room service.

Billy comes back to collect her on Monday and they call down for check out service. I go up and get her suitcases and accompany them down to the lobby. This time she's not fawning on him like before.

As I put the bags down in front of the desk, he hands me a twenty.

"That's alright, sir. It's already been taken care of."

Lori blows me a kiss behind his back as they walk out the door. I'm grinning ear to ear and Betty is looking at me with her *look* on.

"Doing a little growing up, are we?" she says, thumbing through her magazine.

"You might say that," I allow, perhaps a trifle smugly.

"You know not to get caught upstairs, right? Fraternizing with the guests is strictly forbidden."

"I was just doing room service."

"Yeah, right. Room service, my foot. Just be careful. Eddy would fire you on the spot."

At that point the switchboard rings, a call from the banquet room.

"Switchboard."

"This is Graves. I need a bellhop in the banquet room to help me set up the bar."

"I'll be right there, Mr. Graves." I can tell by the lack of flowery prose that Mr. Graves is in a hurry.

"Going to help Mr. Graves set up the bar in the banquet room." I tell Betty.

"OK, Casanova. I shall await your return with breath abated." She replies, blowing smoke over the top of this weeks' Good Housekeeping.

When Mr. Graves called for help with the bar set up, he usually wanted someone to go downstairs and get the booze and the mix for him. I grab the key ring so I can get into the cages in the basement and hurry through the back hall to get his order.

"There you are," says Mr. Graves, looking as harried as ever, "Take this list down to the basement, please and bring the contents back to me here. Please be quick about it, as I have a function scheduled for noon, which is in…" he consults his watch, "exactly thirty two minutes. I will require time to check the order against the list and be sure that you haven't forgotten anything."

It usually took about five minutes flat to get an order together and bring it back up by the service lift, but that was Mr. Graves for you—uptight about everything. I take the list from him and head down to the basement.

As I come down the stairs and enter the cavernous expanse of the basement, I notice the big chandelier is switched on, casting its rainbow of refracted light through the area. I walk over to turn it off, my footsteps resounding on the bare concrete floor.

"Who is there?" comes an unfamiliar voice.

"Bellman. Just getting some supplies for the banquet manager."

As I speak, I come around the corner of some big crates to the biggest one that holds the chandelier. Beside it is the giant chest of drawers that holds the silver service. A man sits on a crate there. One of the drawers is open and a selection of silver flatware has been taken out and arrayed across the surface of a third box, this one covered with a soft red cloth.

He's an older gent, well dressed in a nice suit. He's taken his jacket off and laid it over the top of the chest and his sleeves are rolled up to his elbows. He has on blue suspenders and his tie clip is gold, with a tiny diamond in it. In one hand he is holding a rag that has been stained to a burgundy color by the jewelers' rouge, which lies beside the silver at his elbow. The other hand holds the fork that he'd been polishing.

"Bellman, eh? Well, don't mind me. I'll be another half hour or so. You just go about your duties." He speaks with a hint of an accent. I can't quite place it.

"Excuse me but…are you supposed to be here? I mean, no one is allowed down here but hotel staff."

"Ah! Good for you. Looking out after your bosses' interests—very commendable. What's your name, young man?"

"Rick, sir. Umm, may I ask yours?"

"You want to know my name? Well, that shows you are no fool. After all, I suppose I could be some bum off the street, sneaking down here to steal this stuff and thought I'd just take the time to polish it up, first, eh?" he chuckles. "No, no, don't get angry. I'm just having a little joke. You're right to ask, I should thank you for it. My name is Cymboluk."

Cymboluk? That was Eddy and Mike's last name. I realize I must be talking to the old man—the owner of the hotel.

"Oh, man, I'm sorry Mr. Cymboluk. I'll just get my stuff and get back upstairs..."

"That's all right, don't worry about it. Maybe you want to stay a few minutes, keep an old man company, if it won't make you late getting your supplies."

"Sure. Mr. Graves is waiting for me, but there's lots of time."

"Graves? Good man, just a little bit verbose, if you know what I mean. He'll wait. Pull up a crate. Tell me what a bellman thinks of the place. Be honest."

I look over where he's indicating and find a small box to sit on. He goes back to his polishing, leaving me wondering where to begin.

"What would you like to know?"

"Start with your overall impression of the place; what does it look like, from a bellman's point of view?"

"OK. Well, the tips are good. I can't complain about that. The people are all right to work with. I mean I don't have any great beef with anyone here. Most of them are nice people to work with."

"How about the guests? What kind of people stay here, now?"

"I don't know—working people, mostly, during the week anyway. On the weekends we get a different crowd, out of town folks who come in to shop and party. Great tips on the weekends."

"I bet. So, on a scale of one to ten—ten being the best hotel in town, where do you think we rate in town, with most people?"

"Aw, Jeez. I don't know, Mr. Cymboluk. I'd rather not say, really."

"No, no, don't get me wrong, Rick. I'm not going to hold anything against you. I just want to hear an honest answer to a simple question. You see, I don't get many chances to talk to people without a lot of other people listening in. This might be my only chance to get to see this place without a bunch of bullshit getting in the way. Nobody knows what goes on in a hotel like the bellhops. I know—I was one too, you know."

"You were a bellhop?"

"Yeah, a long, long time ago. I was a bellhop in this hotel. I saw what went on. Of course, it was a whole different class of people came here then. Rich people. But they were people, just the same. They probably did much the same things as people do now. Maybe just on a smaller scale.

I worked here two years when I was your age, maybe younger. My dad came over from the Ukraine. I was an infant. We grew up on a dirt farm north east of here, never had a dime. I worked here to get money to go to school. I could hardly speak the language.

People were mean back then, if you were from somewhere else. They didn't treat me very well. When I quit, I swore an oath to myself that one day I would own the place. Now I do. But what is it that I worked so hard to have? That's what I want to know. You see how important it is, that you give me an honest answer?"

I think about the way I'd felt about coming to work at the Ritz, before I knew anything about the place. I think about all the stuff I'd seen going down here ever since. My answer is plain but it probably isn't one that he wants to hear.

"Well, to be honest with you, Mr. Cymboluk, it's not very high on the scale."

"I didn't think it would be. How bad is it?"

"It's a bit of a dive, sir."

He heaves a big sigh, looking away into the rainbow colored gloom.

"Yeah, I thought so. I guess I just needed to hear it from someone else." His eyes focus back on me.

"Thank you, Rick." His hand goes into his trouser pocket.

"Oh, that's all right, Mr. Cymboluk. You don't have to give me a tip just for that."

"Huh. Nonsense. You're a bellman—take a tip. Consider it a gesture of good faith."

He holds out a twenty-dollar bill. His eyebrows lift when I hesitated more. I take the bill, what the heck, and he smiles.

"You don't strike me as the bellhop type. Tell me you're not planning on staying a bellhop the rest of your life."

"No, sir. I'm going to be a musician. That's why I took this job, so I could buy a new set of drums and go professional. I'll have them paid off in a few months."

"A musician, eh? You'll never get rich at that, you know."

"That's OK. I don't need to be rich. I just need to be playing."

"Huh. Well, there's nothing wrong with that, as long as you are pursuing your dreams. That's what I was doing, all those years, working my way into a place where I could fulfill my promise to myself. Just be careful, Rick how you treat your dream when you get to it. Dreams have a way of dissolving, the closer you come to them."

"Thanks, Mr. Cymboluk. Um, I'd better get going. Mr. Graves is going to be wondering where I got to."

"Right! OK, Rick, well thanks for taking the time to talk to me. Thanks for being honest."

"Yes sir."

I go about my business, unlocking the cage to get the liquor bottles and the pop out and loading it onto a dolly to take upstairs. I lock up behind me and start back toward the elevator but as I pass by the chest of drawers I stop.

"Mr. Cymboluk?"

"Hm? Yes?"

"Would it be all right if I asked you a question?"

"Fire away."

"Why do you do it; I mean, polishing up the silver? You have so many people working for you—why do you do it yourself?"

He hesitates, looking down at the spoon he was working on. Idle seconds go by before he gives a little laugh.

"I don't know, exactly. It's just something I started doing, way back when I bought the place and I found all this down here. I used to think about bringing it all back upstairs, you know; restoring the place to its former glory. But it would never have worked. The world doesn't need a grand hotel anymore. Not here, anyway. I would have lost my shirt.

Still, there's something I like about keeping this stuff shiny. Keeping the lights working. It's...you have a picture in your mind of how something was, how it should be...and sometimes you lose track of how it has changed.

No, that's not right, either. I knew when I bought this place that it wasn't the way it was before. I tried to tell myself that we would maintain it, somehow; keep it from going all the way to the gutter. Then I tried to fool myself into thinking that it was all for my boys, that they would someday fix the place up but they don't care. To them this hotel is nothing more than a money machine, to be squeezed dry. It might as well be a whorehouse, for all they care.

So I come down here and I shine up the silver, replace a few light bulbs. It's too late to do the thing I wanted to do. I saw it too late. So I do this instead. Does that answer your question?"

"Yes sir. Thanks. Maybe I'll see you again sometime."

"OK, young bellman. Goodbye."

I go up the lift and take the stuff to Mr. Graves. He's having a fit because I'd taken so long, launching into one of his scholarly dissertations about the profitability of time, or something. I don't listen. I'm too busy thinking about that old man downstairs, sitting alone in the dark, trying to keep time from tarnishing his silver.

THE GIG

I had been playing a few gigs around town with the band, mostly one night-ers but the majority of the bookings we got were for out-of-town high school dances and the like. It was all good fun and we were getting tighter but it was a long ways from where we wanted to be, which was playing the weeklong con-tracts in town.

In 1970, the Liquor Control Board had yet to allow dancing in bars. This meant that a band didn't have to tailor its repertoire to the dance crowd. It meant, in fact, that we were free to do just about any material we wanted to, provided that we didn't play it too loud for the management.

Those in town tavern gigs were like mini-concerts for us. We could load the song list up with stuff that we liked, and the stuff that the guys in my band liked was decidedly eclectic.

The out-of-town gigs were almost always dances, either at the local high school, or in the community hall. In the halls, we were playing to people who'd been coming into town for the Saturday night dance for generations, dancing the same way to the same music since the turn of the century. They wanted two-steps and waltzes, polkas and the occasional foxtrot. The closest thing to rock and roll in their world was maybe something by Elvis or the Everly Brothers.

Of course, it never occurred to us that we might learn a different set of songs for these occasions and save our more urbane material for the in-town gigs. Instead, we insisted on trying to play rock to a country audience and as a result we got consistently bad reviews from the clients. The booking agents took this as a sign that we weren't ready to play in town, yet. It was a vicious cycle.

The amazing thing was how polite and patient the folks at these country dances were. They seemed to understand that we represented a change in the world and rarely, if ever complained when we launched into a Jethro Tull song when they really had something by The Sons of the Pioneers in mind.

They would mill about, arm in arm, waiting for a beat they thought they could dance to. I often wondered how Elton John would feel if someone told him what a great two-step you could do to his "Saturday Night's all Right for Fighting."

Sometimes it got a little bizarre. We played a dance 'way up north in the Peace River country where the old traditions were especially well preserved. The people there had an old time habit of promenading around the edge of the dance floor until the music started. When the song ended, they all just went back to it, strolling around the outside of the room chatting until the next number started. It was a bit un-nerving at first but after the first couple of numbers we realized that they would be doing this all night.

"What is this, the children of the fucking corn?" Gary stage whispered to me.

At the time, we were booking through an agent who called himself "Rock" Wallace. He was a slick individual with a nose for business and little in the way of any other qualifications. He wore dark wrap-around shades at all times and spoke at a velocity that rendered most of what he said incoherent. We would go into meetings and his secretary (who looked to be about thirteen) would actually translate for him.

They usually went something like this;

(Rock)

"So wethoughtyouseguyscoulddookinthesmallerjointslikethecabaret-sandthehotelsatfrstthenwecantrybreakyouintothebiggerbarsbutouttatown-forst."

(Secretary)

"Rock says he thinks you guys would do OK in the smaller venues at first and then we could try you out in some of the bars out of town."

(Band members, nodding and exchanging looks)

"Yeah, that sounds great, Rock. Any idea when we might get paid for the last couple of gigs? We kind of need the money."

(Rock)

"Yeahahdonworryljusgotsomestufftoworkoutwiththeownersaboutvolume andsomeshitthatapparentlywentmissingfromthegymatthehighschoolbutassoo nasIgetthecheckyouguys'llgetpaid."

(Secretary)

"Rock says he just has a couple of the clients' concerns to deal with and as soon as he gets a cheque, you will paid. Don't worry about it."

The trouble was, the amount of time between our playing the gigs he sent us on and our getting paid for same seemed to be getting longer and longer. We concluded that Rock was using our money to cover some cash flow problems of his own.

We found another agent, an old friend of our bass players' named Ken Chimlak, who also happened to be one of the best drummers in town. Ken worked for one of the bigger booking companies in the city, so he was able to place us in some good rooms in town, but it was too late for the band. The lack of cash flow and career advancement had doomed the enterprise.

In the end, we decided to let it go the way it had begun—by mutual agreement. After one last Saturday night dance, we called it quits.

I was devastated. I didn't know what to do with myself. I'd given up everything to play in the band and now there was no band to play in. I'd moved out of home and it felt weird living in the band house, now.

My drums were nearly paid for but my dream of being self sufficient as a "professional musician" were shot unless I could find another band. If I wasn't playing in a band, I was nothing but a bellhop. In desperation, I went to see Ken.

"I need a gig," I told him.

"You want to go out as a sideman?"

"Sure, yeah. Is there much work for a guy doing that?" It was the first time I'd ever heard the term.

"It depends. If you're good—versatile enough to play a lot of different styles in different venues, a guy can stay busy."

"Busy enough to make a living?"

"Well, like I say, it depends."

We looked at each other in silence for a moment across his desk. He seemed to make up his mind.

"Tell you what, Rick. I've got a gig this weekend. A guy had to cancel out on a casual date I booked in town. I was going to have to fill in myself but it would mean missing my kid sister's birthday. If you think you can handle it you would be doing me a favor. It pays good. I have to tell you, though; this is a high society thing at the Golf and Country Club. It's a three piece, backing a singer. It'll be light Jazz, pop, dance tunes—nice quiet venue. Think you can play something like that?"

"Sure, man, I can do that. Thanks." I had no idea what "light Jazz" looked like from the back of a set of drums but I was willing to find out.

"You're going to have to dress up for the gig, you know."

"Sure. I know that. No problem."

"Ok, then. Here are the particulars. You'll have to get there a half hour early to get set up and get off the stage for speeches and stuff. It pays one fifty. That's 50% over union scale. You *are* in the union, aren't you?"

"Oh, yeah—have to be, don't you?"

Actually, until that moment, I'd had no idea there was such a thing as a musician's union. I made a mental note to join as soon as possible. A hundred and fifty bucks, for one nights' work? Now we're talking.

I agonized over what to wear for the occasion, having no idea what the acceptable standards might be. I could only take a wild guess and work with what I had, which was precious little. I ended up wearing slacks I'd bought for the bellhop job, with a white shirt and a vest I had that almost matched the pants.

I arrived almost an hour early and set up in the center of the little stage there, beside the grand piano. I was a little surprised that they hadn't moved it off the stage to make room for the band. I wondered if there would be enough room for the amps and the rest of the sound equipment.

I hung around a while and when the rest of the trio failed to show, mindful of Ken's advice to clear off the stage for "speeches and stuff," I retired to the bar to wait.

About quarter after the hour, a guy came into the bar and asked if I was the drummer. I allowed as much and he informed me that it was time to get ready, first introducing himself.

"I'm John. I'm on bass." John was a nice—looking fellow, wearing a three –piece suit and horn-rimmed glasses. He looked to be about thirty.

"Rick. Nice to meet you."

We went back into the ballroom where John introduced me to the keyboard player, a dapper man in a natty tweed suit and tie. He seemed a little younger than John but I still felt like the baby of the group.

"Adrian, meet Rick." Adrian looked at me like he'd just gotten on a bus for a long ride and discovered there was a drunk on board.

We shook hands and I settled in behind the kit. I was suddenly aware that there was no sound equipment on stage at all, and that Adrian had taken a seat at the grand.

"Aren't you guys setting up?"

John looked at me curiously as he retrieved his acoustic stand-up bass from behind the piano.

"What do you mean, like with amps and things? This is an acoustic band, Rick. Didn't they tell you? I wondered, when I saw the size of your drum set. Most guys just have little club kits for these gigs."

I was horrified. These guys were going to be playing without any electronic amplification at all, and I was going to have to try to play quietly enough not to drown them out. Clearly, I was out of my depth.

"Wow. So, what kind of material are you planning to do tonight?"

"Standard songbook. All standards, no surprises. She'll call them out and count 'em in. Just follow Adrian, if you're not familiar with something."

'She' turned out to be a lady of a certain age who had been sitting at a table in front of the stage smoking and watching me with a resigned expression. She got up and stepped onto the stage.

"Hello. Rick, is it? I suppose this is Ken's idea of a practical joke."

Adrian snickered. John busied himself tuning his strings.

"OK, Rick, this is how we're going to do this. I'm going to call out the tunes and give you guys a four count. If you don't know the song, hang back until Adrian plays through the head and then come in *quietly*. I suggest you use brushes. You *do* have some brushes, don't you?"

I didn't know what brushes were. I sure as hell didn't have any. I said so. The singer reacted by hanging her head in despair. Adrian snickered. John ran a cloth over his fret board.

"Oh, well, just do the best you can, then but—listen to me, Rick; *do not drown me out*. I need to hear what Adrian is doing, so do not drown him out. Please."

I nodded, wondering what I could possibly play on my huge set of Ludwig rock drums that wouldn't drown out an un-amplified piano.

The first set was an unmitigated disaster. The singer kept calling out song titles that I'd never heard of so, mindful of her advice, I waited until the piano had gone through the verse once before attempting to come in with the bass. The trouble was that the keyboard guy was playing such abstract phrasing that I found it impossible to pick out a melodic theme to follow. Every time I thought I had an idea of where to come in and what rhythm might suit the thing it would turn out to be wrong. I was coming in on the two when I thought it was the one, playing half time when the bass guy came in 4/4, just generally making a fool of myself. After the longest forty minutes of my adult life, the singer mercifully called a break.

She went over to John and had a hurried discourse just out of earshot. I was only able to catch the last thing she said because she raised her voice.

"Well, do *something*," she said.

John ambled over to me.

"Hey, Rick, man—let's take a walk, OK?"

We stepped outside the service entrance and strolled across the loading dock to a couple of dumpsters. He was silent. Trying to frame his words delicately, I thought.

"Not going so hot," I offered.

"No, I wouldn't exactly say that." John mused, "Not exactly hot. Look, you're obviously a bit...under prepared for the gig, right? Sure. Nothing wrong with that, man. You're never going to fly with the eagles if you don't stretch your wings, right?"

I agreed with him, appreciating his kindness in saying so.

"Right, so that's good—we know where we're at, right? What we have to do is figure how we get through the next two hours without losing it altogether, man. I mean, Paula is not that bad compared to some but she does have her limits and the one thing that can really get her wound up is when the drums are too loud."

"I'm doing the best I can, John. The smallest sticks I have are, like 5B's. They just don't do quiet."

"I can dig it, man. I know where you're at equipment-wise. That is a drag. You need to be playing brushes, man. Especially on that big kit."

"I don't have any brushes."

"I know, man. And the stores are all closed. It's too bad, man, because the cats that usually play with us, that's all they do all night, just stir the pot."

I didn't know what that meant either. I was to learn much later that he was referring to the technique of dragging the brushes over the snare in a circular motion, creating a low buzzing sound.

He stood a moment, pulling on his soul patch and hard in thought. Suddenly, his eyes lit up and he looked at me.

"C'mon, man. I got an idea."

He led the way back inside and then took a turn to the left and I found myself following him into the kitchen. I hung back at the door, unsure of what John might have in mind. He approached the chef, who was adjusting the seasoning on a big pot of something that already smelled good. They had a hurried conversation. Something changed hands and the chef came over to open a drawer. John motioned me over.

The drawer was full of all the implements and tools of the cooking trade. Big ladles and slotted spoons vied for space among whisks and spatulas of various sizes. John rooted through it all, coming up with a couple of medium sized steel whisks and a rubber spatula, which he handed me.

"Here you go, man. I bet these things will sound just like brushes. You can use the rubber thing on the cymbals instead of the sticks, man."

I couldn't believe it. This guy was actually suggesting that I play my drums with kitchen utensils. My face must have betrayed my doubts.

"Look, Rick—what kind of music do you think it is we're trying to play here tonight?"

"Ken said, 'light Jazz,'" I recalled.

"Jazz. You know what the basic tenet of Jazz is, man? Improvisation. That's right-improvisation. Some of the old cats used shit like this all the time. Wood blocks, cowbells, car horns—why do think they call a drum kit 'traps'?"

"I didn't know they did."

"It's because, in the early days, cats would add just about anything that would make a noise to their set-ups. Pictures of some of those old guys on stage, man; it's short for 'contraption', man. This is right in the true tradition of Jazz drummers."

The cook had been listening in, watching. I looked at him and he shrugged his shoulders, cocking his head to the side with an; 'I don't know—sounds good to me' look on his face.

"And anyways," John continued, "at least you will be quiet enough for Paula. You do want to get paid for tonight, don't you? I mean, as opposed to having her walk off stage and not come back. It's happened. But maybe, if we can use this stuff to make you sound like what she expects, we might get through the evening."

I reluctantly agreed to give it a try.

"Just so long as I get my utensils back at the end of the night, guys, all right?" the cook said as we left the kitchen and headed for the stage.

I didn't even have time to try my new implements out before Paula hopped up and took the mike. She said a few words to the audience and then turned around to call out a tune. Her eyes fell on my hands, gripping the two whisks with desperate strength. She looked at John, who gave her a shrug and the same look as the cook had just given me.

"Dear god." I think I heard her breathe, and then she said a song title and gave Adrian a four count. He launched into a series of avante-garde experiments in free-form Jazz, snickering quietly. After a few bars, John turned to me and mouthed a four count. I came in on one and kept it simple, just playing the tempo on the ride cymbal with one hand and the two and four on the snare.

It worked. I played that simple tattoo right through the piece and Paula sang a couple of verses, then turned to me.

"Much better," she said.

The set went like that, with me just staying out of everyone's way and making little brushy noises to the beat. The only problem came when I tried to add a little bass drum and drowned out Adrian's solo on some samba-type thing. On the break, John grabbed a cushion off one of the over-stuffed lounge seats and crammed it into my bass drum. I tried it. You could almost hear it. Like someone hitting an ottoman with his hand. Perfect.

John invited me outside again and we walked a ways through the grounds. He was pleased how well his idea was working out but he was on to another tack, now.

"You familiar with the term-"swing," Rick?"

"I've heard about it. 'It don't mean a thing if it ain't got that Swing,' right?"

"Yeah, man. That's what I mean. So, it's, like...a *feel*, right?"

"I guess."

"Well, you ain't got it, brother."

"I don't?"

"Nope. You swing like a rusty gate, man. I don't know how to *tell* you what it is you're not doing. I sure as hell can't tell you *how to* swing. What you're doing is more like a *walking* beat, man. It's flat. It's square. It's not what most of these songs are about, man. Swing comes out of the south, man. It's the end product of the fusion that happened between European and African music. Add a lick of Latin from the Caribbean and you get all these styles-stride piano and honky-tonk and ragtime, r&b and soul and gospel from the southern states and after the first world war, all these players out of the army with *skills*, man. Jazz was bein' born. And the bottom of it was the *Swing*."

I smiled politely, not having the foggiest ion of a notion what he was talking about. He knew it. Sighing, he gave up.

"Look, don't worry about it tonight, man. We're doin' all right now and I don't want you to get all messed up trying to do shit that's not your thing. But you should check it out, some time. Get some Jazz records and give 'em a listen. You can't call yourself a drummer if you can't swing."

It was time to get back. As I sat down behind the kit again, I wondered—one word of what he'd tried to tell me stuck out; Ragtime. Was he talking about the kind of rhythm that Gus did with his shoeshine rag? When the first number turned out to be that kind of feel, I tried emulating some of the rhythms I'd heard Gus doing on the snare drum with the "brushes." John responded immediately with a big grin.

"*That's* what I'm takin' about," said.

Even Paula seemed to notice. Halfway through the song, she turned around and sang a verse to me, and for a bar or two seemed to be actually jamming with me.

We made our way through the next set and a short encore, and that was it. I'd gotten through it and no one had left the stage, although I confess I had been sorely tempted to, myself.

Paula came over as I was tearing down my kit. Motioning to a seat at the bar, she handed me a sheaf of bills. I made some polite noises about not accepting it, in view of my obvious shortcomings.

"Just put it away before I change my mind. I either pay a player for the whole night or not at all. It was touch and go there for a minute, but I can see you have a learning curve, baby-that's why I'm going to give you some advice."

The bartender came over and put a couple of drinks in front of us.

"Complements of the house," he said. He winked at me, perhaps to let me know he was aware I was under age and didn't care.

"Here, darling, you can have mine, too." Paula said, "Now listen. A musician—a serious musician—never stops learning. There is always something new to explore on your instrument, and when there isn't, it's time to take up another one. If you want to be a professional, that's what you must commit to; a lifetime of learning.

You showed me tonight that you are someone who can learn. You walked in here totally unprepared for this gig and you were able to adapt and to find ways to do it."

"I have John to thank for that. I never would have thought of using those things from the kitchen."

"Well, John's a thoughtful person. That's why I like having him around. But all he did was to point you in the right direction. You did the rest and you ended up doing all right. I admit, it was the first time I ever had someone playing *spatula* behind me, but as I say, you never stop learning in this business.

So. If you want to keep doing this, you need to get yourself some education, baby. I'm not talkin' about takin' no private lessons off some chump. You need to get to college and get yourself a *schoolin'*. Oh, I know—all you really want to play is your rock and roll. That's *fine*, baby, I love good rock and roll music. But it ain't the only kind of music in the world. You want to be a player, you have to know *all* the major styles and you need to get fluent in them, so when somebody like me throws out a bosa-nova, you know what to do, you understand?

Now, I know a few people in this business and a lot of the players I respect in this town are teaching at the college. They've got a good music program there and a kid with your skills won't have any trouble getting in. Two years, you will come out the other end with the tools you need to go out and play any kind of gig they might throw at you.

You might as well. After tonight, nobody's going to be calling you up with casual work, 'cause they are all going to be calling me for a reference and I can't lie to them, baby. I won't be recommending you to anyone until I hear you decided to take your work seriously. Understand?"

I found out later that Paula had been a singer in the area for years and knew everybody who was anybody. They all knew her, too.

Adrian was one of the brightest rising stars in the local Jazz scene, with movie scores and recording production credits to his name, while John was *the* bass player for session work in the studios of western Canada. The guy who usually played with them, the one that had to cancel at the last moment, turned out to be Tom Dornan. Tom had spent years playing in local jazz groups and was pretty much considered to be the best Jazz drummer ever to come out of our part of the country. He'd been called away to do some recording in Vancouver.

To this day I don't know if Ken had got it wrong and sent me out to that gig thinking I was up to it, or if he had decided to teach me a lesson. If it was the latter, I learned it.

The first thing I did the next day was to phone the college and arrange to try out at that years' juried auditions. Then I headed out to the library to borrow some Jazz records. Over the next few weeks I took it upon myself to delve into the history of modern music. When I'd exhausted the local library of material, I started on the one at the downtown branch.

I found all the old stuff they had first, remixes of early wire recordings made by FolkArts Records and people from the Smithsonian. Some of it was bizarre, but here and there, you could pick up traces of the music that was to come. New Orleans was the crucible, along with Memphis and Chicago. Early records from the twenties and thirties showed how the bands were forming into what would be the big band later on, the drummers starting to build on their "contraptions", like John had said.

I studied the work of Gene Krupa and Max Roach, Lionel Hampton and Buddy rich. Ed Thigpen became one of my personal heroes. I spent hours with my ears glued to the speakers of my inadequate sound system, trying to make out the subtle nuances of the brushwork through the crackling of the old recordings.

I struggled to understand new and different time signatures and rhythms in the Afro-Latin influences of Dizzy Gillespie and the Cuban sounds of Tito Puente. Sometimes a single cut, like Benny Goodman's "Stompin' at the Savoy," or the great Dave Brubeck Quartet's "Take Five" would give me a week's study.

When the time came to try my luck in front of the jury at the college, I felt I was about as ready as I was ever going to be.

I found the right room, by all the anxious -looking guys hanging around outside. There were a lot of horn players with their instruments in hand and a few guitarists warming up with scales. A couple of guys stood around with nothing but some sheet music-keyboard players, I guessed. I didn't see any other drummers.

When it came my turn and my name was called I went in and sat down in front of a table with three older guys behind it. One man indicated a drum practice pad to one side, so I went over to it.

"Play me a single stroke roll." He said.

I complied.

"Now a parradiddle, please."

I played a few bars of the rudiment.

"That's good, thank you." Said the judge, turning to look at the other two, who both nodded absently and made marks on papers.

"OK, thanks. You can go."

"Um, excuse me."

"Yes?"

"Did I just blow it?"

"What gave you that idea?"

"Well, I don't know—it was so short. Did I do something wrong?"

"No, no. We just don't have a lot of time. You did fine. You'll get official notification in the mail, but you're in."

"I passed?"

"Listen, we need drummers. You passed when you held the sticks right. Don't let it go to your head."

Nevertheless, I left feeling great. I was in. I was more determined than ever to become a professional.

I was working full-time at the hotel, using all my tips to put extra payments on my drum loan. They would be paid off by the time I had to quit work to go to school, but I had no idea what I was going to live on for the next two years. I knew my folks would let me live at home while I was going to school. They had started taking in borders to make ends meet and the place was full of strangers coming and going at all hours. I wasn't exactly thrilled at the prospect of trying to study in the midst of the chaos but without a steady income my choices were limited.

I had applied for a student loan from the government to pay for my tuition and books and one day I got a notice to appear at the bank for an interview. I got there in time, wearing my best clothes and my short haired wig, just in case.

The loans officer was a young guy, probably in training, who seemed about ready to sign off on my file and put my loan through until he came to the part on the application where I had listed my assets. At the top of my list was my drum set.

"It looks like you have some assets here that you might liquidate. Had you not thought of that?"

"Assets? Oh—those are my drums. Can't liquidate them."

"Why not?"

"Well, I'm going to school to take music, right?"

"Yes, I know."

"OK, well, I don't know if you noticed, but my main instrument is drums."

"I see. What's your point?"

"Well, if I'm going to school to learn how to play my drums, what would be the point, if I sell them?"

"Couldn't you buy new drums after finish your studies?"

"I suppose so, but what am I going to play in the meanwhile? While I'm at college, learning to play the drums, like." I was starting to get a bit dizzy.

"But, surely the college has drums for the students to use while they are taking classes?"

"I suppose they do, but that doesn't help me if I need to practice at home, or if I needed to take the odd gig on the weekend to pay the rent."

"You're telling me that if you keep the drums, they could be a source of income?"

"That's the idea, yeah."

"Then why didn't you say so at the beginning?"

It was a rhetorical question. I gave him a shrug.

He signed the papers and gave me a copy. As I stood up to shake his hand I noticed his sideburns had ridden up over the arms of his glasses and popped out at an angle, like little wings. I pretended not to notice.

That took care of my tuition and whatnot but I still had no means of support while I went to school. I had no choice but to move back to my parents' house for a while.

Word got around that I was back in the old neighborhood and I got a visit from my old pal Myles. We spent a pleasant hour filling each other in on the events of the past year.

He'd joined the army, as expected, and tried to make a go of the family tradition but it hadn't worked out for him. Myles had seen the Ed Sullivan Show, too. Somehow the Canadian Military had lost its appeal but he'd stayed with it long enough to get a degree in accounting for free, which he was in the process of upgrading.

I told Myles about my plans and my dilemma.

"Ah, yes. The filthy lucre, or lack thereof."

We were in my room downstairs. Myles was standing by the old chest of drawers where I'd dumped all my stuff. He reached over and picked up my roll of lucky dimes that I'd gotten from Mrs. Russell.

"You must be getting hard-up, if you're rolling up dimes."

I was just about to tell him the story about my friendship with the old lady when Myles interrupted.

"Holy Shit!" he exclaimed, "This is a George the fifth, double struck!"

"What the hell is that, man?"

"This one on top of the roll. Mind if I take it out?"

"Go ahead. What's a George the fifth?"

"This is, man," he said, holding the dime up to the light, "mint condition, too."

I remembered Myles' coin and stamp collection, his dad sending him stuff from all over the world. I guess he knew what he was talking about.

"So, it's worth more than ten cents?"

"Oh, yeah. Lots more, in this condition."

"How come?"

"You always were borderline illiterate. Allow me to elucidate you, you poor ignorant savage-you ever hear about King Edward's abdication?"

"He wanted to marry that American lady."

"Mrs. Wallace, correct. There may be hope for you yet. In 1936, King George the fifth died, leaving the throne of England to his eldest son, Edward. This was a problem for the Canadian Mint, as they had already cast a bunch of these dimes with George's face on them. So they put a stop on the run and prepared to make a whole new batch with Edward's mug on, instead."

"Then Edward abdicates."

"Yup, and the throne passes to his younger brother Burtie, who becomes George the sixth. It's the only time in the history of England that they have three kings, all in less than a year. The guys at the mint throw up their hands and, rather than melting down the George V dimes, they decide to just put a couple of dots on them because they need to get them into circulation. Only time that's ever happened, too."

"So is it worth something, or not?"

"Oh, yes, it's worth something. Not a whole lot but, in this condition...like a hundred bucks, thereabouts. I have guides at home that will tell us. Why don't I check when I get there and give you a call?"

"Thanks, man. I'm glad you came over."

"Me too, man. Good to see you. I gotta go. I'll call you when I get home. Maybe we'll go down to Joe's for chips and gravy later, just for old times' sake."

"You got it. Talk to you later."

Myles left me examining my newfound wealth. A hundred bucks wasn't going to solve all my money problems but it wasn't a bad start. I looked over at the open roll of dimes, thinking about all my visits up to Mrs. Russell's room.

I remembered how she had always tipped me the same way, pressing the dime into my hand, as if there was something special about it. Even on her last day at the hotel, the last time I saw her, she'd wanted to be sure I got that roll of dimes.

My hand was shaking as I reached out to pick up the roll. I opened the end up further so I could pour the coins out on my bed and began examining them one by one.

By the time Myles called, I knew. Every dime in the roll, all fifty of them, were the same, all in perfect condition. 1936 George V's, double-struck, each and every one. There were fifteen more in an old Crown Royal bag that I'd never bothered to roll.

"One hundred ten dollars each, current market value," said Myles, "Chips and gravy's on you, pal."

I gave my notice at the Ritz the next day. Two weeks later I walked out the front door intending to never walk through it again, if I could help it.

My first year at music school was the most exciting, challenging time of my life. I learned how to read music and score parts for drums and other instruments. I learned basic keyboard technique so that I could use the piano to dissect and build melodies and chords and a myriad of other things that turned me from a raw, self-taught rock and roll drummer into a well rounded musician ready to apply my knowledge in any style of music I might be called upon to perform.

I did so well that first year that I received a bursary for my second year and the government forgave my loan.

I also learned that, now that I had the chops to play Jazz, I didn't really want to. It was and continues to be my favourite music to listen to but it's just not my style. I grew up playing rock and roll and rhythm & blues. That's where the heart of my music is and that's what I play, every chance I get. I now have the tools to do much, much more with it, and when those kinds of gigs are too few and far between, I know I can handle just about anything else out there.

A couple of years after I finished college, Joyband got back together. Some of the other guys had gone to school, too, so we approached the new thing with more skills and experience.

It took us a fraction of the time to learn a new number. We found, to our mutual satisfaction, that the thing that had sustained us the first time around was still there-just the pure joy we shared in playing together as a band.

We got the downtown gigs and we did well enough to be called back again and again. We got banned for life from one venue for playing too loud—three times. It was only inevitable that, sooner or later, we would be called to play at the Ritz Tavern.

It felt pretty odd, walking in the front door of the bar, instead of sneaking in through the basement. Gus was no longer there at his shoeshine stand. They told me he'd retired to Florida on his savings. The stand stood empty and silent but I could still hear the rag in my head, snapping out the old time beats.

One night during a break I saw Tiger standing around down there. I went up to say hello but I had to remind him who I was. He peered at me with bloodshot eyes and slowly recognition came into them.

"I always knew you was trouble," he said.

The only person who came down to see me play was Patty, who was now head chef. I sat with her and reminisced through a couple of breaks and while I was on stage I caught her watching me with that crooked little smile on her lips.

Later on we went out for a bite, but that, too, is another story.

One by one the little businesses that had existed to service the customers of the old hotel closed up and disappeared. The last one was the Ritz Shoe Renue, which closed its doors forever in the 1992.

The city named a subway station after her. Ritz Station is a cold concrete hole in the ground. It gives no hint as to what its name meant to generations of citizens.

Those of us who new the Ritz in her last days share an odd sort of affection for the memory of the old place. I guess it might be true of any former grand hotel. In the way of hotels the world over, the Ritz had become a part of the fabric of the city. For me, she had come to represent those old world virtues that are rapidly becoming lost to us in the west.

I think back on my Ritz days and I can see how the time I spent there changed me. The things I saw there and the people I met are part of who I am.

We move through the world, visiting one another for short times or long, each visit changing us in big ways and little. Like guests in each others lives, we leave things behind, and take things away with us when we go.

I can see now that there was no other time in her long history that the Ritz could have wrought the changes in me that she did in that mad decade. The 1970's was a decade of change, but even in the midst of the crazed carnival ride that the cultural revolution became, the hotels' timeless atmosphere provided a unique crucible for the shaping of the man I have become.

I do a lot of travelling now and I stay in hotels new and old in different cities. I have yet to find myself lodging in one that offers a trace of the charm of that old place.

When they demolished the Ritz to make room for a big office tower, the hotel held a big auction sale to get rid of the contents first, including the treasures in the basement. A local millionaire bought the chandelier. The silver service apparently went to one of the other hotels in town.

I didn't go, but Gary did. He bought a box of junk for five bucks, which included a dozen drink coasters from the lounge. They're made out of cork, with the Ritz's logo, a little crown, printed in gold. He gave me a few.

Every once in a while, Gary comes over for a beer and I get them out. We talk about the Ritz and the people that we met there and we laugh deep into the night, and then I put them away for the next time.

The Short Haired Wig, age two,
supported by the author, age 16

About the Author

Neil D. Martin was born and raised in Edmonton, Alberta. He has been a bellhop, a parking lot attendant, a construction worker, a mailman, a professional musician, a sculptor, business owner and an ESL conversation facilitator. Neil was a founding member of Captain Nobody and the Forgotten Joyband.

Neil currently resides with his partner, Sandra and their son Connor in Edmonton, where he crafts custom neon signs for fun and profit.

CPSIA information can be obtained at www.ICGtesting.com
Printed in the USA
LVOW06s0100250214

374986LV00001B/26/P

9 781460 236772